OPEN HEART

OPEN HEART

ELVIRA LINDO

Translated from the Spanish by Adrian Nathan West

OTHER PRESS

NEW YORK

Originally published in Spanish as *A corazón abierto* in 2020
by Seix Barral, an imprint of Editorial Planeta, S. A., Barcelona
Copyright © Elvira Lindo, 2020
Copyright © Editorial Planeta, S. A., 2020
Interior images copyright © Miguel Sánchez Lindo

Translation copyright © Other Press, 2023

Production editor: Yvonne E. Cárdenas
Text designer: Jennifer Daddio / Bookmark Design & Media Inc.
This book was set in Baskerville and Goodlife Serif Bold
by Alpha Design & Composition of Pittsfield, NH

1 3 5 7 9 10 8 6 4 2

Library of Congress Cataloging-in-Publication Data
Names: Lindo, Elvira, 1962- author. | West, Adrian Nathan, translator.
Title: Open heart / Elvira Lindo ; translated from the Spanish
by Adrian Nathan West.
Other titles: A corazón abierto. English
Description: New York : Other Press, [2023] | Originally published in
Spanish as A corazón abierto in 2020 by Seix Barral, an imprint of
Editorial Planeta, S. A., Barcelona.
Identifiers: LCCN 2022034987 (print) | LCCN 2022034988 (ebook) |
ISBN 9781635422528 (paperback) | ISBN 9781635422535 (ebook)
Subjects: LCSH: Lindo, Elvira, 1962-—Family—Fiction. |
LCGFT: Autobiographical fiction. | Novels.
Classification: LCC PQ6662.I563 A62513 2023 (print) | LCC PQ6662.I563 (ebook) |
DDC 863/.64—dc23/eng/20220725
LC record available at https://lccn.loc.gov/2022034987
LC ebook record available at https://lccn.loc.gov/2022034988

For my sister and my brothers,

INMA, MANUEL, AND CÉSAR,

for so many years of good company.

*But are not all facts dreams as soon as
we put them behind us?*

—Emily Dickinson

MANUEL AT NINE YEARS OLD

My sister and I sitting in front of them: my father and his roommate. Manolo and Clemente. The two of them sitting stiff in the pleather hospital chairs with the little attached tray like a school desk, waiting for dinner. The image, too, has an air of school days about it, despite the two men's old age and the oxygen tanks they're breathing through. My father's hair is carefully combed—I've never seen him like this before except in photos from his youth, sent to my mother with romantic devotion. A nurse has taken a liking to him, even if he misbehaves, and she combs him and sprinkles cologne on his scalp every morning. His now quite sparse curls are flattened down with pomade on the back of his neck and they look like tiny snails. Somehow they add weight to his already stern features, which have the frightened look of a ter-rified animal. And he is terrified. He knows death is lurking around the corner, and there's nothing he can do to avoid it. When they let him out, he'll go back to smoking and drinking, and one of these days, he'll stop being able to breathe and he'll die. He's more anxious about dying alone than dying as such; that's why he's latched on to his roommate, Clemente, and the two of them have developed a strange camaraderie.

Clemente is cheerful, fat, and old. He wears his hair in bangs like a rocker from the seventies, or a musketeer gone to seed. He lives in a shelter. According to him, his kitchen-supply business went under, and when—to use his words—King Midas lost his shirt, his wife and daughters abandoned him. For a while he lived with his girlfriend, whom he affectionately calls *my little Polack* on account of her origins, but they were evicted, and she hasn't shown her face in the three days we've been visiting my father. Clemente has integrated perfectly into our family thanks to my father, who got us used to accepting acquaintances of unknown provenance, whether we liked them or not, back when we were kids. He's always been devoted to his bar mates, to the fleeting friends you meet on a roadside bench, to waiters, pharmacists, salesmen, road workers, doormen, distant cousins, anyone you can have a glib conversation with to fill the silence. He's never cared about origins or status, and he's never needed his chums to be interesting. What my father looks for is company, for that immediate relief he feels when he's got someone to talk to and can indulge his innate expansiveness. This is the strongest image I have of my father filed away in my memories: leaning on a bar, veiled in smoke, drink and cigarette in one hand, the other free and gesticulating, erupting in brusque, broken laughter or else in rage if his chosen stranger has unexpectedly back-talked and become his enemy.

A lack of oxygen keeps my father from speaking in long sentences, and for the first time in his life, he has to let the other person talk more than him. My sister and I listen, as we always have, disconnecting. That was our family life: him delivering monologues, and us four children cultivating our inner worlds, and that must be why we all have a tendency to get distracted that makes us seem a bit clueless. Clemente met Manolo at his lowest, and he has taken the reins: he can talk a blue streak with two oxygen tubes running up his nostrils, and tells us, as if it were a prank, how *both of them* woke up hungry last night, and *both of them* rang their bell and called the nurse, who's had it up to here with *both of them*, brought yogurt, cookies, and a little chocolate. When he wants to refer to my father, Clemente often says *our friend here* or *the very same man you see before you*, and as he tells us what he did last night, we nod with wonder at his use of this fusty expression of familiarity to describe the old authoritarian Manolo Lindo. I doubt anyone's ever called him *our friend here* before, and his face looks annoyed, as though it didn't please him in the least to be diminished this way in front of his daughters. But *our friend here*, as his roommate calls him, hardly has a voice left, and in a way, Clemente makes up for his tactlessness by protecting my father, placing himself at his service, and that's something my father's always been a pro at: finding others who put themselves at his service.

In this ersatz couple, Clemente plays the role of secretary. He tells us what the doctor says if she comes to visit while we're away, and he keeps my father's cell phone in easy reach on the nightstand to call us in case *our friend* decides he needs us to bring him something. My sister is used to it by now: if the phone rings at 9:00 a.m., it's Clemente calling to say my father wants us to bring him another checkbook from Santander Bank. We don't know what he wants a checkbook for at the hospital, but we do know if he doesn't get one, he'll throw a tantrum like a little brat. Clemente called the other night because my father needed his denture cream. That was how we found out my father has two false teeth. He's always boasted of his full set of teeth, pristine, unlike those of almost every other member of that malnourished generation that grew up during the war. Oh, and *Manolito's notebook*. Clemente called back, telling us not to forget *Manolito's notebook, please, he needs it*. What he's referring to is a day planner for schoolkids published in 1996, based on the hero of my book *Manolito Four-Eyes*. In it he has written down in no discernible order all the addresses and phone numbers that matter to him. My sister's, mine, and all those people—friends, employers, coworkers—who might help him to locate us if we don't pick up our phones. We've given him others, but he refuses to let go of that child's day planner, with the letters of the alphabet written in his own handwriting on the corners of its pages.

For three days now, Clemente has been a part of our lives, and whether we like it or not, we have to accept him, just as so many times in the past we accepted the vapid barflies my father glommed onto, or the women he established some unspecified relationship with, much to our discomfort.

Yes, there's something about this scene that reminds you of school. The two men's hospital gowns look like schoolboys' smocks. Neither of them has underwear on. They rest their fists on their trays, impatient for dinner to arrive, and when they hear the cart approaching down the hall, they instinctively open their legs in excitement. My sister and I have both been startled by the perturbing sight of the men's squished red genitals on display before us. Ill at ease, abashed, we've leapt up and remained standing the rest of the time, smiling nervously and doing anything possible to avoid another encounter with that sight one would prefer to forget. My father never had a sense of shame: when we used to go to the beach, his behind was inevitably stuck halfway out of his swimsuit. You could always see his underwear sticking up out of his pants—the way you see young people's now, jutting from their low waistlines—and it almost seemed he wished they would fall down so he could make everyone uncomfortable. Time worsened his eccentricities, and nowadays he wears his tie like a scarf and buttons his jacket up wrong. It's defiance—he wants you to draw his attention to it so he can ignore your advice, with the double pleasure of rule breaking and driving you up the wall. He has the soul of an unruly child. These past few months, I've learned that if I avoid correcting his willful negligence and instead go over to him and carefully button his buttons or tie his tie, he gives in, goes soft, feels cared for, and stops rebelling.

Dinner arrives, and the two men eat voraciously, panting through it because they can't breathe. They suck the bones with canine impatience and leave their plates clean like boys during the postwar period.

Clemente is the joker, the wag, the pest on this wing of the hospital: he has a worldly wisdom you don't find in everyone. He tells us the chicken at Gregorio Marañón Hospital is far and away the best hospital chicken in Madrid. My father, suffocating, but not yet resigned to withholding his opinion, chimes in: "Not even close." And Clemente adds, "La Beata is excellent too, but it can't hold a candle to this one. Top-notch." My father nods and tells him very faintly that the eating is also good at Rosario Clinic. This extraordinary gastronomical tourism unites the flush retiree and the vagrant.

Clemente remembers then when he was a traveling salesman and made a tour of the highway restaurants between Madrid and La Coruña. My father, who crisscrossed Spain doing the books for Dragados y Construcciones, the largest public works company in the country in those days, knows more than a few of these himself. Listing not only their names, but also their house specialties, they remind me of a couple on an old game show, *Un, dos, tres*, where the clock ticked down in the background to make the excitement even more exciting.

My father, who came from nothing and climbed the ladder at his company thanks to stubbornness and a head for numbers, used to take his briefcase along on audits of big construction projects all over Spain, and when I would travel with him to keep him company after my mother died, I saw how imposing his presence was. When he arrived at a hotel's reception with his overnight bag, the construction managers were always there waiting for him. More than an auditor, my father had the air of a detective showing up in some one-horse town to investigate a possible crime and out the villain. And often that's more or less what happened. He was ruthless, and could stretch a meeting on until dawn to wring a confession out of someone who'd had his hand in the kitty. Then they'd have to figure out what to do. Later, when I read Georges Simenon's Inspector Maigret novels, I saw similarities in the ways my father and Maigret went about their interrogations. Both detective and auditor felt sympathy for the man who had given in to temptation; it was as if my father, overseeing the accounts of a huge company for so many years, had also been prey to inner turmoil. "I never took a red cent!" he used to say. And I'd answer that this was nothing to brag about, because most people don't steal. He would go to great lengths to prove that honesty was indeed the exception to the rule in a country eaten up with corruption. He knew what he was talking about.

Some of his strange sense of pity for thieves rubbed off on me. My father used to tell my mother softly, because the cases he dealt with were a serious matter, how he'd reached an agreement with some penitent employee, who would pay the company back before resigning in exchange for a letter of recommendation that would get him hired elsewhere. My father held on to some of his files his entire life, as if they were proof of his professional merits. In his last years, when corruption cases were cropping up all over Spain, he liked to say: "Not enough people kill themselves these days." In his opinion, many politicians should have chosen suicide to avoid disgracing their families. According to his peculiar morality, the worst punishment for a wrongdoer was not prison, but shame, and as a man with a certain inclination to violence and coarse utterances, he often praised the decisions of those Japanese who, getting caught in a lie, decided to throw themselves in front of the subway. Hearing these opinions aired so frequently must have affected me, because now, when I see someone in the defendants' bench and think of how ashamed they must be, it makes me shiver; and when people clamor for justice, I can't help feeling a pity not everyone understands in this vengeful society of ours. I imagine if I were facing a prison sentence, I, too, might consider suicide. I'd die, but I wouldn't lose my honor.

It pains me that this verbose blowhard who lives between the shelter and the hospital keeps my father from opening his mouth. We've always listened to him the way a lackey listens to a dictator. Deferential as we were as children to his prolix thoughts about anything and everything, we suffer now from a form of Stockholm syndrome. All my life waiting for my father to stop sucking up everyone's time with his endless, abusive harangues, and now I'm here grieving because he's been forced into silence.

These last two years, old age has made him bitter, and apocalyptic comments pour from his lips. What did we expect? He's a man of the world, and illness has taken him from his natural habitat: the bars, the street, the miles driven between his neighborhood and downtown, crossing the bridges over the freeway. But this wrath that has permanently effaced his good cheer has also let the past bubble forth more crudely. Before, he always spoke of it in a humorous tone that dispersed any shadow of conflict. That was his way, and he encouraged or obliged us to follow suit. Irony buried all our family's nightmares, turning them into a catalog of funny stories. That allowed him to load others down with guilt and elude the burden of it himself. One day he even said: "That day when your mother left home...that day. It had its funny side too, right?" He looked at me, seeking approval, but I replied dryly— Funny, no, Papá, it wasn't, it was tragic for us, for her children. My answer was cruel. I didn't want him to find a trace of complicity on my part. Occasionally, we've dared put the brakes on his storytelling. We've often let him invent and reinvent what life was like before we came into the world, but with time, it's gotten harder to let him go on gilding the traumatic episodes we witnessed.

My father's old. But he's badly suited to old age. That's why he's always angry. In the old days, he could drink anyone under the table, and whenever the family gathered, we were swathed in wine and whiskey fumes and dense clouds of cigarette smoke. Since my father's illness has made it impossible for him to walk or talk without choking, he's started telling the same old stories in versions so different, it's like someone else is telling them. Like many old people, he's plunged back into the world of childhood, and the boy he used to describe as a regular Huckleberry Finn, a scamp who dodged the hardships of the war and its aftermath, reveals himself in the old man's version as a helpless creature who only made it through with deep wounds that scarred him forever.

Uneasily, I think now how, if he'd died before this bitterness overtook him, we wouldn't have met that other self that he had censored so zealously. If he'd died before, all we would have remembered was the superhuman fortitude of the invincible man he thought he was. I know now—there's no doubting it—that his strength was physical, not psychological. Taught to hate weakness, he'd acquired the ability to hide his pain from the time he was a boy. How can you empathize with the pain of others when you've never let yourself feel your own? This negation of weakness was what his own life depended on.

The man in the polka-dot hospital gown with the faltering respiration and the face of a frightened animal came to Madrid for the first time in 1939, just a few months after the end of the war. He was nine years old. He was the son of a soulless captain of the Civil

Guard and a cold, authoritarian mother. My father hinted that on occasion my grandmother raised her hands against her husband. His mother decided that to ease the family's burden, she needed to get rid of one of her children for a while, and she chose the middle one, my father, who was incidentally exasperating, reckless, and prone to mischief. She sent him to the harshest, most devastated, least habitable city in Spain, which Franco's army had razed because it was a symbol of resistance, until hunger and devastation finally defeated its people.

I don't know what part of the country my father arrived from, because my grandparents changed residence frequently, but looking over my grandfather's service record, my guess is he left from Río Tinto. He came escorted by two Civil Guards under his father's command. This image brings back to me another from 1971, because I, too, traveled by train at that same age from Ávila with two Civil Guards. I'd spent some time in the barracks there, where my uncle was a lieutenant colonel. I remember the sidelong glances of our fellow riders on our way to Atocha Station and then in the subway. In my naive optimism, I said when I got home that people had thought I was a princess with an escort of guards in tricorne hats on her way back to her neighborhood after a long absence. My siblings, always ready to bring me back down to earth, refused to let me enjoy this fantasy, and told me people had thought I was a small-time crook, a little sister to the famous bandit El Lute.

My father must have been lonely when he rang the door of one of my great-aunts, a relative of my grandmother's, who lived in the Plaza del Campillo del Mundo Nuevo, at the end of the long slope the Calle Ribera de Curtidores traces down the middle of the La Latina neighborhood. I don't know my great-aunt's name: because she treated my father so badly, he only ever called her the Beast.

My father showed signs of his nervous character (hyperactive, they would say now) from a very young age. He often said he'd been a piece of work, a brat, and that he deserved whatever spankings my grandmother dealt him. But there were reasons behind his alarmist and paranoid tendencies. He'd always assumed his father died in the war, around 1938, until he saw him appear one morning while he was playing in the town square: wobbly, sunburned, with a blanket over his shoulders. He'd have sworn this creature was a ghost or the boogeyman, come to take him away for some caper he hadn't yet been punished for. In the endless seconds it took for the man to reach him, he thought: he's going to drag me off, maybe even kill me. But when the man got close, he recognized he was his father. The shock of seeing him made the boy's hair fall out. It was some time before his precious, abundant, curly black hair grew back, and when it did, it had a white streak that gave him a gallant air, even as a youngster.

A year later, the boy who saw his father return from the land of the dead and who hadn't recovered from it was torn from his family and sent off to Madrid: one less mouth to feed, a wild, savage creature now in the hands of a woman who didn't have children of her own. My father rang the bell on the Plaza del Campillo del Mundo Nuevo, the same square I would visit many years later with his grandchild, my son Miguel, when he was nine himself, so he could trade his Dragon Ball Z cards at the stalls of El Rastro. My hand clutched my son's hand firmly, apprehensively, because he was rest- less, easily distracted, and I couldn't stand the thought of him getting lost the way I had in the village when I was five. And yet, in 1939, no one thought my father, no older than my son then, could stray off or disappear forever in the urban jungle. Our understanding of chil- dren's ages changes, but the wound helplessness leaves behind has never changed.

I never thought to ask my father which building he stayed in during those months. I seem to remember he said once that his room—more like a pantry—faced the back, and his only bed was an old mattress on the floor.

The aunt he called the Beast was a nurse in Maudes Hospital, which had once given aid to Republican soldiers and later treated fighters from the National side. His aunt woke early and left the boy alone with a single mission: to stand in the food line. In a row of beggars, the lonely boy would wait for the rations his aunt was due. Then, with nothing to do, without friends or neighbors to take care of him, he would wander through the city in ruins. In the evening, he'd go find the Beast, because children want to love and they will even cling stubbornly to those who harm them to avoid solitude and win affection. He always remembered the pain of the men wounded in the war, their mutilated limbs and the stench of blood; he had a sharp sense of smell and used to always lean down with his big nose when he wanted to get a better sense of people and things. Now and again, his aunt would beat him. With that strange moral schema he's retained since childhood, he's always said his mother had a right to beat him, but that those thrashings from his aunt were illegitimate. He never reproached his mother's severity, even her cruelty toward him. For me, he used this logic to justify some of the slaps dealt out to my sister and brothers.

My father has always been imposing, one of those men who never have enough room to gesticulate, and it's hard for me to imagine him as small and skinny, hardheaded, underfed, badly clothed, poor, unattended to. I try to visualize that nine-year-old boy, and what forces its way into my memories is the first photo I have of him, from a few years later, standing in front of a chalkboard at school, so handsome and so tall for his age that you can't imagine anyone ever neglected him. Since he's always been expansive, resistant to reflection and silence, I have to make an effort to trace the steps of that child who wakes up alone in a frozen home, maybe not even needing to dress because he never undressed the night before, going outside without washing or eating breakfast in the heart of defeated, working-class Madrid; after two or three mornings following his aunt, he's learned the route by heart, and walks alone up Calle Mira el Río Baja to the Plaza Mayor, crossing toward the Puerta del Sol, taking Preciados to Gran Vía, observant as a fox, following the trail the Beast marked out for him unthinkingly. Sometimes he gets lost in the mass of villagers in Madrid's center; he's briefly alarmed, but then he gets the courage to ask the way, and someone sets him right. In this Madrid full of poverty, orphans, and cripples, no one wonders why a child is asking directions to a place as far as the Glorieta de Cuatro Caminos. He's sharp, his mind clicks all day till he falls asleep, dead tired, and soon he's making his own mental map, adding streets, testing out new routes; from the Glorieta de Atocha, gawking at the broad avenues, he dodges the huge trees on the Paseo del Prado, as tiny in this monumental urban landscape as Hansel and Gretel in the eerie forest. Strong and bold my father was, just like the children in the story, with a fear that, instead of paralyzing him, forced him never to stand still.

No one notices him. In Madrid, under the brutal heel of Franco's boot, countless children are wandering the streets, many of whom will never go to school again; they've lost their fathers, and will spend the final days of childhood as street rascals before their mothers get them a job in some workshop or store. What's unusual about this boy, what marks him out, is how he walks alone, with no friends to cook up schemes with. Not wanting to call anyone's attention to himself, he tries to walk quickly, as if he had somewhere to be or an urgent message to deliver. He walked with that same determined air throughout his life. His destination is his calvary, because when he reaches Maudes Hospital, he sits in the entryway waiting for his aunt and watches the war cripples come and go, and they arouse his disgust and pity; sometimes, when she sends for him, he goes deeper into that horror house and smells the sickness and hears the moans and he thinks nothing at all, or else that this is life, with that extraordinary capacity for acceptance that children have. If someone gave him a toy, he'd sit on the floor and play as if the misery surrounding him were as natural as the landscape.

But a day comes when his forbearance fails. It happens after one of the Beast's whippings. In my mind, I see her as a gigantic prison warden. He comes up with a plan. He studies it down to the last detail because, even if he's impulsive, he's also calculating, and he organizes his steps like a chess player who refuses to let anything escape his control. One morning, he gets up, looks at himself in the little bathroom mirror he has to stand on tiptoe to see, and studies his own gaze: if he puts on a grave face, he can look three years older than he is. He smooths his curls down with water to make a serious impression and buttons his shirt all the way up, convinced he can look like the young man he still isn't with an optimism that he hasn't felt since his arrival five months ago.

He goes to a bar on the square, one where his aunt often leaves him messages or her keys. He trains his child's voice to sound like a teenager's and tells the owner his aunt said the barman should lend him five pesetas. She'll pay him back when she's done at the hospital. With the coin in his hand and his cardboard box in the other, the same one he arrived with—which contains a change of underwear, a sweater, and little more—he skips off to Atocha Station. Along the way, he stops at a store on the corner and buys an apple. It's not a lark: he knows he needs to take something to eat to keep from fainting along the way. He reaches the station and buys a ticket. Surprisingly, it's not for the village he came from, the one where his parents live. I never thought to ask why the ticket wasn't for home, but my guess is he didn't want his mother to see him come back a failure.

He'd heard he had family in Aranjuez. On his father's side. He thought he could ask around for people with the same strange surname as his, and surely someone would help him find them. He'd had word of those relatives, his father's siblings, in letters that arrived home occasionally. He knew they had *fields*, and in his mind, that word, *fields*, sounded like a promise of Eden.

He reached up when he asked for his ticket as if he made the trip every day. Who would raise an eyebrow at a boy that young traveling alone? The country was crawling with lost and nearly destitute children. The train took off, and then, sheltered by his sense of purpose in life, he bit into his apple and stared at the countryside. The other passengers took out their humble lunch pails, and their scent was a torment to a stomach too used to scarcity. There was a constant murmur of conversations. He was happy for the company and the certainty of soon having a home where he could lay his head.

He reached the village, which looked bright and welcoming compared with Madrid. Everything he saw was colorful. He'd heard his uncle was a guard at city hall, and that's where he went. He said the man's name as if there to meet someone who had been waiting for him a long time, even though he'd never laid eyes on him. And everything happened just as he wished. They alerted his uncle, and his uncle came for him and took him home. His mother got rid of one mouth to feed, and now his aunt Clotilde had another one sitting at her table. A table full of cousins and tomato salads from the *fields*, this was my father's idea of a happy ending, and a bustling table full of plates where you could sop your bread would forever remain the best way of calming his inner anxiety.

Life isn't usually so generous, but he's always preferred to focus on the lucky parts and pass over the shadowy ones, and this is how he's told us the story, his story: as a succession of trials in which he's always managed to come out on top.

The miracle is that this family with the strange last name took him in. They were simple country people, austere in the way poverty obliges you to be, but they had fruit and vegetables to eat. They fed the boy, and in the coming months he would grow to nearly resemble the teenager he wanted so much to be. They wrote to his mother, who knew from his aunt that the accursed, disobedient, irritating, and irritable child had run away. The blame fell on his frail shoulders, as was to be expected, and this chapter was remembered as a milestone in the long record of bad behavior that had preceded it. He likes to portray himself as the sympathetic villain rather than a victim. And that's how I've always seen him, almost, up to now, up to this present, when I observe him dressed up as a hospital patient, looking incongruous in his spotted gown.

The pity I'm experiencing is not, or not only, because of his health. We all knew he'd end up paying for his addictions. Now the foreseeable has happened, and he'll die in the foreseeable way, choking on the smoke he's been inhaling since he was twelve years old. This compassion I feel, which he doesn't want to provoke, comes from an idea that's beset me for some time. For all those times I've listened to, transcribed, and venerated stories of Spaniards in exile, suffered for those who had to leave everything behind and forge a new life far from their homeland, I now see in him the tragedy of those who had to stay, to forget the trauma of war that marked their childhood and take their devastated country forward. The lack of victim sentiment in a generation that concentrated its entire energy on *not* doing without, on prospering and reproducing, has meant that there's never been talk of reparation, and even we, these people's children, paid little attention to what they told us on the few times they did, as though it were all a misadventure rather than a calamity.

All my father's suppressed bile, choked back while he struggled to survive and thrive, is now streaming out like a death rattle before he leaves this world. I can see him for the first time now as he is and was: a boy alone in a ravaged city, smacked around by a woman he barely knew, not even sure why she's doing it. What could you expect from him but a hatred for weakness and a caustic insistence on a stiff upper lip?

Only in his ailing dread of solitude can we glimpse the consequences of a trauma that still throbs inside him.

Less than a year after my mother's death, after her long illness and all the other things that had happened to us, my father rushed into a second marriage to a cheerful, moneyed woman, and destiny landed him in her home on Calle Maudes, where the balcony looked out onto the hospital where the Beast had worked. It's a small street, and when we peeked out onto the balcony, we seemed to be in a garden surrounding that peculiar building Antonio Palacios had designed as a hospital for workers. Now, the tragedy is past, and it's just one more government office. Once or twice, when my father was with his second wife, we leaned on the railing and talked and looked at the turrets. He smiled and said: To think of the times I must have waited in that very entryway for my aunt.

I never saw a shadow of bitterness or sorrow in that recollection. It's now, when I see the old schoolboy with his hair combed back and sprinkled with cologne by the nurse, and I realize that the past in all its rawness is coming down on him and there's nothing I can do to help it, that I see my father as a little boy.

Yesterday morning, something happened that's still tormenting me. They'd taken Clemente away to run some test. He'd said goodbye to us—to my sister, my nieces, and me. He was cheerful, but also worried they'd discharge him, because he likes being in the hospital better than sleeping at the shelter, where he says you have to keep on your toes and stay out of trouble if you want to be treated with respect. Clemente says he can't complain, because everyone loves him. Right, my friend? he asks my father. And my father nods, nods with conviction, as if the two of them had spent nights together in the municipal shelter. When Clemente disappears, my father senses that something about his roommate doesn't sit right with us, and he tells us in a thin voice, to put a stop to our unvoiced objections:

"He's a wonderful guy, and he treats me right. And you need to treat him right too. He's a straight shooter, and with all the shady business that goes on in this hospital, that counts for something."

Shady business. Dad, what shady business, we ask. My nieces hear this expression, *shady business*, and they laugh. Their laugh annoys him. It annoys him that we don't take him seriously, that we don't believe what he's saying. He speaks so softly that the four of us have to come close to hear him. He tells us about the days he spent in the ICU. He tells us: I saw everything. Everything? Yeah, I saw everything from the window. What window? Dad, there wasn't a window in there. I saw the trucks coming and going in the back and these guys, they must have been Colombians, were unloading drugs. Cocaine, bricks of cocaine. This place is a front, he tells us, it's rotten, it's full of corruption. We start laughing, but then our laughter breaks off. He gets angry when he realizes we're about to argue with him about something he's so certain of.

I see the doctor walking down the hall and run out to meet her. I tell her what my father's telling me, I ask her if he's maybe lost his mind. In the course of those days, we've begged her pardon several times for my father's behavior: he's acting like a little boy, needy, complaining, not answering questions, refusing to say he'll give up smoking when he returns home. He doesn't like the oxygen tank because he can't smoke with it around, and he wants to die wrapped in a cloud of smoke. The doctor seems unbothered by the ill man's petulance, and these notions of his don't surprise her either. It's normal, she says, many old people can't cope with the feeling when they wake up hooked to a bunch of tubes. Your father was delirious, she continues, and we had to restrain him. These stories he's telling you will go away with time.

I go back to his room. I walk over and say: Dad, you don't have to worry, you're safe in this room. And I kiss him on the head. My sister kisses him. My nieces. And he closes his eyes. Probably he's starting to doubt what he remembers, but at least it calms him down to think we believe him, that his words provoke understanding and not laughter. He's so tired.

Clemente returns, verbose and optimistic. He'll be staying a few more days in the hospital. You all can go, he says, I've got it from here. With dinner on its way, *our friend here* will cheer up soon enough. And we're happy to know my father is in the best of hands. He always had a knack for choosing the right friends.

DOÑA SAGRARIO

Having one grandmother is advisable. Two is a bit much. Two grandmothers in action can turn any human being into a perfect idiot. I only had one; the other died when my mother was a girl. Unfortunately, the one who died was the good one. Or at least that's how I was made to remember her throughout my childhood. The good grandmother died and left behind eight orphans and a halo of saintliness. I grew up believing I was the granddaughter of a saint, and so when I prayed and asked for something—because whenever I've prayed, I've always concentrated on getting something concrete—instead of addressing the Virgin, I would talk with my poor dead grandmother, the one with the cute little face, whom there was only one old photo of, a portrait of a woman from another century. I was right about her: she died so young, she was both a saint and a woman of the nineteenth century.

I tried to be like my good grandmother, because in my family they talked a lot about how beautiful and sweet she was and what a sensation she caused in her village. I'd close myself up in the bathroom, which is where I spent 50 percent of my childhood, performing on top of the toilet lid; I would pull my stiff bangs back from my face and puff up my cheeks and try to see if I noticed any remote similarity between myself and the young woman from the old photo. But no, there was no fixing it: my babyish face, remarkably similar to my face today, was long, with a pointy chin, a roundish nose, and big eyes turned sadly downward. The painful truth is that, at least physically, I looked more like the bad grandmother. No one came out and told me so, but at times I would hear my mother say as much from a distance, chatting with one of my aunts. My mother whispered from a prudent distance to keep from wounding me, but she was bad at faking, and that made me paranoid, and I developed the ability to figure out what people were saying about me behind my back. Especially if it was bad.

Since I tend to get impatient with descriptions of the appearance of characters in novels and I doze off if a

writer gives profuse details about someone's face, I will
sum up my (bad) grandmother's face with an example
from art history: she looked like Pope Innocent X as
painted by Velázquez. In my memory, the contours are
lost, and Velázquez's very human pope is transformed
into the ghastly one of Francis Bacon. All you need
is a tiny effort to change his sex, but not too much,
because my grandmother had the face of a historical
gentleman: take off the papal bonnet Innocent X wore
in the painting and exchange it with a sparse head of
whitish-blond hair with a Christopher Columbus cut,
and you have the spitting image of my grandmother.

The short, straight hair brought into prominence my
bad grandmother's pointy chin. They say that after a
certain age, a person gets the face they deserve, and
that's why, for half a century, I worked conscientiously,
day in and day out, to distance myself from that hardly
favorable resemblance: my character has stressed the
sweetness in these saddish eyes enough to give them a
touch of melancholy, and the childlike smile that comes
often to my lips has lifted my features, erasing all trace
of a grandmother who almost never smiled and who,
when she did, was the opposite of most people, who
look better when they smile: my grandmother tugged
her lips downward, and her prominent chin poked out

a few inches, so that she ceased to embody the pope and came to resemble those classic drawings of miserly Ebenezer Scrooge. This made sense, because, like Dickens's classic character, my grandmother was proud of her parsimony, which bothered her not in the least. So: the face was that of Innocent X; the hair, Christopher Columbus; the countenance, Scrooge, the way you see him in those old illustrations of Dickens's book, which have determined our idea of the miser's appearance forever.

But the bad grandmother must have had something good, you will say, rightly distrusting overly negative descriptions. Of course: she had an exaggerated sense of frugality, sharpness, perceptiveness, strength, intelligence, bravery, slyness, determination, an enviable good health that lasted to her final breath. Because the fear of death neither cowed her nor transformed her like Scrooge, my grandmother died the woman she had always been. She lacked goodwill, but today, when she is as lost as my good grandmother in the mists of the past, I have to admit that saints, except on a few famous occasions, aren't good for much except illustrating prayer cards; whereas those old women we would never call *sweet* old women because they leave this world without ever once provoking an ounce of pity, those old bags who horrify their grandchildren, deserve to appear in one of those anthologies of horror stories that keep children up at night, or in these very pages the little girl is now writing to explain to herself why she has always felt drawn to a person who so horrified her.

My father wouldn't have liked to see his mother described as a mean old witch. I know that. I'm taking advantage of his absence to do so. It isn't calculated, but I'm not the first writer to spill the beans when it no longer matters. My father always defended his mother and her peculiarities, but without bothering to justify her avarice. Just as when you want to stand up for someone who doesn't inspire sympathy, he defended her character, respected it, praised that aggressive fortitude, justified a violence so rarely attributed to mothers, let alone to grandmothers. He admired her as she was. He valued her harshness, her cruelty, even her bravery.

My father wasn't one to waste time reminiscing about childhood. He would talk exhaustively about life in the present, about work, as if he were born in a filing cabinet of the Dredging and Construction Company, but when he did decide to recount one of his memories, he would leave you shaken. When he recalled one of the many times his mother had slapped his face in his childhood, he would accompany the tale with great bouts of laughter, adding afterward that this was the only way to raise a little hellion, a rebel, a skylark always getting into trouble. As a girl, that proclivity for forgiving maternal aggression and that dismissive attitude toward himself both troubled me. I didn't know what to make of them. As an adult, I found them irritating. Now I feel a bitter understanding toward his attitude; it comes naturally to certain children to love their mothers or fathers even when they've done nothing to deserve it.

If my grandmother was never willing to come to the rescue financially, it was because, my father said, she was wisely saving her money for her children's inheritance. As long as there were mothers, he would go on, who went crazy giving their children everything they had, spoiling them, encouraging them to spend senselessly, and driving themselves into the poorhouse, my grandmother was the wise one for holding on to all she had. Her love was aiming for posterity. And who wouldn't adore a mother like that, whose affections were so judiciously turned toward the future?

All through my childhood, I heard about this inheritance that would one day be my father's and, eventually, ours. At my grandmother's house, unlike in most Spanish families, money was discussed even in front of the children: my grandmother would bring up the issue, provoking long, tense, difficult discussions with her children, all men, all smokers and drinkers, all of them hard with everyone else and bashful before their matriarch. These talks occurred amid clouds of smoke and fumes of Fundador brandy, and we children listened to them in a reflexive, timid silence, the way kids back then did, as if on one of those nights, after hours and hours, a contract determining each of our futures were to be signed. Accustomed as I was to listening without a right to reply, I tried to imagine what it would be like to be immensely rich. After all, everything hinted that this was to be my fate. If I was going to be like my grandmother, the one with the fortune, I would have to oversee that guesthouse in the Ciudad Jardín neighborhood in Málaga, hand outstretched to receive the monthly rent of those men who left with a good morning and came back later with a good evening.

My grandmother's name was Sagrario. They were about to name me Sagrario too, but for once my mother put her foot down, and I was christened with my good grandmother's name. A name can change a destiny, can hold disaster at bay. Or maybe I grew up believing the name of my grandmother the saint had protected me from being a replica of the woman who looked like Innocent X, had Columbus's hair, and smiled like Scrooge. But the fear that severe woman provoked in her sons, her neighbors, and her grand-children didn't prevent my siblings and me from feeling a deep fascination with her. The blame, as always, lay with my father, who had convinced us in his persuasive, authoritarian way that Grandma Sagrario had amassed a huge fortune from nothing thanks to her wits alone, gallantly wearing the pants when they proved too big for my grandfather, a Civil Guard and a wet noodle of a man. I admired her the way children admire what they are afraid of and don't understand, with the timid curiosity of a person staring at a wild animal that might bite. Seduced by my father's tale, I longed for the moment when I would see her again during the long journey south we took every summer.

Along the way, my mother would rattle off the list of all the necessities my grandmother wouldn't have in the larder when we got there. My grandmother was rich, but she died without a refrigerator. Her larder didn't have milk or eggs or chocolate powder or fruit or meat or fish or cheese. But despite my mother's efforts to discredit her, that didn't put a damper on our mood. We weren't interested in the details. Flighty in the absurd way children are, with my father egging us on, we thought only of looking in the cabinet and seeing the celebrated packet of Artinata cookies. One packet of cookies, just one a year, which we received like holy wafers, as if we'd never eaten a goddamned cookie in our lives. Anticipating the complaints of my mother, who couldn't stand her mother-in-law, my father would dreamily announce the treasure that awaited us:

"Grandmother's cookies."

Many years later, when he'd become like a son to my father and had grown merciful with his extravagancies, my husband pointed out something I'd noticed but never known how to put to words: apart from their systematic refusal to finish sentences, the men in my family, just the men, tended to leave out verbs. They expressed themselves in a language only those of us who knew them well were capable of deciphering. The more they drank and smoked, sitting there at the dining table—and they were tireless drinkers and smokers— the more the verbs vanished from their sentences, as if, in the mist of alcohol and smoke, the neurons charged with coming up with them had fallen asleep.

When my father announced "Grandmother's cookies," he was contradicting my mother, betraying her, letting her know that even if my grandmother's larder lacked the basics to feed a large family, you couldn't lose sight of the details. The details, for a pathologically tightfisted woman, meant buying a packet of fifty cookies that we, her heirs, would consume greedily that first afternoon, and that would not be seen again until the next year. My father entranced us, clouded our good judgment, turned us into easily satisfied dupes.

The journey from Atazar Dam in the Sierra Pobre of Madrid to Málaga was so long that we had time to sleep, sweat, eat, vomit, sing, and fight, until my father stopped the car and doled out a few indiscriminate slaps, whether we deserved them or not. The journey was so dull that my siblings ejected me from the back seat, and since I was the youngest and had to do as my elders said, I had to cross Spain sharing the front seat with my mother. If my parents argued, which they often did, my mother would put me between them, and that's where I see myself, squashed, with the gearshift slapping against my knee. Sometimes my father would confuse my knee with the knob and give it a jerk. My mother would light my father's cigarettes so he could smoke without missing a dose of nicotine between one cigarette and the next, which made me something more than just a secondhand smoker. When they weren't getting along, she would pass the cigarette to me and I would pass it to my father. As if we were sharing a joint. I found exalting that little act of trust, a consequence of her anger. One time, when my mother had lent me her enormous sunglasses and I felt like someone, a world traveler, incognito, I brought the cigarette to my lips, pouting the way my mother would do at weddings. My father, who could see in 360 degrees, like a chameleon, let go of the steering wheel and boxed me on the ears. The glasses flew off. "That's the last time you get to wear those," my mother told me. From ten years old onward, I sat on the edge of my mother's seat, a barrier between my parents. It was humiliating. They sometimes used me to communicate, like a translator, and I tried to be literal to keep from getting hell on both sides.

We would cross the Meseta after starting the journey at six in the morning, so the heat wouldn't get to my father. He never turned on the radio, because it distracted him. But he loved for his daughters to sing, and we did so as a duet. We were in the chorus at school, and we knew lots of stupid songs, school anthems, carols. From the moment we set forth at dawn, he would start smoking and I would start throwing up. For years,

I had a seemingly incurable fear of riding in cars. My brothers said I vomited to play the victim. My mother would take a few towels with her, though I only gave her thirty seconds' warning: just enough time for my father to slam on the brakes on those country roads where you could drive for hours without seeing another soul, apart from a sheepherder or a soldier, and even that was rare. I remember the dizziness, the anxiety, my mother's hand on my forehead, my eyes looking at the ditch. The ditches. Ditches from all over Spain. One time, my parents told a doctor about how I often vomited even before getting into the car, and he attributed it to something *psychological*. It was the first time I'd heard that word. I was nine years old. What I had was psychological. I didn't know what that meant, but I interpreted it in the same way as my parents: *The girl is a lunatic.* It would never have occurred to anyone in those days that it might be normal for a child to get sick, even before the car was put in gear, because she'd gotten up at dawn and been smothered in the scent of gasoline and cigarette smoke before she'd even had breakfast. I still haven't gotten over it to this day. My father sometimes got the sense that we weren't breathing as we ought to and would open the windows. In winter, the icy air would rush in, and my sweat would freeze, making a strange accompaniment to my anxiety and shivering.

We only went to my grandmother's house in summer. We never spent Christmas there. Maybe because doing so would have obliged her to shell out more than she was inclined to. Or because spending the holidays alone didn't bother her. My grandmother was too calculating to know the meaning of melancholy. Incapable of sadness, but not too cheerful either. That could be considered an advantage. Her attitude and virtues were those of a chameleon: she was observant, still, slow moving. If she saw something interesting, she could quickly strike, stretching her hand out the way a reptile stretches out its tongue. Unlike Scrooge, my grandmother never got a visit from the Ghost of Christmas Future telling her to reconsider her stinginess.

I remember there was one August, I would have been eight or nine years old, when we stopped in a bar in Despeñaperros and heard on the radio that members of the Lute gang were hiding out in Ciudad Jardín, where my grandmother lived. Afterward, my brother Lolo, who shared his name with Lute's brother, assigned us each a name of one of the goons from the gang. His name stayed the same; my other brother became Lute; my sister was Charo, and I was Toto. They found it hilarious that I had to take a dumb man's nickname.

I struggled to play along, consoling myself with the thought that it was better to be Toto than no one, but all the while, the notion that a band of gangsters was marauding around my grandmother's house terrified me. My grandmother had turned her precious house in Ciudad Jardín into a pension, with rooms in the attic and in the basement, and was perfectly happy to give lodging to whomever, as long as they paid in advance. Being the widow of a captain of the Civil Guard didn't mean she was a puritan or traditional, but you couldn't call her modern either. My grandmother was out of step with all times, not immoral, but amoral, with principles invariably subordinate to her own economic benefit, irrespective of any political or religious inclination. And so it wouldn't have been surprising to get a nod from the Lute gang as they crossed the salon on their way to the guest rooms. My father felt the same way, warning us about it from the first time we heard that the most infamous criminal gang in Franco's last years was wandering around his mother's neighborhood. He was sure, though, that if they paid even one day late, she would soon be threatening to call in the Civil Guard.

In his own way, my father inherited that absence of moral judgments, and he was absolutely fascinated by thieves. Years later, I had the chance to interview Eleuterio Sánchez, Lute, by then a free and cultivated man.

I told him how much my father had admired him, though out of respect, I held some things back, because what my father valued was not his extraordinary rehabilitation but the earlier part, the ups and downs of a small-time thug, a goon whose face was splashed across the front pages of the Franco-era newspapers thanks to his repeated escapes from the Civil Guard. My father, son of a captain, took the criminals' side as a rule, with a seemingly secret inclination to rule breaking, taking pleasure in the evildoing of others.

When we entered the city, my father would say: "Málaga."

Not:

"Now we're in Málaga."

His mind was full of words, and he would come up with titles for the different chapters of our lives. It was his way of telling us to appreciate what was before our eyes, and it impressed me deeply, because his verbless phrases made places desirable and worthy of admiration.

Despite the traumatic experience of carsickness and vomiting, I have good memories of those trips. Crossing Spain on country roads back then, you got to know the landscape, as if you were nosing in on someone's daily life or innermost secrets. There was a combined familiarity and the promise of adventure. A pastor in winter, wrapped in a blanket, raising his crook to greet us; a soldier hitchhiking, and my father giving him a lift toward his destination; a melon vendor who filled our trunk with melons; and endless little animals crossing our path as night drew on. If one of them had the bad luck to die under our wheels, my father would wrap it in a towel and hold on to it to cook it with rice. My father loved animals as much as he did hunting them. Now and then, he would stop next to a river and cast his line, and if it was summer, we'd sit down beside him: my siblings would put the bait on the hook and we would stay absolutely silent to keep from frightening the trout. We were children with few fixed desires, with few demands, repressed compared to others our age. Intimidated and fascinated by a presence—his—that made the atmosphere tense and led to sibling rivalries, with struggles and tattling.

We always stopped at the same bars. Maybe memory deceives me, but I recall people at the bar greeting us as if they recognized us from before. Or maybe it was just my father's attitude, the way he could jump right into a conversation, drawing on his stock of commonplaces and paying excessive attention to what others were saying, however hackneyed it was, provoking distrust at times in people not used to anyone paying attention to them. He would drink a brandy or two before getting back on the road, and we had the sense—and this would leave a mark on me—that talking with strangers eased the inevitable tension of family relations, which were complicated or constricted by the roles we'd been assigned since childhood.

I was intrigued by those eternally shuttered houses with their neon signs out in the middle of the fields. They seemed to have come straight from one of my fairy tales, warm refuges for children lost in the forest. If not, why would something so beautiful be standing in the middle of nowhere? *The Mermaid Club*, I said aloud, and my brothers laughed, and my father smiled and told them to keep quiet. And I got the sense, the way younger siblings often do, that words like that, like *The Mermaid Club*, concealed some mystery I would have to solve on my own.

We got to Málaga, and once we'd parked the car and I'd vomited on the sidewalk, I'd notice the sticky, dizzying scent of the orange blossoms decorating the courtyards in Ciudad Jardín. My mother would wipe me off with a towel, murmuring that her mother-in-law probably didn't have detergent. In my grandmother's garden stood the tallest tree in the neighborhood, and almost everyone was familiar with that big old house with that impressive araucaria. It's still standing today, though the house has lost its decadent charm, with its gravel lot and its redbrick pillars.

Doña Sagrario, *Doña* to everyone in the neighborhood, used to wait for us sitting down, very stiff, on her porch in her wicker chair. She was always there, vigilant, sincere, a *doña* to the core, armed with her big black fan. I often imagined her—I'm not making this up—with a rifle across her lap. I must have gotten this image from the Westerns we used to watch on Saturday afternoons, which often featured some toothless old man sitting on a rocking chair on a porch with a rifle. My grandmother had good teeth, but for me, she was that old man. I never felt she belonged to the female sex. Or to the male one, for that matter.

When we arrived, my father would parade us in front of her, nudging us to give her a kiss. She would remain impassive, with no indication she might hug us. This kiss was the only physical contact we would ever have with the woman with the fan.

As we approached, we never saw a rifle, but the fan was always there, and she waved it with a determination capable of doing away with anyone who threatened her property. My grandmother feared no one and would resort to violence if need be, never feeling an ounce of remorse. In a corner of that pretty gravel courtyard she watched over from her porch, my uncle Paquito would take quick, short, clumsy steps, feet turned out like a duck, walking round and round in a circle, sometimes clapping cheerfully. My uncle was in his thirties, but remained an eternal child, with pale skin and a tubby build, hair shaved (or maybe he was just bald), in a tank top and striped pajama pants, never properly dressed, destined as he was to live forever confined to the courtyard of his home. Fat and white, with a smile pasted on his boneless face, he reminded me of the Michelin Man.

Our presence overjoyed Paquito, and he would emit shrill shrieks that never quite turned into words. As long as we were there, he had a cheering section and playmates for his mysterious, solitary games, while the routines that helped him grasp the world were momentarily suspended. Paquito had never seen what lay beyond that gravel courtyard, or any other children, for that matter, besides us.

"Good old Paquito."

Good old Paquito, my father used to say. He'd kiss him twice on the head, resting his long arms on the milky shoulders of that big baby, his little brother. We would watch their strange encounter with curiosity: the astute, attractive, nervous brother who'd taken on the world on his own terms, and who suffered from the clumsiness common to big men, hugging a big slobbering baby who lived in a fenced-in, routine universe.

Paquito expressed his joy with guttural sounds, and would follow our games slowly and awkwardly. Then he'd get tired and go sit in a corner, crossing his legs like the Buddha, hitting his back against the wall over and over till he found peace. We gave him kisses too. Paquito was the lone angelic figure in a house otherwise immune to tenderness. You could always find him where you least expected to. Sitting alone and inscrutable in a chair in a bedroom; or you'd walk into the bathroom and he'd be standing there, striped pajama pants around his knees, paralyzed as if he didn't know what you were supposed to do after you pee, waiting for his mother to come help him, exposing guilelessly the one part of his body that revealed his true age.

Paquito was the Baby Jesus in that house, one of those oversized babies you see in Baroque paintings. He always dressed the same, his exposed arms the color of candle wax, verbally inexpressive, devoted to his indecipherable habits, respected the way you respect the child of God. My grandmother used to make up nasty names to call her children and grandchildren behind their backs, but not that child she gave birth to when she was already in her forties, he was always just Paquito. Paquito. She clearly respected her offspring, even if it never occurred to her to try and somehow stimulate him to communicate with others. God forbid anyone say something unpleasant or cruel about the boy. My father, to describe his mother's ruthlessness when she took justice into her own hands, told the story of how one time she heard the cleaning lady mock Paquito, so she grabbed her by the hair, and dunked her head into the mop bucket, nearly drowning her. My grandmother would listen along without interrupting, just nodding, and when my father got to the end, she smiled with a strange contentment, lowering the corners of her lips and pushing out her chin.

There were other stories that her children attested to: the one about the militiamen she chased out of the Civil Guard headquarters with a frying pan, because there was no one but women and children left inside; the one about the other servant she found stealing from her purse and choked until she confessed; and other ones I couldn't understand back then, because my father recounted them in a low tone, very abstractly and without verbs, calling his mother an expert "contrabandist." I didn't know what a contrabandist was. All I knew was my father spurned his mother's inclination to do deals under the table, and it was this rejection of dirty dealings that led him to avoid her so much as a child. That was the only trait of hers that repelled him. Not her beatings or her coldness. Something similar that happened when he was in the military pushed him away from his logical calling as an officer in the Civil Guard. Naively, he arrested someone he shouldn't have. His superiors upbraided and ridiculed him, and not knowing how to control his anger, he threw his tricorn hat to the ground. It was only thanks to my grandfather that he didn't go to jail. He often boasted that he'd never given in to the temptation to steal, even if he often had the chance. He admired gangsters because he was personally incapable of breaking the law.

We burst in upon the customs of that dark house of filthy odors and austere furnishings. After eating the famed packet of Artinata cookies, we were sent out to the courtyard. In the living room, there was nowhere for the children to play. If you stayed inside, it was to sit in a chair in the dining room and listen to endless stories about money or witness conflicts between the brothers that their mother seemed to provoke. She had a strange way of talking, failing to mention anything that didn't pertain to her finances, no matter how important it might be. She went to Mass early each morning, with the first ring of the bell, to ask God to intervene in her problems with the renters in her apartments or her guests at home. God clearly listened to the pleas of that mammonist, because that fortune she'd amassed through saving and scrimping never ceased to grow. If she crossed the bridge on her walk through Málaga at dawn on her way to church and saw a man who'd hanged himself from the railing, she would tell you about it the way most people would tell you it's a chilly morning outside. She wouldn't pause or suffer for the suicide's fate, she'd just carry on with her unvarying habits and her private conversation with God.

My father used to listen to her in silence, with a shy respect he reserved for no one else, except, perhaps, his company's head or its engineers, conceding her an unparalleled authority. That might have been a consequence of terror left over from childhood. My other uncles showed her the same suspect submissiveness. Armed with a glass of brandy in one hand and a cigarette in the other, they used to sit around their mother, inflamed by family conflicts I could never grasp, like three teenagers disputing a mother's love they'd never actually known. Paquito, sitting in his chair in the corner, smilingly revealed his alienation from all spite.

Now and again, a neighbor would interrupt their gathering, coins in hand, asking to use my grandmother's phone, one of the only ones in the neighborhood at the time. We didn't see it that way back then, but it's extraordinary how all those neighbors would talk in a near scream, the way people did in those days, about the most private of matters, arguing or saying sweet nothings with us right there next to them, forced to lower our voice out of respect for these people who had paid to talk. The men would use that time to refill their drinks and dream up the shows of devotion their mother demanded in exchange for money that would only materialize after her death.

I don't remember the pension's inhabitants well, but I do remember their comings and goings and the jokes my grandmother made about them. She told stories about a gay couple, "the butterflies," about a Manchegan businessman passing through, about some druggists who rented the basement for years, using it as a laboratory and inventing a syrup with more energizing properties than Ceregumil, the famous syrup from Málaga. I doubt it was a coincidence that so many oddballs came together in my grandmother's house. Her lack of interest in other people's lives attracted those who had something to hide.

———

One guest who caught my attention was a certain Fernando. He might have been thirty, but of course for me he was old. Looking back now, you couldn't really say clearly what age he was. Fernando was sanctimonious, a blessed bachelor, dressed like a seminarian in mufti, and he used to rub his hands together and smell his fingers in a way that was repulsive even to a child. He had thin hair, was neither tall nor short, neither handsome nor ugly, just the kind of person you can hardly remember five minutes after they've left the room. He did, though, have a conspicuous, soft way of talking, with a fine Andalusian accent that distinguished him from our noisy and vulgar neighbors in Ciudad Jardín.

Fernando was an Andalusian dandy. An Andalusian dandy who tried to pass himself off as a penitent rake. His story wasn't secret, my grandmother told it as soon as he walked out the door: he'd burned through an inheritance he had lucked into on his mother's side, and was kicked out of the family home for his profligacy. In a kind of makeshift restraining order, his father offered him a monthly allowance if he never had to set eyes on him again. Little Fernando, as my father called him, inspired in me a great deal of pity. I imagined him as an orphaned prince, disinherited and expelled from the court.

Fernando was a rich kid, a layabout, but there was something fastidious about him that intrigued us children, who couldn't grasp how strange he really was. I thought he was my grandmother's butler: he acted like an assistant or factotum. If my grandmother ordered him, *Fernando, make breakfast for my grandkids*, he would do so; she also sent him on errands, and you would see him returning home in his short-sleeved, white shirt with his pale, slender, hairless arms poking out, swift and diligent, shopping bag in hand. Three days into our stay, we'd just sit down at the table in the morning and wait for Little Fernando to bring us chocolate milk.

To the frustration of her sons and the bewilderment of her grandchildren, Fernando sometimes offered to buy my grandmother underwear, since he was going downtown anyway. A new pair, Doña Sagrario, I suppose it's about time. I couldn't imagine a man buying women's underwear, let alone Fernando buying the kind my grandmother wore, which I knew so well from seeing them hanging up every night on the shower rod: flesh-toned, enormous, recently washed and turned inside out to let the frilly part dry. When I went to pee before bed, I'd close my eyes to keep from seeing them, but in the end I could never avoid it, and in thrall to one of those morbid superstitions that tortured my mind, *If you don't do it, your mother will die*, I'd sometimes get up, kiss them, and run away.

My father used to laugh at Fernando. He thought he was a wimp, sexless or a repressed homosexual, clinging to an authoritarian grandmother from a need for protection or order. My father never said *repressed homosexual*, that wasn't the language of his time. Nor did he say *faggot*, at least not in front of us, but children understand these things perfectly, especially when their parents try to whisper them. Once or twice, I got the idea that he wasn't just gay, but was also my grandmother's lover, and so I, who had never gotten and never would get even the most minimal sex education, was forced to contemplate the unsettling image of those two human beings caressing each other or whispering loving words when they were alone.

My father used to laugh, to cackle about all this. Nothing could be more like his wily mother than forcing one of her renters to act as her servant. It was a swindle what my grandmother was doing, or not quite a swindle, rather the perks of the old woman's razor-sharp wits. After all, how had she made her fortune? Striking while the iron was hot, scheming, bending the law.

In his meek manner, Little Fernando became the go-to man for everything. He was the one to give my grandmother's medical update when her children called. It's not that my grandmother couldn't answer the phone: she just preferred to let Fernando handle it. She saw him as part imbecile, part angel descended from Heaven, and you had to admit it was something, taking care of an old women whose stiff, unemotional character made living with anyone else impossible. Little Fernando went to the bank, to the grocery store, accompanied her to the doctor, and if he made it home on time, would even go to Mass with her, very early in the morning, still in his white alpaca suit. Little Fernando went out every night until dawn, but my grandmother never informed her sons of that detail.

In 1973, my father took us around Spain. Our point of departure was Palma de Mallorca, where we lived at the time. I started vomiting on the boat during the night crossing and kept going across the Iberian Peninsula—my father had included Portugal in our adventure too. In photos, we seem to be in a bad mood, a little dirty, always in the same clothes, sitting on the hood as if to prove that we'd really made the journey by car.

The reason for including Portugal in our route, said my father when my mother was no longer around to confirm it, was to thank the Virgin of Fatima for the success of the open-heart operation my mother had undergone just a few months before. I was never aware that the trip was a pilgrimage of any kind, let alone one motivated by my mother's surgery. I doubted the Virgin could do more than the surgeon and I already had.

I remember her gossamer slenderness after the operation. She had bought jeans and blouses with flowers embroidered on the front, and in her fragility, she seemed rejuvenated, a new mother, with a girl's body, moving through the world with reserve, unsure of her place among the living. I can see her now, if I want, on Super 8 film, on a reel my brother found digging through my father's things. She looks like she's flying as she walks, more modern than I remember, with huge glasses that cover her small features and draw out her characteristic square chin. She is teetering on white platform shoes, patent leather, maybe, and she looks at the camera, at my father, with her new, grave face, the face from after the operation, the new character that overtook her, as if the scalpel had altered her heart's sentiment more than its physical substance.

We crossed Spain through Ayamonte to Málaga, envying the people we saw living their day-to-day lives in the villages we passed through, unconsigned to our nomadism, our existence constantly in flux because my father, no matter where he was, needed to feel he was just passing through. We reached Málaga as we did every summer, but by '73, we were starting to be different people. Because of my mother's illness, we'd had to go without her, while she was spending a few months in the hospital. We'd gotten used to what my father seemed incapable of, taking responsibility for a woman in extreme vulnerability. I'd started thinking magically. I had the tendency anyway, but my neuroses worsened when I thought I might lose my mother, and countless tics overtook me. But there were no diagnoses then, just crude character judgments: That girl's a lunatic.

I relieved my fears through mortifying repetitions: touching the ground three times, scratching the wall, winking, cutting the light off and on, staring at the sun or else looking backward while I walked. My mother was apprehensive as she observed these eccentricities and thought she could extirpate them through criticism, around people she could call me out in front of, making me feel ridiculous and weird. She couldn't imagine they were the consequence of an anxious character afraid that whatever security she knew was doomed to collapse. Carping about my conduct only made me cling tighter to these wearying routines when I was alone. Sometimes it takes half a lifetime to look at yourself with compassion. Fifty years—that's half a life. When I was fifty, I spoke with a therapist about my old childhood compulsions and how they worsened after my mother's operation. She listened attentively, with a knowing and comprehending smile, looking at my former self rather than my present one. Do you know, she asked me, how children can become prisoners to their obsessions? How tiring it is, how much time can a child waste trying to hold disaster at bay when they should be playing, enjoying, observing life unreflectingly and with joy?

I remember the afternoon I walked out of that session. I was alone, I would be alone the entire night. My husband was in New York writing a novel. I walked home, as in those old days, when I bore my solitude on foot. I walked from Chamartín to Cibeles, calmly, feeling the night fall over me. I wanted to remember who I'd been as a child, to touch my face as it had been then. I'd already used my memory that way before, I knew it from a strange experience I'd shared with a boy kidnapped and held for months in Colombia. In the unlit room where he was kept holed up, he would draw on his life from before, imagining conversations with his parents, his friends. He tried to recall them literally, gesturing along; he recollected entire days of freedom, using memory rather than speculation. He reproduced these scenes from the past with extraordinary detail. He told me this was what kept him from going insane.

When your life is filled with too many absences too early, you have to try to keep from losing faces and voices to the fog of memory. Photos aren't enough. You have to concentrate on rescuing those moments teetering on the verge of oblivion. They say forgetting is healthy for the brain, but what if you're afraid of losing the few things your memory conserves? I hate how lazy minds turn people into the heroes of three or four cherished stories and that's enough to reconcile with their memory and make us believe we are keeping them alive. However painful, however obsessive this is, for years, I've been trying to hear the timbre of my mother's voice, her whispery way of singing, her peculiar gait, her smile. I struggle with moments my memory censored because they were too heartrending, but there's no point in ignoring them. I wish I could control the pain some episodes produce in me, but I'm more afraid of the past vanishing. There are traumas that come not from a single brutal experience, but flare up slowly and form part of our character. If I erase my trauma, will the years of my childhood vanish?

———

Suddenly, transported by the state of mind my long steps brought about, I saw myself so clearly, I thought I could take the girl I was by the hand, splitting in a way I never had before. I felt so close to her that I could smell myself, smell the sweat of that child upset because her obsessions barely let her live. I passed my hand through her short, stiff hair, stroked her face with its snub nose and the chin always raised a bit, ready for something; I looked into those big, melancholic, slightly downturned eyes, the mouth with the little scar on the bottom lip, the robust, gentle, cinnamon-colored body, seeming sunburned no matter what the time of year, the belly that wouldn't flatten out till adolescence. Still walking, I took that child in my arms. Come here, you ugly little thing, I said. With a strange feeling of tenderness, I became my own mother, giving myself the protection that had been stripped away by the need to become a caregiver at nine years of age, a girl who thought she was capable of saving her mother from pain and that depression she fell into as she held her daughters' hands so they could pull her up or she could take them down with her forever.

Lost in thought, I felt I was watching my rescue after a life unguarded. My meeting with myself was private, no one else would ever witness it. Who could I tell about it? I walked all the way home with the girl I used to be.

We were other people on that trip south in '73. My brothers were teenagers. They squandered their energy in fights that ended with one standing on the other's neck. My sister read in solitude, and I wandered around the yard in Málaga imagining my grandmother had died and everything there was mine. Paquito was old and wrinkled. Hairless, he kept walking in circles around the araucaria until, like a dog, he found a place to sit down and rock. My father tried to find some point in common, something to tie together all those private yearnings and that aloofness, wanting us to believe, as we had as kids, that his choice was the best for us. But by then, we were skeptical. We were staying with a woman who'd balked at lending us money for my mother's operation. A million pesetas we needed. And my mother, forced to be there, to play the good daughter-in-law, was reserved, with a hushed but evident rancor.

Fernando went on setting out our breakfast. It seemed so natural, we nearly forgot there was a time when it was otherwise. He served us, picked up afterward, and went diligently out to run errands. I don't know where he ate. He was like a cat, subtle and elusive.

You might find him anywhere in the house, and that kept you on alert, fearing Fernando or Paquito might pop out and frighten you. Them or one of the other weirdos who lived there.

Those summer days in Málaga made me dream of my inheritance from my grandmother. She inflamed us with her promises and the way she blackmailed her sons when they conversed, and though I didn't know what it would feel like when I eventually became rich, I had read enough literature, high and low, to want my future wealth to be not just abundant, but also full of beauty, sensuality, enthusiasm, adventure, with fewer trips by car and lots of long breakfasts in bed. I didn't see the point of an affluence that reproduced my grandmother's stinginess. My mother used to try to drag my father to the beach bars in El Palo to avoid the indecipherable food my grandmother made us. She always kept a pot on the stove with chunks of meat, of doubtful provenance, my mother said. She called it *odds and ends*. At lunchtime, my grandmother would portion out those odds and ends, flinging them at my brothers' plates as if they were dogs that had to jump up and fetch them. She never threw me any odds or ends, and that saddened me, even if the odds and ends themselves I found repulsive.

My father laughed, trying to downplay her barbaric manners, but in my mother's face, her ecstatic smile,

her beauty, her delicacy, her dignified rancor, I learned
to distinguish between elegant and coarse.

The perennial conversations about money were
now punctuated by dense, wounding silences, fruit of
this hard, unfeeling old woman's refusal to lend my father money for his wife's surgery. In the course of her
never-ending recovery, my mother permitted herself a
resentment she had previously suppressed; that huge
scar that split her torso from top to bottom gave her the
strength not to fake it any longer, and her silence was a
constant, unsettling reproach.

Little Fernando appeared promptly at sunset.
With the lights left off, the shadows in the room would
thicken from the smoke my father exhaled, and maybe
his brother too. His costume for the evening had a
dazzling appearance in the dark salon as he waited,
yearning to discreetly step out. Little Fernando's bright
alpaca suit shimmered like water when the last ray of
sunlight fell on its fabric. It was uncertain whether this
image clashed with his morning nature or whether the
man who set our breakfast out was the imposter. When
he left, the adults would say a polite goodbye. And once
you heard the gate creak, my grandmother would say
dryly and unemphatically, as always with her outrages,
that she'd once had to slap him across the face, when he
gambled away at the casino the monthly allowance his
father had sent him. She said she'd do it again if need

be. Afterward, Fernando repented and fell to his knees before her, begging for the old woman's forgiveness.

A firm hand was what that boy needed, she and her children agreed, and he'd found it under the tutelage of an old maid who could tolerate any vice except wastefulness.

Paquito died a few months later, the same way he had lived, retiring and innocent, never uttering a word, with no idea that his inability to suck in a breath was a prelude to death. We didn't go to the funeral, and we never returned to that house.

My father, incapable of managing a house full of teenagers, called my grandmother to come enforce order after my mother's death. She arrived one morning in the company of Fernando, who arranged her clothing in the closet before returning to Málaga. Her presence was unsuited to our apartment in Madrid. It was as if she didn't fit in the hallway, as if she might get stuck there, and you'd run into her there one night on your way to the bathroom. I tried not to cross her path, which was easy, because you could tell she was coming by her deep, sonorous gasping. I couldn't help but see myself as an orphan at the mercy of an old woman who would do anything she could to chill my father's feelings for me. I was the one who spent the most time at home, and I was apprehensive and unstable and terrified of being alone under the same roof as her. Her presence seemed to snuff out the light of my mother's memory. Away from her world of guests, neighbors, and tenants, she sighed constantly, like a wild animal in a cage. One fine day, she said she couldn't bear us anymore, and she left. I don't remember what nickname she gave me, just the ones she gave my cousins, but I did hear her tell my father she didn't like me: *I don't care for the way she's always looking down*, she said, *that girl gives me a bad feeling.*

Just over a year later, my father remarried. My mother had said he would: *He's going to marry a blonde.* And he did, but a blonde in the same way any woman who wants to can be blonde. My siblings drifted away, for one reason or another, while I stayed home, pretending to study, though I spent my days wandering around with a boyfriend I convinced to skip work and go along with my indolent routines. My life was floating off toward who knows where. I had no goals, no vocation, no will. I wrote bad poems on an Olivetti, not thinking much about them, on my father's stationery, with his name in the left-hand corner. My poems, my father's name. The typewritten letters gave them a professional look, and these works revealed a previously unknown political awareness. In the main, though, I just wasted time. If most adolescents are on the lookout for ways to satisfy their sexual urges, I was in the prior stage, trying to find and identify some trace of that desire to then fulfill it. I had started a degree, but I rarely showed up at school. Like an office worker, I'd go out to have a coffee at midmorning with my boyfriend, pulling him away from his work to make him a party to my laziness, and every day I promised myself I'd break free from that all-consuming sloth. I'd come across some old classmate who'd turned to dealing drugs, or else a friend of my mother's who'd look at me with unconcealed grief, thinking she had the right to pity me.

My father would come home every day to have lunch with me. For that brief period, he'd put on his pajamas. Estrella, our eternal maid, would prepare our meal. He had kept her on because he wanted to retain some order in the house, even if I was the only one who still slept there. After coffee, he would laze about briefly before leaving with his new wife, apparently free of regrets. His wife, platinum blonde in the way any woman who wants to be can be, was kind to me, and despite my mother's insistent pleas from the beyond that fidelity demanded I boycott their marriage, I ended up appreciating her. My aunts trained me not to love her, but I did.

When my father left, I'd stay behind, mistress of the house, unable to put a name to all that I was feeling, the hateful solitude, the hopelessness, but also relief, because the period of illness and death was over. Alone, like a retired adolescent unsure what to do with herself, vexed by a formless mass of time I couldn't manage to put in order, I wondered if I might gather the strength to finish a few vague poetic projects, or if that talent that had barely shown its head would eventually come to nothing.

One afternoon, while my father was putting on his suit jacket and slipping his tie into his pocket, a classic gesture that was entirely his own, the phone rang. I answered, and on the other line was a voice from beyond the grave. What I mean is I'd erased this voice, my grandmother's, from my mind, like one of those actors you suppose dead because they've vanished from the screen, and then you're surprised one day to see their obituary in the newspaper. My father had realized his mother was unredeemable, and he was the only one who ever went south to see her, and I assume he called her once a week. The nearly dead woman asked, "Is your father there?" and I passed him the phone, realizing later that as I did so, I looked down in that way she always hated and that gave rise to a nickname I never learned.

My father spoke with her. He asked how she was, and then fell silent, staring at the floor. He asked me to bring him a chair. He sat down, listening, face resting on the palm of his hand, like a child pondering a problem he'll never solve. When he hung up, he told me he had to go to Málaga the next day. I knew it wasn't her health. I guessed—what else?—it had something to do with his inheritance.

During the years when my grandmother had disappeared from our lives, our conversations, and our memories, Fernando was the one who took care of her. Her sons relinquished to him a mother they couldn't get along with. This accord worked splendidly for all involved: the man whose father had ordered him to stay away from his family home redressed his orphanhood through an old woman who gave his life order. In their way, they were like a common-law couple, with a relationship founded on a trust no one could compete with. He listened to her, happily looked after her investments, accompanied her to the doctor, bought her panties, handled her paperwork and domestic duties. That he remained a tenant, paying for a room rented

by the month, seemed like another grift from that de-
crepit vampire determined to turn a profit from every
personal relationship.

But Fernando, that enigmatic, feline man we
watched scurry off in his alpaca suit every night during
the summer of '73, hadn't wasted his time. With the
patience of a scrupulous counterfeiter, Fernando had
besought little loans from his protector. When Doña
Sagrario had slapped him across the face, he hadn't
changed his ways, rather the contrary, and the thought
that she could improve or reform him convinced her
to go on supporting him. She thought she held the
reins, while all along he'd taken his time and observed
her from up close. Astutely, he'd detected the one vice
stronger than her will: greed. Not only did Fernando
not stop going to the casino, he tricked her into giving
him money to gamble with. Naturally, he gave her the
lion's share of his winnings. And they must have won at
first, and instead of slaps in the face, there was jubila-
tion. And then, as always, statistics must have won out,
and so they lost and lost and kept on betting to make
up their losses. I don't know how many mortgages she
took out on her apartments before getting to the beautiful house in Ciudad Jardín that was supposed to be
mine once everyone died. In those years, my grandmother had disappeared from our lives and seemed lost

in some beyond before the phone call that afternoon that revealed everything.

My father tried to catch the rogue, but he'd vanished along with her money. The casino in Marbella had banned him, and that was the last thing anyone knew. They tried to pursue an embezzlement charge, to get his brothers to pay some of what he'd swindled, but it had all been perfectly legal: the old woman was in her right mind; she'd spent a life of sacrifice and greed, scheming and scraping to amass a small fortune, and toward the end, she'd tried to make it grow by putting herself in a grifter's hands.

Hot on the villain's trail, my father found out that Fernando had a record. In his youth, he'd gotten away with selling laboratory equipment belonging to the University of Valencia, and had gone on to commit several other felonies, destroying people's lives without leaving behind a trail.

My grandmother died soon afterward. Once she could no longer talk about money, the blood congealed in her veins. Later, my father, a whiz with numbers, managed to square her debts. I don't know who went to her funeral or what cemetery it was in or if she's buried next to my grandfather or Paquito. I never asked. My father swore that when he and his brothers were standing by her coffin before it was lowered into the ground, a nail shot out of the wood, and the other two men stepped back in terror. He cracked up when he told the story, but if it was really true, I thought, he would have been the first to take off running, from fear of the dead in general and the special dread his mother provoked in him.

My uncle Angelito called one Holy Thursday to tell my father to hurry and turn on the TV: he'd spotted Fernando chanting with a chorus of Benedictine monks. The hood covered part of his face, but those inimitable, timid eyes had to be his. He's trying to pass himself off as a monk, my uncle said, taking for granted that this new identity was also a farce. My father didn't see him; maybe the camera didn't turn back toward him, but we all found something fitting in this new profession, and were certain he was hiding out in some monastery pretending to be a friar.

We never thought about our inheritance during the years when my grandmother was dying, but knowing that the money was gone extinguished a dream that stoked our childhood fantasies. There would be no inheritance. Surprisingly, the end of this saga, which my mother would surely have relished, gave rise to no resentment on my father's part. His whole life, he'd been strangely lenient about his mother's behavior. Why did he protect her from our barbs if she always treated him so coldly? Why did he joke about her cruelty instead of trying to understand it? Maybe to avoid the terrible conclusion that the person who brought him into the world and was meant to love him unconditionally hadn't even been capable of love.

I wouldn't say the loss of that money made me rethink my indolence, my lack of motivation, but it did make me realize I should be earning something, not to save it, but to spend. I'd been raised to think the opposite, to be strict, to scrimp, but I wanted cash in my pocket so I could blow it. And strangely enough, I got the chance. Through my sister, I met a guy who was teaching a broadcasting workshop. I told him I was studying journalism, and he invited me on board. While it lasted, I'd go to the studio on Calle Huertas, enthralled with the subject and relieved to be skipping class. When it ended, I stayed on the radio. On the radio and at the nearby bars. They paid me next to nothing, and I spent what I made without ever leaving Calle Huertas. Later, after I'd learned the basics and they'd given me a raise, I spent that too. My father was proud. He had blind if basically unjustified faith in me. From time to time, he'd insinuate that I'd inherited his mother's initiative.

I hated that. I didn't want to resemble my bad grand-mother in any way. If his mother had a talent for mak-ing money, I used my ingenuity spending it.

I've found something I wrote about my first days on the radio:

I first went on the radio at six in the morning one spring day in 1981. I took the doorless, jerky freight ele-vator to the eighth floor of the building. There, in that makeshift editing room, where I saw someone writing now and again, Izaguirre, my boss, a gigantic Cuban exile, was waiting: he handed me a huge pair of scissors and supervised me while I clipped out stories from the newspapers we would read on-air. I adopted his accent from a childish urge to please, so we recited the local news in the tones of Havana. After the first mission of my life as a journalist was over, I went downstairs and had the first coffee and pastry of my career in El Diario, a bar on Calle Huertas. There, between taxi drivers and deliverymen, I watched the sun rise, and leaning my elbows on the zinc bar, I felt like a big-time professional reporter.

My grandmother's vanished legacy, her brutal avarice, dragged me up out of idleness. To go on being a spend-thrift, I had no choice but to make money.

POPPY

Across the blackness that came over my eyes
I see the flickering light of these words even now:
"And Jesus said unto him, Verily
I say unto thee, To-day thou shalt
Be with me in paradise."

EDGAR LEE MASTERS
Spoon River Anthology

There are souls that have
Blue stars,
Parched mornings
In the leaves of time,
And chaste corners
That harbor an old
Rustling of nostalgia
And dreams.

FEDERICO GARCÍA LORCA

I have no memories, no past, before my life in the Sierra. I'm the girl who arrived here. Its name means poor, the Sierra Pobre. I don't remember any trees being here in 1966. The mountains that hugged the immense wound of the dam were gray and stripped bare. At first, there were no children either. It was a solitary summer, and wind and sun alike burned you. Behind the house was a brutal precipice that descended to the reservoir. Dad didn't let us go close to it, but when he left for work, we kids all got on our bikes and rode down to the edge. They had fun riding me on the handlebars and submitting me to the so-called Chinese Torture, jerking the grips back and forth and skidding until it seemed we would tumble down the gulley. I was attracted by my playmates' bravery and grit, but I always wound up crying. I never said a word, I knew what we were doing was forbidden, and that if I spoke up, Dad would slap the other kids and they would call me a snitch. I already had a reputation as a tattletale, so I kept my mouth closed even when I shouldn't have. After a few days, some workers came and put up a fence. The same fence you're now peering over more than fifty years later.

I was impatient for more girls to come, because my sister Inma kept her nose in her books and my brothers, Chechi and Lolo, couldn't play without getting into a fight. But sometimes, when there were no other boys around, Chechi would be nicer, and take me to explore the hills around the village. The newly installed streetlights quivered when you touched them, and we used to dare each other to touch them and feel the current. Electroshock, we called this, and no one could get out of it. My brother used to go around with a glass jar looking for snakes, grasshoppers, beetles, and any other creature that could be found crawling through the arid brush, and I would watch, scared but riveted, hugging my doll tight. Occasionally he ventured down to the Lozoya River and left me sitting there on a rock, watching him intrepidly descend that slope, sometimes crawling on all fours like an animal, down a narrow trail he had discovered. If I lost sight of him, I'd get scared he wouldn't return. I didn't know how long I was supposed to wait before telling Mamá he was gone. He always showed back up with a triumphal smile and a treasure, some critter he would try unsuccessfully to tame.

The village seemed purpose-built to hold a scale replica of civilization in all its shame and glory, like a Noah's ark stranded in the mountains. Its inhabitants occupied a place assigned according to their status: barracks for the single laborers, cramped apartments for those with children, detached houses for mid-level managers—we lived in one of these—and big houses for the engineers. At the top of the settlement, almost touching the sky, was a cross, grave and unadorned, crowning the humble church whose lone concession to frivolity were a couple of chichi stained-glass windows. The school—two rooms where every child studied till age sixteen—stood flush with this little house of God. From the highway you took to get here this morning, the village seemed like nothing more than an insignif-icant white dot on one of the shelves of the mountain, but back then, remember, when we got home after a rough ride on rocky roads, we had the sense that life in that village with no history and an uncertain future was as vibrant and intense as in the big city.

We were pioneers in the reservoir. The other children didn't start showing up until near summer's end. They arrived the same way we did, in a modest car trailing a huge moving van that wove dangerously over the steep and badly paved roads that still didn't have guard-rails. The children—soon to be my friends—came behind their sofas, beds, toys, and appliances, with their mothers—around fifteen of them, women of resilient and vigilant character—and, eventually, the swings, which we saw put up in the town square with immense expectation, with the almost scholarly attention typical of old people who notice a new building or some other change in their neighborhood. Around the playground with its beds of gravel, we formed friendships, and when suspicion and envy poisoned them, our mothers had to beat them out of us, unless we confined them to quiet conversations at night. Peace among the children in that tiny park depended a great deal on those women.

I don't know if Mamá was weak, but she always seemed so to me. She emanated a fragility—not physical, but inward—that I could never explain but that must have been evident enough, because my neighbors and aunts treated her as if she might shatter at any moment. I noticed this with apprehension, and any pain she ever felt, from a simple cold to a burn in the kitchen, filled me with a deep sensation of insecurity, a foretaste of disaster.

———

One evening, Mamá and Papá went to El Atazar, the village that gave its name to the dam, to look for a woman, a shepherdess by trade, who they'd been told could help them out around the house. Her hometown was visible from where we lived, tucked away in the valley like one of those distant hamlets in a nativity scene, put there to give a sense of perspective. Chechi and I spent the whole afternoon sitting on a rock and thinking if we looked closely enough, we would see our parents' car go down the hill. Chechi had asked for binoculars for Christmas for the very purpose of keeping guard.

They returned at nightfall with María in the back seat. In my eyes, María was a woman, but she couldn't have been older than seventeen. She was a goatherd who'd lost her mother, and she was timid and especially fearful around men, because her father drank and vented his rage on her with horrible beatings. When she heard Dad's proposition, she didn't hesitate: she jumped into the car with a change of clothes and the bed linens she had started sewing for her wedding, even though she still didn't have a boyfriend. Papá sealed the deal with her father, and María was ours. Things were like that back then. María didn't talk much—she wasn't used to conversing—and she always had a smile on her face.

She was pretty, even delicate, given the hard life she'd lived. She had a precious head of abundant, curly hair that cascaded down her back, and her body was bony, fibrous, the body of someone who'd grown up sleeping in the cold, watching the sunrise in the open air, communing with the stars and her dead mother.

She never watched the TV, because moving images made her woozy, but she liked me to go to the kitchen and tell her what the movies were about. I used to pester her, *Come on, there's nothing to worry about,* but something about the device scared her, like she thought the characters would jump out and grab her. That's what she said, anyway. I don't remember much of my past before her. Just those first days of solitude and discovery, when there weren't any other children there and the fence hadn't been built, or the afternoon when we stared down in the village waiting for the herder girl to come. María liked to play with the children, chasing them around, and she'd laugh when she knocked them over and held them down on the ground. The country girl she'd been came out at those times, the person she still was, really, even if she liked sitting next to the radio in the kitchen and drifting off into pensive ecstasy. The voices and songs on the radio were the only shelter she'd known since she was a girl.

———

By the time school started, I was a legendary figure in the village. A mix of derring-do and innocence led me to ring each doorbell of every house and ask when all the children would arrive. I see myself now at five years old, ringing the doorbell to a house my father had told me three girls were supposed to move into. Mamá was shy, and told me not to be a bother; Dad was expansive, and encouraged me to go make friends. For a month, I went out every day, full of stubborn hopes. The lady of the house invited me in, and we talked in the kitchen, where she set out milk and cookies. A prisoner in my role as the youngest daughter, I found freedom in this conversation with an adult: I could express opinions and observations without fear I'd be made fun of—that's always the most painful thing for the child who's last in line. A precocious talker, and surely a pretentious one too, I aroused curiosity and tenderness in that mother waiting for her daughters to arrive. Then they did, and they listened to me no less charmed, and fought over which of them was really my friend. I don't know the origins of this allure, this unexpected popularity.

Mamá was jealous of my relationship with this other mother. I could tell instinctively, the way children grasp this kind of reality. Everyone in our house was jealous, and this made the atmosphere permanently tense. Our place in the family tree was so conclusively

assigned that all of us yearned to escape ourselves and
be someone else.

There was no knowing what living in that village
meant before winter. The mountains turned grayer
and the clouds came so close, it seemed you were walking among them. I learned to read and write early,
but I'm not sure how, because I barely went to school
that first year. Mamá couldn't stand seeing me all little
and struggling against that cold, of a kind she'd never
known. I'd spend the mornings at home, giving classes
to my dolls, teaching them all the things they didn't
know; and when lunchtime came, I'd wait for the girls
less fortunate than I to show up in the square so I could
join their games, never explaining my absences.

At first, the snow brought the children a splendid
promise: of shelter, serenity, and a change of routine.
School would close, and we'd spend the whole day in
our pajamas. I lived the life of the boy from the only
story I owned, *The Paper Doll*, who had a fever, as I
often did, and was bored and cranky, and cut a paper
doll out of one of his mother's books. The doll came
to life and took him off on extraordinary adventures.
In the end, it turned out to be a dream, it usually does
when hijinks turn dangerous, but it was a sweet dream

for the little boy, whose homebound reveries were so much like my own. An apprentice Don Quixote, I cut out my own paper doll, thinking it would wake and carry me up to the stars, as in the book. The snow was a fitting landscape for this kind of illusion. Magic silence inundated the Sierra, coating the gray countryside, bundling it in a white blanket. But the snowplows, the trucks, the endless activity of the bustling workers, turned much of it to mud flats and stole away the enchantment. In rubber boots, the children returned to school as a flock.

The school was uphill from the houses. We had to climb to get there. In the winter, it was night by the time class ended. The children who lived in houses would walk down together in tight groups, protecting each other like sheep gone astray, leaving behind the workers' kids to return to their apartments. Dad said some mothers liked this rigid segregation. They saw it as conferring status, and were thankful for the separate plazas and pools for the sons and daughters of men of different means. Dad never tired of insisting we go play with the other kids. He hated people who put on airs. He also hated those who were a step above him. His lack of formal studies meant he'd struggled since his teenage years, and even in his commendable position, he knew there were other jobs he could never aspire to. He had a knack for numbers, and certificates from the various schools he'd attended as the itinerant son of a Civil Guard, living hand to mouth. Civil engineers were his bêtes noires. He hated engineers. When I was around, he talked about them softly and in code, because he knew I was a danger: I learned early on that the easiest way to hold an adult's drifting attention was to repeat something my parents had talked about at home. Besides, they thought I was a snitch. They shut up around me, but I spied on them, hiding behind the living room door at night and seeing their shadows on the sofa lit up by the television's glow. My father drinking, cigarette smoke settling over him like fog in the darkness, my father talking, always talking, with words and with his hands, analyzing the fine details of the dam project, the promotions, the miseries, the work stoppages, repeating his colleagues' last names, the same last names as the children at school. The next day, if it wasn't so cold and my mother had decided I could safely attend class, I'd tell the teacher during recess some phrase I'd overheard so she would give me a potato chip from her bag. The crunching sound she made when she ate her chips made me slobber like a dog; she'd look straight ahead, ignoring me, but then prick up her ears at some detail, often invented to appear more interesting and assure me of my reward. If these schooltime conversations reached my parents' ears, the punishment was severe. Lolo started calling me the Gossip Queen of Atazar. I began to imagine some engineer would come to our house one day and kick us out of the village, and it would be my fault: I had a deep sense of guilt, the kind that can cripple a child, but the engineer never came. Their reprimands worked for a while, but then I would open my big fat mouth again. That's just me—now what about you?

Dad was contemptuous of those who'd had it easy, daddy's boys who'd gotten everything handed to them. He was suspicious of university degrees, almost as a rule, and hated idlers, bigwigs, and anyone else he had to bow to every day in that segregated universe. In the privacy of home, where he reigned like a beloved leader, he would stew over his revulsion for authority.

He was paternal with his workers but servile with those above him. He dodged the humiliation of obeying by bragging about his achievements. It wasn't his intention, but he taught me to disobey. From the time I was little I just had to follow my whims. That may be one reason I didn't have to work as hard as my brothers.

Dad was a bit of a braggart. Or just a braggart, period. He'd had no one but himself until Mamá came along, and then us, and he saw us as an achievement that reaffirmed him and made him a man. We were his identity. He often said he'd have liked to have eight, nine, ten children, a battalion at his orders, with him playing the feudal lord, but mother couldn't keep giving birth. He liked to tell us about his adventures as an untamed boy, pulling away from his mother's cruel hand and running off, dodging beatings from his aunt in Madrid when he was nine, winding up in the English hospital in Río Tinto at twelve because he'd fallen down an embankment running from a goat he was playing bullfighter with. He liked to boast of his disobedience, how he'd started smoking when he was twelve, how a boy from the seminary had touched him on the shoulder and he'd given him one in the kisser, how he was the first one to jump in if there was trouble, but this song and dance about his dauntlessness didn't stop him from reigning over us with an iron fist; he didn't make excuses for it or offer explanations, and seemed blind to the inconsistency of his position, as though he believed he was the one and only boy in the history of the world who would ever have a right to get into trouble.

He was deprived of so much because of a firm conviction on his mother's part: that he was smart enough—and he was—to make his way alone. This made him resentful, bitter, and that came out in his arbitrary, illogical character. He prided himself on being a model father, but his example was far from instructive. He knew how to give orders and how to love, but in an intense, roughshod way that was sometimes elating and other times unfair. When my sister failed math, he bought a chalkboard, the same size as the one in the classroom, and hung it in the entryway that summer. He made my brothers sit with my sister, thinking that it wouldn't hurt them to get a jump start on the next year's lessons, and I went along too, very diligent with my notebook and pencil, though I had no idea what I was supposed to write down. Other children from the village square also came, and like attentive students, we set out our chairs in rows of two. Summer afternoons, and him writing equations on the chalkboard. Cigarette in hand, pants drooping, chalk sliding around on the slate, making numbers that looked like letters, letters that looked like numbers, and combinations of letters and numbers that looked like hieroglyphics. When he finished, he would ask us: "Understand?" And the same dense silence floated in the entryway as in a classroom when no one can jump in to save the rest. "Nobody gets it?" he would ask, incredulous. And, reliable as always, I would raise my hand. "I do." The children would laugh. Lolo would whisper, "Ass-kisser," and Dad would return to the charge with another puzzle, striking and inscrutable, that struck me as the fruit of inspiration. He would look at us, then briefly and admiringly at his work, incapable of any explanation that would clear up the mystery. Then he'd walk off, saying, "That's it, we'll try more tomorrow."

I can say in all honesty that they loved each other then. The amorous tension was palpable, and had nothing to do with us, but they never declared their love. People back then didn't say *I love you*, and they didn't kiss on the lips, or at least never in front of their children. Anyway, Dad was the classic bon vivant who acted like a puritan at home. When people kissed in movies on the TV, he would turn it off. My parents had less of a social life than the other couples in the village, who would go to the club at night for a drink. Maybe it was because Dad was jealous, pathologically so, and he couldn't have taken one of his colleagues offering my mother some token affection. The engineers and priests were the most dangerous, because if things got out of hand, he'd struggle to stand up to these authorities. He was frightened of priests, who supposedly snuck into men's houses when they were away to "take confession" from their wives. He was obsessed with that. He would bring it up from time to time, telling Mamá quietly the name of some woman who had *taken confession* in private. I know all this because I heard it, but I can't remember the words used or how I could grasp something so distant from the world of my childhood. These mad stories of betrayal and infidelity swirled constantly through his mind, and sometimes his obsessions grew contagious. This one in particular unsettled me: I couldn't imagine what a priest would do with a woman, or a mother with her husband's coworker, but I became aware of the profound significance of *obscenity* long before I learned the word.

Dad ate and talked at the same time, as if one side of his mouth was reserved for food and the other for words. In his delirium, he may have thought that by presenting my mother with these tales of aberration, he could nip temptation in the bud. His paranoia would have been comical if the threat of infamy and betrayal weren't so real to him. You could see Mamá there, ignoring his dark side with a measure of irony, busy with her domestic routine, almost cloistered off from everything but her family; always waiting for that gruff, handsome man. The balance of power was asymmetrical, and you could feel the latent peril Mamá suffered through. She had deep roots in her people and land, and she had left her village to marry a drifter with no real sense of warmth. She was prudent and timid, and he was her only proper contact with the reality of their new, nomadic life, passing through cities and villages—Tétouan, Cádiz, Málaga, Ciudad Real, Guardamar del Segura, Tarragona, Buitrago—so fast that she never got used to the shifting landscape and had to make do with a window where she watched her children come home from school. He was a blowhard, and never admitted how afraid he was that all this could disappear.

So they loved each other. With the dangerous love of unequals. She loved him more than life, more than us, and put up with his fits and injustice. Dad used to lock the bedroom door at night, and I would knock and knock and no one would answer. I never understood why they turned their backs on me. Eventually, bored and wounded, I would go to bed.

You didn't know what life in the village was until it got so cold it burned your face. At seven in the morning, when it was still dark, I'd hear the racket of trucks full of workers headed to the job site from my bed. Winter left the roads nearly impassably muddy, and in summer the traffic raised huge clouds of dust. *María*, the men would shout, meaning our María, because one of the men had fallen in love with her and the workers had gotten into the habit of shouting her name to the four winds. Their shouts grew indistinct as the trucks rounded the corner, *Maríaaaaa*, but a trace of sound would float awhile in the air, like a vapor trail behind a plane. María hated them turning her name into a joke and everyone knowing that someone was courting her. If we brought it up, she'd smack us on the neck. At that same hour, you could also hear the boring machines shaking the earth. The dam was always present, with those horrifying noises that sounded like the mountain might split in two and the frequent accidents the workers sometimes lost their lives in. I knew Dad wouldn't get killed by a high-tension cable or crushed under some load, but it horrified me one solemn Sunday afternoon when a worker came to inform us of a death and my father had to leave to notify the man's wife.

The monumental, perilous labor of building a dome set on its side to restrain the flow of water combined with my father's irrational fears: of storms that would make him unplug the appliances and force us to hole up in one room while the sky darkened over; of winds that roared like a hurricane and rose up violently without warning, like the one that caught me on my way home from my friends' house. At seven, I was nearly weightless, and I felt it lifting me off the ground, and I cried and grabbed onto a manhole cover in front of my house. I shouted for Dad, but couldn't hear my own voice, and I lay on the ground and waited for him to notice I wasn't home. Alarmed by the howling wind, Dad stepped out onto the porch and saw me stretched out at the top of the steps, hands clutching the ring of the manhole lid. I saw him come running, pants whipping backward to reveal the outline of his long, bony legs. He picked me up and squeezed me to his chest, as if he, too, feared the wind would carry me away. From that day forward, I thought he could hear my thoughts.

His fear of heights never went away entirely on that house overlooking the abyss. His fear that we'd get lost or drown. That the night would swallow us up on our way home from the neighbor's. Dad's fears stifled him. Not even he realized the effort it took to maintain his reputation as a man of bravery. Sometimes he smothered his fears by lashing out. He would fly into a rage to relieve himself of some ancient fear whose origins we knew nothing about. You remember, of course you do, that time he hit Inma because some friends took her off exploring and brought her back later than expected. As soon as it started getting dark, there he was standing on the corner, walking to the bend every now and then to see if any lights were approaching in the distance. He took long strides, he was terrified. What would he do if he lost her? I watched him in dread and expectancy, wanting to be with him, feeling how his nerves overpowered him. At last, the car appeared, and Inma got out, smiling and innocent. She was barely twelve years old. He motioned for her to finish her goodbyes and walked with her into the house. He took her to the bedroom and throttled her. She cried, she didn't know what she'd done wrong, and I ran back and forth from the bedroom to the kitchen, where Mamá was, but I was disconsolate because she wouldn't say a word.

I don't know if that was the first time, but that night I scratched the wall close to my bed. I scratched it, it set my teeth horribly on edge, but I kept going. If I did it three times and then three more times, that would never happen again. When I thought the ritual was done, I went and got in bed with my sister. We slept snuggled together, the way animals sleep in the open to stay alive.

Inma was the first to go off to boarding school, then Lolo, and by the third year, all three of my siblings were gone. I was jealous, because I thought their lives were more exciting than my own, but at the same time I enjoyed being an only child, coddled by my parents, who would never have a small child at home again. Inma stayed in a neighboring village, Torrelaguna. In my imagination it was a big city. On Friday afternoons, I would wait anxiously for her, because she always brought me a gift from the kiosk, a picture of flowers or maybe a book of cutouts. She told me how cold it was in the dormitories, it gave her chilblains on her feet, and there were horrible nuns at her school who made the girls shower with cold water. In our house, which the newfangled heating system kept piping hot, it was hard to imagine a life that hard. For me, my sister was a saint. She was five years older, and that condemned her to the bitter trials of an adulthood imposed too early. In our parents' eyes and mine, she was no longer a girl, and she gave in and accepted that with resignation. She used to read at night, because at her school they didn't allow her to, but I was needy and always went to her bed and forced her to turn off the lights and tell me stories. The tales of saints and martyrs from the books and movies they fed her at school had poisoned Inma's mind, and if her presence relieved my nocturnal fears, she sent my imagination reeling with those legends of torture and woe. To calm me down, she used to say a child should never fear the darkness, because Jesus is always there by your bed, watching you while you sleep. I didn't need some man with a beard and tunic sitting at the foot of my bed. I used to pull my blanket up to keep from seeing him and stretch out my hand to scratch the wall. I was far more trusting of my guardian angel.

With my siblings gone, I grew closer to María. I'd sit down to eat with her in the kitchen, and we'd listen to the music program on Radio Intercontinental and to

Elena Francis's show, where she answered letters from
women who wrote her. María would sew the sheets for
her wedding-to-be, and I'd ask her if she was going to
marry El Motos, as they called the worker who was in
love with her. But María was aiming higher. "I'm going
to marry," she would tell me with aplomb, "someone
who's got a butcher shop or a fish stall, and I'll wait on
the customers there, I'll be good at that." I'd ask her
about us, about me. Where would I fit into her future?
She told me children grow up, why get upset about it,
but no need to worry, I could always come visit wherever I might live. No, I said on the verge of tears, I'll
never leave the village. She tried to reveal to me a future I wanted to ignore: one where the dam would be
finished, and everyone who lived there would move
somewhere else, with streetlamps, movie theaters, and
fish stalls. "Then who's going to live in this house?" I
would ask her anxiously.

If the radio announced a song she liked, that we both
liked, María would shush me, and if it was dedicated to
all the mothers out there, she'd cry, looking at her hem-
stitch in concentrated grief. "María, was your mother
pretty?" She told me her mother was more beautiful
than the Virgin Mary. I always found that compari-
son strange, because I'd never thought of that virgin

on prayer cards as a woman. Mamá's hair was short and teased up. She dressed soberly, unless there was a celebration, then she'd don her sleeveless black dress, her pearl necklace, and her white coat. For me, that was the ideal image of maternity: Mamá in her white high-heeled shoes. Mamá told me María couldn't remember her mother, who had died when she was five years old. She said this without thinking of the effect it might have on me. I never realized a mother could die. That mothers die. Just like villages that reach the end of their purpose, and the houses empty out and the wild animals of the Sierra take them over.

From our brief but significant conversations while we ate, I figured out María got paid to be at our house and to clean and take care of us. For me, this was a great disappointment: I thought she was there because she wanted to be. I got upset and asked her: "María, if another woman paid you more than Mamá, would you go take care of her kids?" She would laugh and reply: "What kind of question is that?" The two of them, María and my mother, made me think with apprehension of the future. Everything was fragile, perishable. At school, apart from cursive, I don't remember learning much of what you could call *education*. One of the strange assignments the lady there gave us now and then was to memorize a song before class. This task thrilled me. My head was full of songs I heard with María, and boleros my mother would sing. Mamá didn't have a voice for *coplas*, her range wasn't dramatic enough, but she would murmur boleros softly, as if they were lullabies. Every song she sang seemed soaked through with memories. Our aunts liked to tell the story about when she was single and she entered a bolero contest in Málaga at the fair. She won with the song "Noche de Ronda." That memory overwhelmed my father. Everything she sang sounded earnest and melancholy. She tried to think of some innocent song I could memorize for school. One afternoon in June, we were sitting next to the fence that overlooked the dam. Mamá, it's the end of the school year! I told her, as if that demanded something special. And she taught me a song that has always been with me, in her priceless, timeless voice, which the years have never managed to efface:

> *Poppy, lovely poppy*
> *My soul will always be yours alone,*
> *I love you, my little girl,*
> *The way the flower loves the daylight,*
> *Poppy, lovely poppy,*
> *Don't be thankless, love me back,*
> *Poppy, poppy,*
> *How can you live so alone?*

I tried to understand the lyrics. The words' poetry wasn't enough, I needed something literal. I wanted to ask her if she was the poppy in the song, always alone, writing letters to her sisters, waiting at the window for me to come home, lonely until Papá was done—and he was only really hers at night, in the shadows, when they didn't know I was there behind the door, rancorous, because the two of us were fighting over the same man's love. Or was the lovely poppy me, the little girl in a future when everyone had faded to nothing, as I'd heard they would?

When my brothers came home for the holidays from boarding school, everything turned risky, fun, surprising. They did handstands, and the soles of their shoes left streaks on the wall; they did bridges and smacked their heads on the floor; they pounded on each other nonstop, or shoved me, or pulled me by my wrists up in the air, provoking respect and admiration among the children in the village, who lived in a happy routine throughout the school year. My brothers seemed rougher around the edges, as though they were back from the army rather than from school. Dad would leave them be, until he finally got fed up and smacked them both across the face or led them to their room by their ears. They didn't cry like me and Inma: they turned red, accepted the blow, and soon enough they were back to normal, out for trouble. You didn't feel bad for them, you envied them, especially because Dad took them along on his adventures, fishing at dawn or to the job site, where he gave them hard hats to wear while I had to wait outside, condemned to live forever in the protected universe of girls. I was half a boy. Mamá saw me that way too, thought I was less feminine than my sister and didn't burden me with ribbons, bobby pins, or other frills. I always kept my hair short, stiff, *à la garçonne*, she'd say. I wanted to wear a tutu to my first communion, but she bought me a habit, a novice's garb, because that was the fashion, even if the nuns said something else, and when we went to the photographer in Madrid, I put on a devout, God-fearing face, but even in the photos you can tell it's fake; I didn't believe, and I never experienced any religious crisis like the other girls. Dad wasn't religious and didn't go to church, but other no less extraordinary beliefs filled his head: in ghosts, and supernatural phenomena, especially extraterrestrials. God had never done a thing for him. He had no need for God.

––––––

María didn't want to watch when man landed on the moon. She spent that whole night hiding out in the kitchen, afraid to feel the earth shifting beneath her feet. Papá was elated, predicting a future of revelations, and this fed María's fears and mine. Our porch was packed, because Papá had invited friends and family over, and neighbors dropped in to chat on that night that seemed never to end. We children ran back and forth, I served Dad the occasional brandy, and with every glass he drank, while the night got darker and darker and you couldn't see the ground past the porch, his fantasies turned from silly to delirious. He entertained himself with dreams of future space voyages, with moving vans transported by rockets. Who knew, maybe one day we'd see an astronaut step out of a rocket and plunge the Dragados y Construcciones flag into Martian soil. Was that any different from when we arrived at the top of these mountains? Wasn't it just as hard, or harder, maybe, because the technology was dicier, when all those trucks full of machinery and workers had taken those roads full of mud and dust to build the first barracks by the reservoir? Our first workers, he said, now intoxicated by his discourse, were no less heroic than the astronauts, and they, too, had put their lives at risk. Making it here had been harder than landing on the moon. They might as well have filmed the same images right here. Take off my helmet, give me an astronaut's, and I'll jump out of the jeep onto the ground like if I was floating.

He passed from blind faith in space voyages to a be-lief in deceit and conspiracies meant to dupe us, and with his storyteller's gifts and his penchant for pulling back the curtain, he took us from place to place, from one absolute truth to another. If someone doubted his latest absurd theory, this intolerable insolence made him cling tighter to his fantasies, defending them with undue ire. When someone contradicted him, we could feel his tension and my mother's alarm, because she foresaw the outburst of rage that would ensue, and we'd wish the person arguing with him would just give up, the way we gave up every day, trained as we were to tell him he was right.

The next day, I still wasn't sure if man had reached the moon, but I was convinced that we lived there any-way, that the soil we trod was made of moon rocks, and that we were just as lonely as those privileged figures floating above the planet, the rest of which seemed very far away up here in the Sierra. Wasn't it a lunar surface where María took her goats out to pasture? We chil-dren passed the time pretending we were descending the slopes in our spaceship, and we emerged as though floating into a universe of endless night.

———

When everyone left the village, not just the dam workers but even the maintenance crews that came later, the mountains gained distinction, a bit like hallowed ground, and on certain days, became propitious for sightings of aliens. I suddenly see Dad again, getting out of a bus full of tourists brought in to witness a UFO landing. What better place for it than this lunar landscape? Ten years might have passed since you left. The visitors sat in a circle in that rift in the mountains. Expectation and uncertainty were in the air. The guru readied his followers; Papá's voice was there, deeper, like the bass that accompanies a singer, solemn but sometimes breaking into laughter, constantly interrupted by drags on his cigarette. He was heftier, thicker around the middle, but had the same incorrigible spirit, the same gift of gab, the same embarrassment as he tagged along with this docile group of believers, trying to belittle the spiritual experience of people hoping to glimpse something more than stars in the sky.

Dad told them about his years at the dam, and managed to distract their attention from the extraterrestrial expert at times as he recited his memories of the harsh conditions on the work site. He always behaved the same at group rituals, at Mass, at the movies, at a funeral; something kept him from sharing the respect or reverence that others had. This irritated Mamá, and upset and saddened me a bit too.

He did and he didn't believe. The existence of a judgmental God so unnerved him that he traded him out for Martians. He hated the mere possibility of divine authority.

Going to work every morning at the dam, he told his companions on the UFO excursion, was just as dangerous as going to the moon. Even driving down that hellish road in a truck back then meant putting your life at risk. Those workers would have wished they were astronauts. More workers died here than astronauts in the whole of history. And who remembers them? Who commemorates us when they pour a glass of tap water? I'd sign up here and now to go up in a rocket before I'd climb a power line.

I watched him at a prudent distance, the way I used to spy on him and my mother when they watched *Belphegor, Phantom of the Louvre* on TV, suppressing the urge to run over and protect him by hugging him so he'd shut up. But I didn't want to scare him, upset him, or have him turn cold on me. My father, my poor father, always a sucker for magic, seduced by the supernatural, fighting off his fear of ghosts.

———

He returned a few years later, maybe three. He got out of the car with a pretty, rather flashy blonde woman with a thick fur coat over her shoulders and a pair of high heels so poorly suited to the Sierra that they twisted as she walked on the gravel. Suspicions flooded my heart, a panic as I realized why they were together, and then despondency, only somewhat consoled by the emptiness of the terrain and the way life was suspended in this place where nothing changed but the seasons and the daily shift from light to dark. He showed her the town square, the club, the church, my school; unusually reserved, pensive, even, he answered her questions from that remote place we enter when memories start to throng. He didn't go near our house, out of respect, perhaps, or because he was afraid the presences that go on inhabiting places from our past might catch a glimpse of him.

This morning, before you took the curve into the village, I had the feeling someone was coming. I'd heard the warning from speakers telling tourists not to park next to the dam. It's a woman's voice, metallic, not really human, and every time the recording starts up, it echoes through that immense cavity cupping the reservoir, making it seem as if the mountains themselves were speaking. Normally, hearing that strange tone and worried they're being watched, visitors get back in their car and head off for some authorized vantage point to look down at the reservoir. This morning, I had a feeling. I went to the little patio beside the kitchen, where the bricks formed a lattice to let the air through, and I stood there staring at the road, the way María did back when the trucks would pass and the workers would shout her name.

As soon as I saw the car, a sense of familiarity rushed over me. The driver's arm was hanging out the window pointing out details of the dam, just as Papá used to do, remember; he was a confident driver, and let go of the wheel to gesture, draping his arm over the door, cigarette always between his fingers, or maybe leaning his head on his hand, as though the urge for a catnap might come upon him. I had a vision inspired by that frenetic hand and the car's lurching as it sped up and braked to the rhythm of the conversation. You got out of the car. Chechi was driving. There was no mistaking him. He jumped up onto the porch of our home. Moved by the same impatience, the unquenchable thirst for adventure and activity, still, still audacious. He wanted to get there first. You were in the back seat holding hands with your husband, who observed the surroundings and observed you, wanting to read your emotions.

———

This is the fence, the fence I always told you about, you said. Dad had them put it up when we arrived. Fifty years ago. So there weren't any trees. No, there weren't any trees. But I liked seeing everything all austere like this. Children don't judge what's pretty or repellent the way we do. Anyway, there was a beauty here. What do you think, Antonio, do you like it? It's not just that I like it, it's that it makes me feel something. I like imagining you here as a girl, with your stiff hair and the same smile you have now. Memory's a strange thing: in my memory, the cliff overlooking the dam was just past the fence, but it's not really as dangerous as all that. What do you mean, it's not dangerous? If you fall here, you're done for, it's a sheer drop all around. The roads weren't like they are now, they were basically dirt. I remember the trucks seeming ready to tip over under the weight of the workers standing in the back, even now I can see them all packed together. They must have been so young, and when they rounded the curve by the house, they'd shout María's name, and she'd act angry, but deep down it must have stroked her vanity, because every morning she'd hide behind the lattice in the patio by the kitchen and wait for them to pass. Here's where we hung our clothes. That's where we kept our firewood. It was full of mice, and María used to thwack them to death with a broom so they wouldn't scare Mother. She was a mountain girl. Look, that's where María took her goats to pasture. She'd drive them down the hill from the village to the banks of the Lozoya River. I'd like to find María, but how? Dad says she married a fisherman from Torrelaguna. He went to see her once or twice. It's funny, a guy who seems so aloof, and then you find out he never lost touch with the people and places that marked his life. He did all that alone, you didn't find out till later how he'd followed the map of his feelings on these excursions. He knew where everyone wound up, María, the electrician, the owners of those bars where the highways cross, those bars he liked so much.

The dam is an impressive sight, a massive engineering project seen from a tiny town. Now the village looks like something from a John Ford movie: one-story houses in the middle of nowhere set in an awe-inspiring landscape. You imagine a woman waiting on the porch. Or a man sitting there with a rifle. It's a scene from a Western, a village from the Mexican frontier. A place where the men come on horseback, looking for vengeance or a bounty. It's Juan Rulfo's Comala. Or Spoon River, and on every porch is the soul of someone who disappeared and has a secret to tell that left its stamp on their life or death.

————

You walk around the house and you like it as much as you did when you arrived. That day in the summer of 1966. Almost as lonesome then as it is now. Childhood inflates the dimensions of its surroundings, but the humble beauty of the house remains unchanged. You're happy, it's a deep happiness, like a conquest, bringing your husband here and letting him know the strangeness, the singularity of this village built just for us. You ring the doorbell, but no one answers. It's empty now, except in summer, when priests come to perform their spiritual exercises. What would Papá say if he knew priests had overtaken his home? Look, you tell him, taking his hand, this was my room, the girls' room. And then, you and your husband shield your eyes with your hands to see if you can make out what's behind the glass. In the darkness is me. By my bed pushed against that stippled wall where, if an archaeologist scraped away the many layers of paint, he would find a little girl's fingerprints. Are you still doing it? Are you still warding off fear with embarrassing rituals? Are you still talking to Dad, even though he's dead? Some people never do go away. Look at your face now, your eyes, shrunken with time, melancholy but no less alive, and try to figure out what time has done to you. You suffered. You've known this since you were a girl, your soul was divided between joy and all-consuming unease. Did you ever figure out how to express it? Did anyone listen to you? Why did you come back, what are you looking for? If you fantasized about rescuing your little girl's soul from some ancient threat, you won't find that imperiled child here. The village was the place where nothing had happened yet, though the tension was always palpable, and it's strange that you remember it, the tension of two people who, even with four children, managed to preserve their complex, possessive intimacy. Maybe unconsciously, your anxious spirit could sense the tragedy before it happened. But they loved each other then, in the imperfect, prejudicial way a jealous man loves his wife and his wife, weakened by love, gives in to his madness. Despite her growing vulnerability, her heart still beat with a steady rhythm; he kept his deliriums under control, and life marked out a straight path for him: head of the family, enthusiastic worker, loving husband.

You pull away from the window, and I watch you walk to the square. At the top of the steps, before you lose sight of our house, you see a concrete manhole cover. A ring sticks out of it. You kneel down and grab hold of it. Look, you say, I told you. The wind nearly carried me off and dropped me in the reservoir. The hand was mine, but much smaller, the hand of a seven-year-old girl. I didn't want to leave. Not living is not suffering and not knowing. I watched you leave in Dad's new car, behind a moving van where the workers loaded the few things they cherished: a bit of furniture, austerity for a nomad's life. There was a year left before the dam went into service. María moved to another house to take care of another girl who would learn the love of a nursey-for-hire. Friends came to say goodbye, and they cried because the girl who became a legend just a few days after arriving was now leaving.

And I stayed here. My hand is next to yours. You can feel it, I know, because the warmth of the metal binds you to that moment when we shouted Father's name without shouting.

LOOKING AT THE SEA

I'm sitting on a throne like a Catholic queen, my feet don't touch the floor, and while I wait for the Mother Superior, I sing softly, the way I always do to calm down or because I'm happy or sad. I sing all the time. *Chiquitina, chiquitina, the boys say when they see me pass, poor chiquitiiiina wishes she could touch the moon. Chiquitín, chiquitín, chiquitín, chiquitín.* The teacher says I'm too young for her class, and she's sent me to the Mother Superior. I've never seen a nun so superior, and so I'm as nervous as if I was about to meet the pope. It's my first day of class. I've been to lots of schools, but not too many classes. I haven't been to many classes because as soon as I get a touch of fever, my mother lets me stay home and climb in bed with her, and we sleep to our heart's content. My brothers have always gone to school, my sister too, especially these last two years, when they were in boarding school. This year, playtime's over, my mother's informed me. Munchausen syndrome by proxy? Because there were times when I did feel like going to school, but she'd touch my forehead and say I had a touch of fever, and she wouldn't even bother mixing my chocolate milk. I'd climb out of my bed and into hers, and we would sleep there while María cleaned. At some point, María would come to the bedroom and wake us, *Mister is coming home, mister is coming home,* because my father sometimes came home without warning us, and my mother would jump up, get dressed, and run to meet him. Me, with my touch of fever, I'd go back to my own bed.

The teacher asked for the new girl. That's me. It's always me. I've stood up, and after looking me over, she asked me how old I was. I told her nine, and all the girls started laughing. Then she said, Oh no, no, this won't do, you can't be here, you're too young. And she sent me to this Mother Superior. A girl a good deal taller than me has come with me. We've walked down a huge hallway with a floor of colored tiles so shiny they dazzle me. The sun pours splendidly through the windows, and the place doesn't feel like a grammar school, it's like a palace. And the chair is a throne. *Chiquitín, chiquitín, chiquitín, chiquitín.*

I'm looking quite elegant. My mother's finally let me grow my hair out a bit, and it's long enough to put it in a ponytail like that of the singer and actress Marisol, even if it's still short and stiff. My brothers say it looks like my father's shaving brush. I admire Marisol so much I sometimes feel like she's possessed me; I smile with her same panache, and I've even adopted an Andalusian accent. No one realizes, but there have been times, just a few, when Marisol has emerged from inside me and I could pass for her perfectly.

I don't know why I'm waiting on this royal throne. I can't imagine what I've screwed up. I haven't had time, I've barely been at the palace an hour. I have one uniform for summer and another for winter. I got them from the seamstress at this luxurious school. My father says it's the best school in all of Palma. He always says this: I send you all to the finest schools.

My sister is in the older girls' palace on the hill, and I'm in the one for little girls. My school looks like the one from Malory Towers. I've read the whole series, and I've often daydreamed of being a boarding student. My sister tells me not to idealize it, because she was a boarding student in Torrelaguna and they made her shower with ice-cold water. She got chilblains from the cold on her feet, and the older students, who were almost as bad as the nuns, forced the younger ones to be their maids. That didn't happen in Enid Blyton's boarding school novels, because it was an English school and in English schools the children have mysterious and exciting adventures. I've read a lot. I know what I'm talking about.

I've never been alone with a Mother Superior, and this one must be the most superior one at this school, something like the queen bee. I don't know if I'm supposed to kiss her ring when she comes in or what. When I change schools, I try not to be noticed, or at least not at first. Later, when I'm feeling confident, my mother says I overdo it.

The nun comes in, and at first she disappoints me, because her clothes are almost like mine, a blue short-sleeved uniform, the summer uniform. She has no ring for me to kiss, what a bummer, she doesn't even have on a headdress; her hair is clipped and graying, but her resounding voice is impressive, as though she'd swallowed a microphone and was singing at Mass. I've got a soprano voice, that's what the choir director at my old school said, my voice is so high it could shatter the windowpanes. I told my mother and she said, "I'll see about getting you out of that choir." I've never tried to break glass, but I think he's right, I could if I wanted to.

———

When the Mother Superior comes in, I jump up, and she tells me to sit back down, and so I hop back into my seat. Mother Zaforteza, that's her name, tells me I'm too young for the grade they assigned me to. My brothers always say I never grow because my parents baby me too much, but this was the first time my own teachers were telling me the same thing right to my face; and nuns to boot, though I've never met one before this morning and only know what they are thanks to my sister, who tells me at night how horribly they treated her. If I knew this word, I would call the nuns *bitches*, because they made my sister's life hell, but I still don't have the vocabulary I need to call things by their names. My sister has populated my nightmares with nuns. I dream of flying nuns, hovering over my bed like bats in their habits.

I'm ashamed to be so short. I don't know who I got it from. Lots of people ask. My mother's tall, my aunts are tall, my cousins, my sister, even a cousin who's two years younger, all of them are enormous except for me. My brother Lolo says this proves I'm not my parents' child, that a gypsy left me in a basket on my parents' doorstep. And I cry, I cry, it hurts so bad to know he's right, and I throw myself in my mother's arms, and even as she consoles me, I can tell she's not convinced: Come on, don't be silly, don't pay him any mind, he just says that to make you mad...And my doubts remain.

Mother Zaforteza says I need to repeat a grade, and I can feel my chin quiver and a tear falls, so fat it leaves a blotch on my new uniform. She tells me it's better to do it now than to get to the end and then flunk and get held back to the end of time. I'm utterly disconsolate. If I don't start growing, I'll repeat the same grade over and over until I'm an old dwarf sitting there surrounded by little girls.

Mother Superior stands up and says she's going to take me to my new class. We walk down the palatial hallway again, but I don't enjoy my surroundings this time, I'm as sad as when my mother dressed in mourning because my grandfather had died. My grandfather was enormous. They say they had to make a custom coffin to fit his gigantic body. Some people get buried alive. My brother Lolo tells me that to be sure someone's really dead they have to leave them in the coffin for a few days at room temperature. If they start to rot, then they're really gone, and it's off to the hole. Anyway, for resurrection purposes, the soul is what counts. I don't know how I'll tell my mother they're keeping me back.

I'll have to do it when my brothers aren't around, so they won't make fun of me. Mother Superior opens the door to my future classroom and everyone turns to face me. They're as short as I am, and this soothes me. At least this year I'll feel like one of the girls.

The desks are turned in to face each other in groups of four, like restaurant tables, and I love that. Again, I feel like a student at Malory Towers. There are huge windows that open onto a forest, and on the top of the hill is Bellver Castle—magnificent, my father calls it. Look at it, kids, magnificent. It's so wonderful that for a moment I forget my misfortune, because, as people say, I make the whole world laugh. I feel fancy, and I smile again, possessed by Marisol's smile, though I don't know if these girls, no bigger than I am, get it. It's not the kind of thing people notice at first. These girls sound like they're sighing when they talk, and when they finish a phrase they say *but...* and I do it too, to fit in. In three days, I'll talk just like them. My mother can't stand how I try and change my accent at every school I go to, she hates this *but...* but it's the only way for me to go unnoticed. After two weeks, no one can imagine class without me. And this is true even though I don't attend too often. Mamá hates how my father instantly convinces me that whatever city we've just arrived in is the best one in the world, and the new apartment is the best, and my new school, and my new friends. My mother wants to be sad sometimes, but my father won't let her.

I like it here better than on the continent. I don't say this to kiss up to Dad, but because it's the absolute truth. My father takes us to the beach every weekend. I vomit several times along the way, but it's worth it. I spend the day in the water. I only get out to eat my potato salad and my fillet and then I go right back in. If you go right back in after eating, you still won't die. I'm living proof that the old wives' tale about needing two hours to digest was made up by pharmacists. My father says the best thing about Mallorca is everything is free. He won't even buy us a Coca-Cola. I dream of being older and bathing in Coca-Cola, like Cleopatra.

When night falls, we get in the car, dusted with sand, looking like croquettes, and I sleep the whole way back, waking up only to vomit. At night, I pretend I'm exhausted so I don't have to shower. My bed is full of sand and smells like suntan lotion. My shoulders itch and burn like they're being poked with needles. I like lying backward in bed, with my feet up on the pillow, so the last thing I see before I fall asleep is Mark Spitz. Since I was little, I've always had a little plaster Jesus over the headboard, but my mother let me take him down and put up the Mark Spitz poster that came in *Lily Magazine*.

Mark is a bare-chested Olympic swimmer, and his seven pure-gold medals glimmer in the darkness. I see him smile under the light from the streetlamp. I've realized that he's looking at me no matter where I am in my bedroom. I've even hidden under the bed and stuck my head out suddenly, and there he is, watching. When I enter my room, I feel like he's been waiting for me. I'd like to marry Mark Spitz one day, but I haven't told my father, because he'll oppose it, he always tells me to stay single so I can be his secretary. There's a lot of pressure on me. I keep Baby Jesus in the nightstand, and sometimes I take him out, give him a kiss, and put him under my pillow. He's always cold, and his skin is like the pristine arm of the doorman's daughter that I see years later.

The teacher—who doesn't look like a nun, because she wears a miniskirt and plucks her eyebrows—tells me that at this school, you don't take the books home, they stay on the shelves in the classroom. My mother definitely won't believe that. She'll think this is another one of my stories and that I've lost them. For now, I'll take my empty satchel home and bring it back to keep from having to explain things.

Those first days, I go back home alone, but I don't feel bad for myself, because I already know my future. I've lived it many times, and I know this solitude won't last long. When I turn onto our street, Calle Quetglas, I see my mother in the window waiting for me. My mother has never met me outside school the way some mothers do, but she always has a window in every city, strategically placed to keep watch because she's so frightened of losing me. She's like a lighthouse keeper. When I was five, I got lost in the village after dark, and all hell broke loose. A kindly man in a beret found me crying by a fountain and took me to the home of my grandfather, a sort of big shot who was mayor before he died. After that day, I was told a hundred thousand times about the boogeyman who lurks around corners waiting for unruly girls to come so he can take them away forever. I don't know what disappearing forever means, honestly, no idea, do you disappear just for your family or do you disappear for yourself too, like those women magicians put in a box and they vanish like stardust? But I do know I was the one who got blamed when it was my brothers who took off running and left me behind. I couldn't run fast back then because my legs were even shorter than they are now, but recently, when I saw a rhythmic gymnastics competition on TV, I told myself I had the body of a Russian gymnast and was probably cut out to be an elite athlete. I'll need to train a little, but I've got what it takes.

What I can't stop thinking about is how I was supposed to know that the kindly man in the beret wasn't the boogeyman. How can you tell them apart? I just got lucky, because when I took his hand, I didn't look at his face. In my desperation, I would have gone off with Frankenstein's monster if he'd shown up there. Anyway, my mother doesn't come to school to pick me up in this new city, but she's warned me that I better be turning the corner of Calle Quetglas at 1:15 or it will kill her. If she doesn't see me, her heart might start pounding and she'll get really sick.

Since we came to Palma, she's gotten sick several times. My father says it's nostalgia, women get it all the time, and he doesn't pay her any mind, but she lies down in bed sometimes and puts her hand on her chest. She's had several attacks of this nostalgia. Nostalgia is something bad. My father says he's never felt it in his life. But when he leaves, my mother says that's not true, he had it in Algeria and that's why he came back. I think she's right for once. My father went to work in Algeria, but he couldn't stand being away from me. I get it. My parents always want to be with me. There are times when I'd like not to bear this responsibility, but they won't let me. I was going to go live with them in Algeria, I had a spot reserved at the Lycée français. My brothers were going to stay at their boarding school in Valencia, but not me, I would go with my parents and study at the lycée. I spend a lot of time thinking about what my other life would be like at this lycée, and I feel a French girl possessing me. I could have been French, but my father couldn't stand the distance and he came back, so now I'm Spanish forever. The morning he turned up after months without seeing us, I hugged him and sat on his lap and stayed like that the whole morning. He seemed like he'd come back from the dead. He spoke softly to my mother, using words I didn't know, he didn't want me to catch anything, but I got the drift. I know them well. My father was afraid they would fire him for coming home to see me. But in the end, they didn't, because he's indispensable.

I knew it, I knew it, not even a year has passed and I'm already Mallorcan. I say *but...* at the end of every phrase, way more than the other girls, I talk in a sing-songy voice, I eat cake with chorizo, sandwiches with olives in them, like that was normal, I leave my books on the classroom shelf, I've learned to dance the *parado de Valldemosa*, and I want a Lacoste shirt because I've been invited to two birthday parties and I'm the only girl without one. Someone asked me how many colors of Lacoste shirts I have, and I didn't know the answer because I'd never heard *Lacoste* in my life. Now I know everything about Lacoste and all I need is for my mother to understand that I need it. My mother says those shirts are for tennis champions, like Manolo Santana, not little girls. She's wild about Santana. One day she told the cleaning lady: I love a man with big teeth. I didn't know a woman could like a man for his teeth.

When we're alone and my mother starts to feel nostalgia, she calls my father at the office, and he hurries home as soon as he can. One night she got worse, and he had to make dinner. It was sad to see my father cooking, because he's never done anything in the kitchen and he smears oil on himself and doesn't even know where the frying pans are, and his ashes fall into the potatoes as he fries them. He burned himself. It's sad. Thankfully my aunt came from the mainland to cook for us so he never had to do it again.

I can tell it's not a good time to bring up this problem of repeating a grade, so one day passes, then another, and since no one seems to notice, even I start to forget I've been held back, even if it's the biggest embarrassment for a child's parents, at least that's what my father says. When the secret comes into my head and I can't stop thinking about it, I tell myself if I just let time pass, they might just forget what year I'm supposed to be in. Luckily, since my mother is getting sicker by the day, no one seems to care what year I'm in or what I'm doing or what I should be doing. I crouch down to touch the floor three times before I enter a room. If I don't, maybe they'll find out my secret. I also switch the lights on and off three times. I look at the sun when I walk. For a year now, I've been picking at a zit on my nose. I blink or I furrow my brows. I do this when I'm alone, and quickly, but my mother knows, even if she's in bed, and I hear her shout: Stop with your nonsense! She told me if I keep tearing the scab off the zit they'll have to operate on me and amputate part of my nose.

One day at lunch, my father told us he was taking her to Madrid and the rest of us would stay here with my aunt. Inma started crying, and I did too, I didn't want to be left out. The morning my mother left, I took the elevator down with her. There was a chair in it, because she constantly panted and no longer had the strength to stand. I wanted to sit on her lap, but my aunt told me I needed to understand she barely had enough air to breathe and I was making it harder on her. No one tells me she's going to be gone two months, so I'm sad, but not as sad as I would be if I knew. While my parents are away, my aunt and I sleep in my parents' bed and my aunt tells me stories. They're old stories, ones I heard back when I was little and got lost, "Rumpelstiltskin" or "The Princess and the Pea," but the poor woman doesn't know any stories for older kids, and anyway I can tell she'd rather I was little. My father's the same, so when I'm with him I have to pretend I'm two years younger, but I also know he'll be mad if I repeat a year. Sometimes you can't figure out what people expect from you.

My aunt's started coming to school to pick me up, and I'm ashamed to see her by the entrance with her coun-trified shoes. I have friends now, because I talk with a Mallorcan accent and that's opened a lot of doors for me. At first, my classmates thought that my aunt was my mom and that angered me, because my mother is younger and prettier. I told them she's my grand-mother, I don't want to go into explanations about how she's taking care of me because they had to take my mother to Madrid so some eminent doctor can op-erate on her. I don't want anyone to know anything about my life. My aunt, whom all my classmates call my grandmother, makes me flan from a box and farina and bean casserole. I help her, and I make dinner on lots of nights, because here in Palma we've learned everything about modern cooking. Modern cooking means dishes with sides: frankfurters with ketchup, mustard, and instant mashed potatoes. Where'd you learn all this? my aunt asks, astonished, and I feel like a child prodigy, because in these years, nobody yet uses the term *gifted* children. She's the only one I pretend to be Marisol with, because she doesn't laugh, she takes me seriously and applauds and sees the resemblance perfectly when Marisol possesses me and blossoms forth. I sing to her *Cabriola, qué bonito es mi caballo.* I wish she was my grandmother. I don't tell anyone at home I'm repeating a year, and at school, I say my aunt is my grandmother. Living a lie is hard.

There are times when I forget I have a mother, and then I think, How can I? My father calls from Madrid every other day to talk to my aunt. At first, they let me on the line, but now they can't, because my mother gets excited when she hears my voice, she can't even talk, I hear her crying. My soprano voice might kill her.

OPEN HEART

The girl who's smiling into the camera will only be a girl a few more months. I know her future so clearly that it pains me not to be able to save her from what's about to happen. She smiles at the professional photographer who has gone from house to house taking family photos he will place in a strange montage: a hippieish image of the Virgin Mary, Saint Joseph, and the Christ Child for the holidays. It's the first year they're not going to the village for Christmas, and my parents want to be present on top of the TVs at my aunts and uncles' houses. The girl would have liked to go spend Christmas and New Year's as they do every year, beside her uncle the baker's warm oven. Expansive and gregarious, the girl is in her element surrounded by fifty people, with aunts, uncles, and cousins, on nights when the children sing until their voices are scratchy and they run on the icy village

streets in the morning and bundle up under seven
blankets whispering one last secret in their cousin's
ear before they fall asleep. The girl still doesn't quite
understand the nostalgia her mother feels, so far from
her family, but sometimes an inexplicable melancholy
possesses her. Melancholy is a faint shadow falling over
her character. The girl smiles easily. Smiles tug her
features upward, and only her eyes remain stubbornly
downcast, as though announcing an unstable tempera-
ment shifting between two extremes. She has a series of
diffuse memories about her brief past. The landscapes
of the places she's lived in mingle, and there's a feeling
that life is a constant arrival and departure, and she's
resigned to that, and knows you have to adapt quickly,
without protest, to new homes and new accents. The
girl talks like a Mallorcan. She picked that up in a
matter of months, and now she can't imagine life away
from the island. It seems like she's always walked down
this street to Señor Jaume's store, the way she's doing
now and does every afternoon to get a sandwich of *so-
brasada* and olives. Her best friend on this street is missing an arm and has a false one made of plaster that
resembles the arm of the Virgin Mary or Baby Jesus.
Sometimes they play ring-around-the-rosy, and the girl
knows loyalty demands she hold her friend's statue-like
hand. In these moments, her soul trembles with fear
and compassion. As if presenting her with a gift, her

friend shows her the stump, and the girl touches it. She touches the furrows, like at the end of a doll's limb, formed by the skin at the tip of her elbow. The girl will dream for nights on end that her own arms fall off like ripe fruit from a tree. This is, without a doubt, the most palpable tragedy the girl has known. This, her mother's melancholy, and the anxiety that drives her to compulsive behaviors like scratching walls, winking, or pulling off the scab from her cholera vaccine until it gets infected and a doctor has to pay them a house call. Her compulsions come and go, torturous and shameful, and get worse every time her mother utters the word *compulsion*.

One day, her mother's weakness receives a concrete name: heart. Her heart doesn't beat right, and that's what makes her sad for no reason. That mysterious organ behind her left breast that the girl leans against many nights when she falls asleep, even though she's too old to be held like this and her older brothers make fun of her.

It's because of her heart that her mother has to go see a doctor on the mainland. *Eminent*, they call him. Her mother's never left home before, so the girl is plunged into preliminary orphanhood—a rehearsal. She doesn't talk much with her mother on the phone, who's too weak and gets emotional, her aunt says. There will be time for that later. Time passes, it runs like a greyhound, and two months have gone by when her father announces it's time to go see her in Madrid.

It's one of those long afternoons at the beginning of spring. The apartment is new, brightened by the last light of day, there's barely any furniture, but there are people everywhere, the same aunts and uncles and cousins who drink and sing around the oven at Christmas. But now they're whispering, the way you do at a funeral or Mass. They're everywhere. In the kitchen, the women are making dinner; in the living room, the men are smoking; in the hallway, others come and go. The girl can sense a life is about to end: hers, as a girl. She doesn't want to enter the room they guide her toward, she wants to wait for her mother on the island, and for her to come back without all the song and dance a return implies, for her to just be there as though nothing had happened, leaning on the windowsill like always, supervising the walk home from school.

The girl resists, but her father's firm hand leads her in until she's standing in front of the bed. The woman she sees there isn't her mother. Her mother was tall, with the kind of generous breasts mothers have, a place for you to sink your head and seek solace when someone's hit you, where you can nestle in and muffle your rage. Her mother wore her chestnut-brown hair teased up, she had small, lively eyes, a round smile, big white teeth. Her mother had a sweet voice, a slightly raspy, melodic voice that sang boleros in the kitchen. No, this isn't her. The woman lying in the bed has yellowish skin, a ghastly color. Her yellow hand rises, trembling, trying to touch the girl's face. The girl is supposed to give this strange woman the succor of a yearned-for embrace. She is supposed to, but she stays there at the foot of the bed, cruel without intending it, unable to keep from resenting this mother who doesn't look like her mother.

One of her aunts loses patience. Kiss your mother, she says. The girl reluctantly brings her head close to the white-haired head of this woman, who sobs instead of speaking. My daughter, my daughter. The girl rests a hand on her body and touches something hard and pointy. It's hard for her to accept that it's a hip. The hip she knows, the round, fleshy hip, no longer exists. Her siblings are there too, standing frozen before this unknown woman. The aunt they love most, with that character that might seem cold to anyone who doesn't realize that love is there too when you wrap your kin in their shroud or wash the bodies of the dying, pulls down the sheet and opens the nightgown of that ancient forty-two-year-old who vaguely resembles their mother. Look at the poor thing, look what she's had to go through. A fat, red scar runs down the woman's trembling torso, a centipede with endless black feet on either side that wriggles or retracts when the sick woman's reedy voice utters the names of her four children and looks at them with frightened eyes from a world that is no longer that of the living. You have to take care of her now, someone says. When the girl hears this, two feelings invade her that will never go away: responsibility and danger. Responsibility is a pressure in her chest, and the danger is death, which sinks its claws into the back of her neck.

Night enters the room. No one turns on the lights. The adults come in and say their goodbyes, caress the sick woman's forehead, murmur a last bit of advice. The two daughters stay sitting on the other bed in silence, knowing their mother wants them close. They lie down, and the older sister hugs the little girl, who is trying pointlessly to suppress her tears. Don't cry, don't cry. The woman sighs and sobs, says things they can't understand. When weariness overtakes grief and then goes quiet, a soft noise becomes audible. It's rhythmic like the ticking of a clock, but something about it is weird. It keeps changing speed, like a broken metronome. The girl gets up and does as she's seen others do so many times this afternoon, wetting the corner of a washcloth in the glass of water and running it across the woman's lips. Thank you, dear. The voice in the dark is delightfully familiar, as if not seeing that yellow face with the sunken cheeks helps bring back the person she loves. It's my heart, the mother says, don't be scared, what you're hearing is my heart. She says this as if she, too, had to get used to that sound that seems to be constantly attesting to her precarious presence among the living, the days stolen from a future she won't be around for. I'm hot, she says. The girl's sister gets up and pulls back the bedcover and the two of them, the girl and her teenage sister, stand there looking at her without seeing, listening to her heart, willing to do anything to keep that heartbeat in the world. Just as she accepts the challenge of a new city or a new accent, the girl accepts that her childhood days are numbered, and without much argument, the way sensitive children face adversity, she passes her index finger over the head of the huge centipede sleeping on the neck of the old woman who, when she's touched, becomes her mother once more.

My life has changed so much I don't even recognize myself. In the mornings, I look in the mailbox, and there is almost always a big envelope addressed to me full of homework sent by the nuns from Palma. I go upstairs, do it all so quickly it's funny, seal the envelope, and go out with my aunt to send it back. Tossing the envelope into the mailbox is the best part of my day. It's the only reason I do my homework. Now I'm the one sitting by the window at lunchtime watching the children coming home from school. My father says Mother Zaforteza was understanding when she heard my mother didn't want to be apart from me anymore, she said it was reasonable and that I could finish the school year from here. I would have been pleased as punch if they'd told me a year ago I could go to school through the mail, but this is the first school I've ever liked going to. When they said we had to leave the books in the classroom, they won me over, and don't get me started on dancing *jotas*. I also love drawing Venn diagrams on the floor. When it's nice out, we go up the hill with a knitting needle to grill chorizo on a grill set up by the nuns, if they even are nuns, I don't really know. For the first time, everything seems easy, and I can look out the window at my leisure and stare at the magnificent Bellver Castle.

But now I'm stuck in Madrid because I have to take care of my mother. I do whatever I can so she'll get better and we can go back to Mallorca. I get up, juice her three oranges, and take it to her in bed. I've gotten used to the noise of her heart and I hear it beating at night like a ticking clock. My aunt, the aunt who's here, forbade me from sleeping with my mother because she says her scar isn't healed and I might pull it open, but when my aunt's light goes out, I go climb in bed with Mamá, and she likes it, or at least she doesn't complain. Since I can't lie next to her and can't spoon her, we stay on our backs. Sometimes I count her stitches because they're big and fat, like worms about to pop out of their hiding place, hard, black, and stiff, and I put powders on them so the wound will heal. I've learned her medications and I bring them to her on a plate three times a day: hydro-quinidine, acenocoumarin, Valium...My mother has plastic valves in her that Dr. Rábago put there, and that's why you can hear her palpitations. Dr. Rábago is much more eminent than Dr. Barnard, but he's never in the magazines because there's so much backbiting in Spain. I imagined Dr. Rábago just as handsome as Dr. Gannon, but the other day I was in his office with my mother and I got a glimpse of him and no, not even close. My father told me on the phone from Palma that I shouldn't leave my mother for a second while Dr. Rábago was *auscultating* her. My mother said to my aunt, *that man, that man.* And they both burst out laughing.

The hairdresser's come over and has changed her hair back to its normal color, so she looks like my old mother again, even if the skin of her face is yellow and her hands smell weird. She walks around the house with me. We come and go up and down the hallway. She's wearing a long robe with blue flowers that hangs to the floor; she bought it so she would look decent when Dr. Rábago saw her at the hospital, and now, with her brown hair combed back on the sides, she looks like a patient in the movies. We play cards in the afternoon. My aunt likes to bet money, but when she realized I always won, she stopped betting. She calls it *dumb luck,* like I'm dumb for winning. My mother says later, she's a skinflint, a skinflint. Everyone talks bad about everyone else behind their back, and later they pretend like they get along.

My father bought a TV for this apartment everyone will come live in when the school year in Palma is over. My father bought this apartment with the money he won in the lottery when I was born. My brother Lolo jokes about it, he hit the jackpot and got the crackpot all in one go. He means me. He's jealous of me, that's why he attacks me. Madrid is full of empty lots. In front of my house is a huge empty lot, and past it is Madrid and the Corte Inglés department store. My father says there's not another apartment in all of Madrid with views like these. Velázquez would pay to be able to stand on our balcony and paint. For a few days, the fog has been so white you can't see anything, like in London. I miss our old furniture from the house in El Atazar. They say it's in a garage on the side of some road. It makes me sad to think of the furniture there without me. This lottery apartment is almost empty, just a sofa, a table, and some chairs my father borrowed from the office. When we sit down, the green pleather sofa is so straight and stiff, it feels like we're in a dentist's waiting room. When I sit at the table to do my homework, my mother says: "Here's the boss."

The other day I went down to the mailbox to get my envelope, and when I opened it at *the boss's* table I saw there was a letter from Mother Zaforteza. My heart was pounding like my mother's. Mother Superior said my work was good, but I should put in a little more effort, because she could tell, since I was repeating a grade, everything was coming easy to me and I was rushing to get it done. I heard my mother coming down the hall and thought about eating the letter, the way I saw a killer in some movie do to get rid of the evidence, but when I put it in my mouth, I started retching, so I shoved it down my panties. Later I went to the bathroom, tore it into pieces, and since it wouldn't sink when I flushed, I had to take an abundant crap on top of it. My aunt, the one who's like my grandmother, sings us a song that makes us pee ourselves laughing:

> *One day I went to take a crap*
> *And two million worth of shit came out*
> *That's what I call taking a crap*
> *Not those dumb pieces of shit*
> *Who go to take a crap*
> *And can't shit out shit.*

We love her a lot. Sometimes more than we love them.

My father came to spend the weekend with us, and my mother asked him why he was so dark. From being out in the sun, he said, and that was that. But it turned out the sun had burned his chest too. He brought a bottle of whiskey in his suitcase and put it on a bench where our future bar would go. My mother asked him since when had he stopped drinking brandy. The other day, he said. Then, like a magician, he took two glasses from his suitcase and told me from now on, he wanted a couple of ice cubes. I've always made my father's drinks. Brandy in a big glass after dinner. I love this because when they don't see me, I wet my lips with his drink, and I take it to the sofa with my nose sunk in the glass. Now I'll have to pour his whiskey. My mother doesn't like this change to whiskey. She threw a shoe down the hallway at him last night. I heard it thud against the floor. And the next day, my aunt said: "You didn't have to throw a shoe at him, it wasn't that bad."

We're back in Palma and I feel more like the new girl at school than I did the first day I arrived. Someone told my classmates that my mother was sick, and now they all give me pitying looks. Since we've been back, my mother has thrown more shoes at my father. Or things that sound like shoes. A lot of times, my father comes home late. I put the record player on loud in my bedroom and concentrate and pretend that when the song is over my father will be back and sitting down to dinner. But one song passes, then another, then another. Then my mother comes and gets into my bed. When my father arrives, my sister or I set out a cold, dry plate for him that I've prepared. After that,

I have to sleep with my mother. It's over, Mark Spitz, I can't sleep turned the wrong way around to look at you. My mother's chest trembles as it rises and falls, but it doesn't make as much noise as before. Sometimes I hear her cry and I'd like to disappear and come back when it's all over.

There's a girl in my class, Margarida, who stained her seat with blood, and they sent her home to her mother to tell her why. Your mother should explain it to you. My friend Assun Planas told me that it happens to all of us, sooner or later. I don't know if it's because we're short or what, but I can't go bothering my mom with this nonsense about bleeding. One day, without any warning, everything changes at my house and I hear them laughing in the bedroom, and they tell us they're going out that night. My mother has bought blouses with flowers embroidered on them and bell-bottom pants and since she's so thin, she looks like she's floating. I put on her white high heels while she's getting ready, and she dabs a little Chanel perfume on her finger and wipes it behind my ear. I'm happy, because I know that tonight, my parents will sleep together and I'll get to sleep with Mark. Once I got up to go to the bathroom and I heard my mother say, "I love you too, but you're a brute." I had never heard anyone say I love you except in movies.

At school, everything's easy, and nothing matters that much, because I know I'm leaving, even if I haven't told anyone yet. Some women in regular clothes came to class the other day and gave us tests of numbers, comprehension, memory. A few days later, they gave us a sealed envelope to take home. The first thing my mother took out of the envelope was the bill. Pay, pay, pay, always the same, thank God Dragados is footing the bill for this damn school. Now every time I hear my father say he's paying for the best schools for us, I laugh and think, liar. My mother has it in for this school and I don't know why. For this school, for whiskey, for me being Mallorcan, for me setting out a plate for my father when she shuts herself up in our room and lies down in my bed. She gets irate with me because I sit down with him and listen to him the way she does when she's well. He talks to me about his colleagues, their projects, the budgets. I do a good job of paying attention, just like in class, but I can hardly understand anything he's saying, and my head separates from my body, I can't say where it goes, but I'm still there, with open, unblinking eyes.

The women were there to give me an intelligence test and make a psychological profile. They analyzed me up and down, gave me exact scores, and wrote at the bottom of their report:

An intelligent girl who would do better in her stud-
ies if she could overcome her highly emotional character,
which keeps her from completing her work in a manner
suited to her abilities.

My father said that he already knew I was intelligent, look who I got it from; my mother said they didn't need to pay all that money to find out I could get distracted looking at a housefly.

The end of the school year has arrived. I've gotten my report card, and I have to bring it back signed. My grades are so good, you'd think they were someone else's, but supposedly that doesn't matter, because I repeated a year, even if I never remember what I learn. I could take the same class for fifty years and everything would sound new to me. My head is like a torn sack. I open the report card for my mother so she won't see the first page, where it says what grade I'm in. She puts on her round glasses and says, Well, you studied hard this year. She doesn't know that I couldn't study because the books are always on the shelf in the classroom. They barely know anything about me.

The afternoon when we dance the *parado de Vall-demosa* for the graduation party, I look to the stands the whole time to see if I can spot my mother and aunt, but I never do. The applause is uproarious. I love applause, it makes me want to cry and bow and for this to be the end of my life. When we're walking to the courtyard, Mother Zaforteza puts her hand on my shoulder and asks, "Don't you have something to tell me?" I shake my head no. I want to hug her, because for me she truly has been superior, but I can't, I would have to explain too much. She tells me, "You know we'll be here waiting for you."

I leave the other girls behind. I never will say goodbye to them. Maybe they'll call me one of these days and the phone will ring, ring, ring, in the empty apartment and no one will answer because I'll have disappeared. When I turn onto Calle Quetglas I see my mother and aunt. They mixed up the hour and now they're walking toward the school. It was the only day my mother was going to see the only school I ever liked, and now she'll never do it. I cry a little, and they ask me to forgive them. Then we stop and buy ice cream. My mother looks like she's floating. She's beautiful, delicate, you'd think a gust of wind could snap her like the stalk of a flower. I take them by the hand, my mother and my aunt, the same one people on this island think is my grandmother. Soon I forget the disappointment, which is minor compared to other ones. My mother is proud of me this afternoon and recites my grades aloud. She doesn't know what year they're from, but she's happy about them. Maybe everything will come out when my father signs me up for school in Madrid. The idea terrifies me, and I blink my eyes three times three times, that makes nine.

When we go on board the boat, night covers the city like a curtain falling over the place I was coming from and wished I was from. I've taken a Dramamine and feel my eyelids drooping with exhaustion, even though the cool air is hitting me in the face. Leaning on the railing, I hear my mother sing a song by Jorge Sepulveda. My mother says she likes how he sings, but she doesn't like him as a man. I don't understand the difference, but she mentions it often. She likes Gregory Peck as an actor *and* as a man. She sings softly, afraid of hurting her heart, but after so long, she's finally singing again and I will never forget that voice. I know the lyrics, I know almost all of them, and I identify with them completely:

> *Looking at the sea, I dreamed*
> *You were here with me,*

I don't know what I felt, looking at the sea
But I cried when I remembered my lady.
The luck I lost some time ago
Will come back I know,
Will come back to me
While I stare at the sea.

And though it might look that way, because I'm on the verge of tears, what I feel isn't nostalgia. Once again, I'm obeying my father, and no, I don't feel any nostalgia.

THE SEMPERVIVUM

I'm going to tell you a dream
I had last night
A dream that must be
Tucked away in the warehouse
Of dreams
From 1978:
My mother was living
Unbeknownst to me
In an apartment in Estrella
Right across from our neighborhood.
Someone was looking after her,
A friend.
I was trying to remember
Her number
But I could only recall
The first three digits.
At that point

I started asking myself
When's the last time I saw her?
Why haven't I called her
In all these years?
Is she angry with me?
Did she read about me
In the papers?
Ay,
I know she doesn't want to see me.

I see how her friend's hand
Rests on her shoulder
Consoling,
Knowing.
And I hear her voice,
The voice of my mother,
Always so weak,
Whispering:
Why,
Why did I have children?

I want to tell you
That I ruminated on this dream
The whole day
While writing my article
And the dream continued
With me calling my sister

And she talked to me
About class
In ninth grade
And I said,
If you're going to retire
Now who cares?

And the dream went on
We were eating your rice
And talking about fears
Of the future.
I was afraid for mine
More than yours
But I didn't tell you.
And without knowing why
My dream crept
Into this fear.
And it hurt me
Opening a wound from another time.

I sat in front of the mirror
To make myself up
The way women do
In poems written by women.
Languid,
Like the heroines of novels
Always do.

My eyes reflected
An intense look
Like when I'm listening
To things other people say,
That look that provokes
An always unsought
Disconcertment.
Women in novels
Look for themselves in the mirror.
And I could see a fifty-four-year-old woman,
Face defeated,
After a day
Fleeing a dream
Thrown up, I thought, by the waves
Breaking from the nightmares of 1978
When my mother
Died.
But no.

It was me observing myself
The way I only observe others.
When I realized the dream
Hurled me back to a
Far more remote
And willfully censored
Year:

I came home from school one midafternoon
And I hadn't yet removed my satchel
When my sister said:
"Mamá's gone."
Gone?
The four of us sat,
Four
In the chairs in the living room.
In silence.
We all looked smaller.
My hands in my lap
Clutching the handles
Of my schoolbag
The way a little girl does
When she's awaiting punishment.

Three days later
I went to look for her with my aunt
We crossed Madrid
I don't know where
Or where we were heading
I don't remember where
The apartment was.
My mother was sitting
In a chair
Looking out the window

With her back to the door
Just as she's appeared
Since then in my dreams
Remote as a ghost.

Now and again she sobbed
And between sobs
Uttered a phrase
Hard as a stone:
Why did I have children?
They haven't called
Not one of them has called.
She talked as if I
Weren't right in front of her
Ignoring
My presence
I wanted to go closer
Touch her
Sink down in her fleshy
Lap
But I was afraid
She'd reject me.

My mother returned home.
Returned.
And life went on
As usual

Until her death
A few sad scenes
Overlay others.
After 1978
My memory did a good job
Blocking out
The black years
That would have kept me
Years later
From loving you.
Loving.

The woman who appears
In dreams
Isn't the dead mother
She's my mother
The one who left home
And blamed for abandoning her
The one who had been abandoned.
Her friend told her
"Don't say that,
She's just a girl"
But it wasn't true
Not anymore
My parents made me
An adult
At ten years old.

Time
Which enthusiastically
Works to
Alleviate pain
Heals no wounds
It stores them
And brings them back
On the day you least expect it.

Today, at fifty-four
I can still feel in my hands
The handles of my brown
Purse.
And I ask myself,
Mother, why did you come to me last night?
Mother, I finally understand
The origin of the dream,
Tell me,
This is the last thing I'll ask of you:
What are you warning me of?

The moment came when everything fell apart. My extreme fidelity, my faith in them, my sweet innocence. Also that magical element I thought I possessed that made me believe I could save her, save them.

A racket of glass and ceramic shattered against the floor pulled us from our dreams. My sister and I got up and went running to the living room without knowing whether someone had broken into our house or was trying to kill us. We found her next to the walnut bookshelf grabbing the little decorations, the ones she'd been collecting the whole time they'd lived together, and throwing them at his feet. In her long blue robe embroidered with flowers, firm, resolute, trembling, but this time without crying, she bit her lip to keep from succumbing to sorrow. She, my mother, who had been waiting till three in the morning for him to come home, insomniac, victim of obsessions, determined that this time he'd get what he deserved. She didn't want to hurt him, didn't know how to hurt him, because the decorations, so few in number and so treasured by her, by me, fell not on his head, but at his feet. At the feet of a man who looked at her stunned, standing by the door, tie badly knotted, pulled aside as though thrown on slapdash to feign normality in the unlikely case of an encounter. My father said nothing, he watched immobile while this racket continued, waking the neighbors, probably, and did nothing to protect his face from any shards that might fly up. His hands at his side, holding an overcoat under one arm.

My sister grabbed my mother by the arm and dragged her off to our room, where she now spent most of her days. I stood in front of him. At the dawn of my adolescence, overcoming my own immaturity and asking him, What are you doing coming home at this hour? Sensing how this phrase, one a wife or mother would utter, stayed there floating in the air, ridiculous, improper, after I had left. And I repeated it to myself several times in bed, weeping with rage because I'd been forced to utter a phrase that wasn't mine to utter.

That is the moment when everything breaks, the way a tacky little porcelain Lladró figurine with its eighteenth-century character breaks, the way a Murano glass ashtray breaks, a Manises pitcher. Nothing special if you consider how many years they'd been together, but a lot if you realize that it was only relatively recently that my father had put our nomadic period to an end and they could finally think about purchasing decorations that would stay on the same shelf forever. The next day, when I went downstairs to go to school, the eternally gruff doorman said, Hey, what happened last night, the neighbors have been asking me. I shrugged: Nothing, one of our shelves broke. And I walked out free, ready to let the outdoors embrace me.

But the future has to put time in order, turn life into plot, and it chose that very night for its significance and brutality as the start of a period of distancing, a rupture that would push me toward adulthood, with fury, with rage, and with remorse, dispossessing me of my childish gentleness and turning me into something strange, a person unknown even to myself.

I am fifteen years old on that morning when I take off for school with my folder of notes under my arm. Carrying a backpack now would be childish. My friend comes out to meet me every day. Together we cross the empty lots between my neighborhood and the Madrid that lies beyond the border of the freeway. We aren't afraid to take a shortcut through this hostile zone. We've grown up in a world of empty lots and unfinished parks. Half our perspective is taken up by an open sky with a glimpse of the big city far off. My mother doesn't know I walk to my school in El Retiro, she doesn't suspect that my friend and I are saving our bus fare for an adventure, an escapade, even if we suspect we're not brave enough to actually do it. If my mother knew I was walking through the same area where some guy assaulted Estrella, the cleaning girl, she'd be pissed. But I'm not afraid. All of a sudden, I'm not afraid of anything. Even though I saw Estrella come in with a busted lip and messed-up hair, crying and wiping her nose on the back of her hand. Her boyfriend, Juaco, and she hatched a plan that same afternoon, and the next day, she took the same path. The guy was waiting there, and he tried to assault her again. She shouted, Juaco came out of his hiding place, and the two of them beat him like a rug and dragged him off to the police station at knifepoint. I'd like to be that brave and have a boyfriend as cool as Juaco; I have fantasies of something like that happening to me, and coming out triumphant.

Estrella has taken the baton from me, and in these times, she's the one helping my mother cope. She tells her stories of a world my mother doesn't know, about houses thrown up in Vallecas in the middle of the night, poverty in the outskirts, quick wits, working-class Reds, bravery, survival. Estrella lost her mother when she was young, same as my own mother, and she loves her father and takes care of him and has sisters she can trust and a boyfriend she's in love with and will marry soon, when their government-subsidized apartment comes through. Her story could be like my mother's except that this girl with the gypsy traits and dark black hair, the brazen accent and shiny dresses, is zealous and tenacious, and talks shamelessly of her desires and the sex they have in the dusty little bedroom in the house her father built at night in the seventies, behind the back of the Civil Guard.

My mother listens to Estrella and sometimes seems to want to give her advice—to reflect, to keep from letting her recklessness get the better of her—but she wavers and then decides it's better to listen. She's attentive, curious, meditative, maybe envious of Estrella's shamelessness, which fills the whole house as they move from room to room, bellowing homey, off-color expressions my mother's never used in her life. Prisoner of a timidity and a correctness that she's incapable of defying, my mother is eternally astonished at the younger woman's impudence.

Estrella tells me goodbye in the mornings as if she knew I were hiding something. Sometimes she looks at me and says: You're a strange bird. She found my Communist Youth card and told me a better hiding place so my mother wouldn't see it. They legalized the Party during Holy Week. The two months undercover that preceded it were hard on me. But at home, I'm still undercover. I joined because of my brothers' influence. I have assorted confused political preoccupations that I can't manage to express because I know nothing about theory, but my concerns are contagious, and now my friend Raquel shares them—the girl I'm now walking quickly with up Avenida del Mediterráneo—and she's gotten a membership card of her own.

I tell her what happened the night before, more to blow off steam than to console her, to reassure her about our project of running away when we turn eighteen. A month ago now, Raquel's mother left their family home and went to live with an old lover in a small apartment even farther from downtown than ours. Since then, Raquel's been doing the cooking for her father and siblings. She doesn't complain much. She's smarter than I am but she doesn't know it; she understands all the things I can't wrap my head around and lets me copy off her science exams. I read, I write. And she admires me, she thinks I'm a poet or artist. She thinks I'm cultured.

Sometimes Raquel goes to see her mother, who lets her in when her lover isn't there, and she thinks she can see a shadow of doubt, of penitence, a desire to go back, because the apartment is run-down, horrible, depressing, and the new guy is unbearably jealous. It upsets me to imagine that gorgeous woman I've seen so many times walking happy and carefree through the neighborhood without her children now imprisoned by some man in a distant, unknown neighborhood. It never occurred to me that a mother could cheat on someone and move out. My mother left one time, but she did it to get my father's attention, even if in the end it was I and not my father who went to find her.

My mother let me register for public school, as long as it wasn't coed. I dragged my friend there with me. When we go back, I walk her home and then she walks me home and then I walk her home, and in between we waste a lot of time. There's always something to talk about, so we call each other on the phone after. I'm the only person in the neighborhood who knows her mother ran off with another man. My mother heard a rumor at the hairdresser's and asked, but me, I'm quiet as a grave. Last year we cut our arms and mixed our blood. We already think it was stupid, but what's done is done. It was even stupider when we touched our rings together and shouted: Shazam!

It was hard for me to convince my mother to let me go to public school, but I was stubborn: I couldn't keep up the farce of private school any longer. I was ashamed to show up at the Communist Youth meetings looking like a prep. My father's better off than the fathers of my comrades, and that creates conflicts for me. I'm political now and I need to show consistency.

My mother doesn't trust me. She hates that I'm growing up. But there's no denying it: I have a pair of breasts round and firm as Reinette apples, and they're sore all the time and I try to hide them by hunching over. Not long ago, a friend's father was taking me back home one night, and he stopped the car for no apparent reason, looked at them with a smile, and said: Well now, you certainly have changed, I bet you're already getting busy with your boyfriend. Getting busy. It was repulsive. I was reading *The Catcher in the Rye* at the time. When I got to the part where Holden Caulfield's trusted teacher makes a move on him, I thought, This world is rotten. I think that often, that this world is rotten. Sometimes I'd like to end up in the hospital with depression like Holden Caulfield, and that would be that.

I still went to Mass until recently. How a person can change from one year to the next. I passed through a spiritual moment, encouraged by Don Felicísimo, the school chaplain, who gives Mass at a church in my neighborhood. If you went to his Mass, he raised your grade, and a good religion grade brought up my average. I thought he was a nice guy, but then one day in class I asked him if it wouldn't be better to wait until we were adults so we could decide ourselves if we wanted to get baptized or not, and he slapped the daylights out of me. I didn't expect it, honestly. I should have paid attention to my father, who always used to say: The further away a priest is, the better. Shove it, imbecile, is what I thought at the time. In the days before I got slapped and became politically involved, I would leave Mass on Sunday and stop at a stand these hippies had on the way home. I'd taken a liking to a wooden cross they had, and I kept looking at it, but I couldn't afford it. Suddenly my science teacher came up behind me and bought it for me. I was breathless. When I got home, I engraved his initials in it with scissors, L. E., Luis Ernesto. Not long afterward, they fired him for inviting boys to the movies and feeling them up. After that, if anyone asked, I told them it was my initials, E and L, but backward.

Despite what my mother might have thought, I haven't missed guys since I started public school. In principle I like them, but I also think it's gross when I open

my mouth and their tongue slides in like it's trying
to inspect the gaps between my teeth. I like it when
I imagine it but not when it's live and in the flesh. It's
true I haven't had much experience with sex. On Saturdays, after the political meeting on the ground-floor
offices of the Communist Youth, we turn off the lights,
put on music, smoke, and feel each other up on the ter-
razzo floor, which is grainy with sand from our boots
and makes my hair stand on end. Until a better pros-
pect presents itself, I let Manolo the Goon feel me up.
It's unrequited—I don't touch him. I know he's popped
a boner, but I think, Sorry bud, that's as good as it's
gonna get. He's a cute guy, a looker, actually, but his
nickname turns me off. And it fits him too: he's a goon
from head to toe, and even though he's nice and he's
as into politics as I am, it's just an uphill climb for me,
trying to like him. While the meeting's on, Manolo
smokes Ducados, but as soon as the lights are out and
the debates over, he rolls up a joint. He's a hash expert.
I see him around sometimes in the square with other
goons like him arguing over the quality of their hash.
I've taken a hit just to fit in, but the smell of it turns
my stomach. Manolo, his tongue, his hair all smell like
hash. That also makes me think there's likely no future
in our relationship. The other day, he was touching me
down there, fumbling around, and all of a sudden he
asks me: Does it hurt? And honestly I didn't know what

he was talking about, I had quit paying attention long before.

There's a chick in the Party—not the Communist Youth, but the actual Party—and even though she's just two years older than me, she's already a woman of the world. Amanda has an exotic face, like an Egyptian cat, and curly hair that she lets grow wild, like an Afro. She normally wears these hippie Indian dresses that hang down to her feet, and she doesn't wear a bra. Her boobs sag a little and bob under the fabric when she walks, when she talks, when she smokes; I'd like to have a pair like that and not mine, which seem made of pure marble and start right at my collarbone and make me look hunched over and fat. In wintertime, Amanda doesn't wear a duffle coat or shearling like the rest of us. She puts on a sheepskin vest with wool on the collar that hangs open. Whether it's hot or cold, her boobs are out flopping around. One time my father saw me with her in the plaza and I had to introduce her. My father went all gaga, but she was more gaga than him. It was embarrassing.

Amanda's got a black boyfriend. He's the hottest guy in my neighborhood. By far. When you see them on the street with their matching Afros, their ponchos, their leather shoulder bags, her snow-white boobs quivering under her dress, and him, tall and thin, seeming to float as he walks, they look like an apparition, like a scene from a movie. Just walking through, they seem to transform my neighborhood into the background of a record cover: they're a couple that ups the ante, because next to them, none of us, not even I, can make the cut. The other day, I don't know why, I told my father that if I ever fell in love with a black guy in the future, I'd marry him. Maybe I was trying to clear the way. My father looked at me uncomprehendingly, and the third time I defended this hypothetical matrimony, he said, "Great, go marry a black guy if you like!" And I thought, Of course I like.

Sometimes Amanda says to me: We're going to meet up and fuck in this apartment someone's lending us. I have to pretend this information is something natural for me, like if someone told me they were going to their friend's house to water the plants. I don't think I've ever said the word *fuck* aloud. F. U. C. K. It's not that I never had the chance to, but I'd like to just be able to say it blithely, fuck, damn it, son of a bitch, shithead, for fuck's sake. A lot of the guys in the Communist Youth say *for fuck's sake*, but before this past year, the only time

I'd ever heard it was coming from the surly-looking drunks I saw in the village bar when I went looking for my dad. Sometimes in the bathroom I practice swearing, but I can tell my pronunciation is too prim. I also get up on the toilet and shake my torso to see if my boobs vibrate, but no, I'm like a concrete block. My brothers have always told me I have a complex, that I'm a Goody Two-shoes or a spoiled brat.

I don't know how this instantaneous friendship came about, but I've started following Amanda everywhere: she walks so fast that I'm always behind her, running like a little dog. You look like her dog, Raquel said. She's jealous. But since she started cleaning houses, Raquel hardly goes out. Amanda says: Come on, let's go to my place, and I go to her place. My mother would say: If she asked you to jump off a bridge, would you? I follow Amanda blindly. She lost her mother a few years ago, and her father is paralyzed because the Fascists beat him up for being a union organizer. Her house and her life— it's her and four siblings—are run by a family council. This council meets once a month to take stock of their money situation and their conduct. I try to imagine how my life would be if, instead of parents, I had a council. Sometimes, seeing how things stand at home, I dream of having a council to run my life for me. But maybe the four of us would come to blows the way they do at Amanda's house. I've seen her hitting her siblings, watched them pull each other's hair, seen the sisters shouting. One says: Don't you dare touch me, you fucking lesbian! Then the other shouts back: Stay out of my way and stick to fucking your black boyfriend, you tramp, that's all you ever think about anyway!

Amanda looks at me sometimes, and a mischievous grin rises up one side of her mouth. I don't know why she's taken a liking to me, I don't feel I can really compare to her. When she looks at me like this, the way she might look at a little girl, I feel horribly embarrassed. She says to me: Do you masturbate? You should masturbate. And before I can make myself answer, she gives me advice the way a mother would, You really need to start masturbating. Who am I supposed to think about? I ask. Who the hell told you to think about anyone? You just do it, because you like it, because you want to come, so you can be independent of any man. Lots of questions remain there floating in my mind, like, for example, whether she masturbates so she can be independent of her boyfriend or whether she needs to masturbate after f. u. c. k. i. n. g. that boyfriend. That boyfriend! But I don't ask anything, I don't say yes or no, I just observe, I observe without opening my mouth those fights to the death between sisters in that house governed by a family council, with that father that stares at them, remote, in his wheelchair. He's a sad sight too.

Amanda makes me feel like a complete idiot, but I keep going back to her because she fascinates me, enchants me, and fills me with self-doubt. Sometimes we go together to a meeting of the Communist Youth on Calle Peligros, because I'm in charge of propaganda in my area, even if I don't know who decided that. I don't dare admit that I've hardly ever gone downtown: just to buy clothes with my mother and eat pancakes with whipped cream at the Nebraska restaurant afterward. Last year my Saturdays were spent going with Raquel to a bar in Goya where they made hot dogs. We'd eat two in a row for twenty pesetas and be back in our neighborhood in half an hour. I spend my whole life pretending to have experiences. It's exhausting.

We sit in the last row during the political discussion, and Amanda talks to me the whole time, jumping from one subject to another, from a skipped period to skin fungus to her sister's fucking girlfriend to her poor mother. When Amanda talks about her mother, her eyes mist over. Have you gone to the gynecologist yet? she asks me out of nowhere. To the gynecologist? I think. But even though she seems very interested in the question, she doesn't wait for my answer. I don't say I did or didn't go. I don't know what we're doing there anyway, we could be at one of the bars in the neighborhood where we wouldn't have to talk in whispers like we do in school. The delegate who's teaching us slogans has called us out several times. I'm super-embarrassed, but Amanda half grins and asks him straight out: Dude, what's your problem? She's free, she leaves the meeting, and I watch her disappear into the dark, narrow streets of downtown, she isn't going back to the neighborhood, I run off after the Number 20 bus because my mother is surely already sitting by the window looking at her watch. The Communist Youth newspapers are weighing me down, and I don't know how I'll keep them hidden at home until I can take them where they're supposed to go. If the 20's late, I'll catch a taxi and tell them to drop me off a block early so Mamá won't see me from the window. Everything I save walking through the empty lots to school I blow on taxis.

I'm forced to play many roles. With Amanda, I feign experience, in the Party I try not to be a petty bourgeois, at home sometimes I forget all that and sit down to watch a movie with my mother as I did when I was a girl. We watch it holding hands. I feel a long-lost peace. Then I get into her bed for a while; it's not my father's bed anymore, they sleep separately, and we talk about things that have nothing to do with the outside world. We focus on the film, on the actors, on the plot. My mother likes Gregory Peck. She talks about him as if she knows him. She thinks he's not just a great actor, but a good man. She must imagine he comes home on time. Not like some men. My mother doesn't go out much. She's always afraid her heart will start racing. The afternoon she went with my sister to see the film *Cría cuervos*, she came home sad and wouldn't tell me why. My sister told me what the movie was about: a girl who thinks she has superpowers, and her dead mother, who wasn't taken care of as she should have been by the girl's father, appears to her at night. For me, it's obvious that my mother sees me in that girl, and it's hard for her to accept me as a fifteen-year-old, she liked me better before. She's thinking about when I'll be an orphan even though it hasn't happened yet, and it makes me suffer, because I can't stop growing, getting uglier, pulling away. My old powers of turning her despair into joy stopped working a long time ago.

My sister goes to the movies with her boyfriend, and then she tells me the plots at night. We sleep on a sofa bed, and at night we pull the two mattresses snug. We sleep together, my parents sleep separately. We can spend several nights on the plot of one film, because I ask her for lots of details: about the costumes, the dialogue, the settings. Then I fall asleep before she can finish. She gets mad because she says I make her waste a bunch of time when all she wants to do is read. She spends the day reading because she's studying literature in college, and then she lends my mother the books the department assigns her. They whisper behind my back and then fall silent when I enter the room. They don't let me in on their secrets. Once I heard my mother say: One of these days I'll go, but this time it'll be for good.

My mother barely leaves the girls' room, as they've called our room forever. She listens to music there, reads novels, and makes incredible flowers out of white bread the way a neighbor who gives floristry classes taught her. She's also started reading from front to back the newspaper my father brings home at night. There are days when she's going through a silent spell and she doesn't come out to serve my father his meals and I have to do it instead. Then she gets jealous because she hears us talking. And don't get me started on what happens if she hears us laughing. She'd like for her, my sister, and me to be a single unit, and for me to take her side and leave him his dish and his wine and walk off without speaking a word to him. But I don't know how not to love my father. She taught me to love him above all else. Even if he's late, even if he doesn't take care of her, even if he leaves us things to do that he should do himself. And I listen to him. Or I try to. I act out the strange part of the girl substituting for her mother. I don't like it, and sometimes I hate both of them for it.

Chechi's hair is wild and wavy now, and he wears beaded necklaces. I'm the only one who seems to notice he smells like weed some days. When I smell it, it makes me laugh. He looks like Jim Morrison. Lolo leaves his room in the mornings now with a beret on, like Che Guevara. My sister Inma has plucked her eyebrows so much they look like two lines drawn with a pencil. My mother won't let me pluck mine or even my shadow of a mustache, which is driving me crazy. My legs are so hairy Chechi tells me I look like Pirri, the soccer player. We spend lunch listening to a cassette of protest songs Lolo puts on whether we want him to or not, and he listens closely, looking gravely down at his plate, as if being with us were a waste of his time. The only person whose life is open and sincere is my sister. The rest of us lie one way or another; we say we're going to one place and then we go to another, or we say we've been in class when we've gone to the movies, or, in my case, El Retiro. Lying isn't always necessary, but you get used to it and then you can't stop. Sometimes I run into my brothers on the street during class time and we say nothing, as if we didn't recognize each other.

I'm the gullible one in the Party, and at home they treat me like a little girl. I go along with it because it suits me. But at my school, the school my mother chose because there were only girls there, I'm a hell-raiser. I feel like a tomboy at times, and I hang out with other girls like me. We wear hiking boots, flannel shirts, corduroy pants. I like playing the boy when there are girly girls around. We smoke between classes, and on certain afternoons, we go take a nap in El Retiro. Once, while I was asleep with my lips cracked, a guy came and gave me a kiss. I could feel his damp, fleshy mouth and his spit, with the snail trail it left behind. A shiver ran through my pubis, a brief and fleeting excitation, but it went away when I opened my eyes and saw he was a young beggar, a lost crazy who laughed and revealed his chipped teeth.

There are men who wander around El Retiro looking for girls, and we make fun of them, we point and jeer at the little flaps of flesh they show us; like banshees we scream that theirs is little. We fall on the ground laughing. But I don't have any other dicks to compare them to, because I've never seen any other ones in person.

Sexual promise is in the air; we feel excitement for what's to come, and it permeates everything: the philosophy classes where Victoria, a big, chubby, sarcastic, shameless teacher, talks to us about liberty of thought and the search for pleasure. We are astonished, yearning to go outside and uncover all mysteries once and for all. My mother couldn't imagine this subversive doctrine she delivers to us without the need for any boys to pervert us. It would never pass through her mind that my old physics instructor, Delia, comes to class in a Russian cap and wears a patch of Lenin's face on the lapel of her austere leather jacket. Delia walks between the desks as though mustering troops, and I try to keep from crossing eyes with her because I understand her no better than if she were speaking Russian: zilch. Then there's Domi, Domiciano, the trickster, the meek-looking teacher preaching revolutionary ideas. He's infected us with his love for Spinoza, whom we haven't read, but whose thoughts he relays to us regardless of what we're talking about or what the topic of the day is. We shouldn't joke about human actions, he says, we should try to understand them. He looks at me, or I think he looks at me, and I lower my eyes because I don't know if he's aware of what happened the other day.

Some classmates from another homeroom told us the literature teacher, Don Feliciano, rubbed his groin on the edge of the desk to get himself off while he was giving lessons. Somebody's got to teach that pig a lesson, we told each other. I don't remember who got the big idea in their head or if it was a collective effort, but we colored the corners of all our desks with chalk. That afternoon, we listened more attentively than usual to his soporific monologue, recited from memory. Affected, trite, pretentious Don Feliciano in his impeccable cheviot suit with his watch chain dangling from his vest. We watched in shock, seeing that the rumor was true, and while he rambled on about alliteration:

The princess pursues across the orient's sky
The vague firefly of a vague inspiration

He kept discreetly grinding against the edge of each desk and staining his pants front with chalk. Those verses reminded me of my father's deep voice; he recited them often when I was a girl. And I was unsettled by that blend of childhood memory and perversion:

Ay, the poor princess with the mouth of rose
Wishes to be swallow, wishes to be butterfly,
Thin wings to have, beneath Heaven to fly

He saw our smiles, sensed there was something mocking, malicious, sly in them, and turned on his feet, like a dancer doing a pirouette or in a chameleonic reflex, mannered but inquisitive, shocked at the looks on our faces. Then, for some reason—maybe because deviants live in fear of their deviancy being found out—he looked down at his zipper, saw what had happened, and started shouting hysterically: "Whores! You band of whores!"

———

We celebrated this triumph—there was no getting around it, our prank had been a resounding success—but the euphoria dissipated as I made my way home, and when I arrived, I was pouty, deflated. My mother asked: What's going on, something's up. I felt almost feverish. I thought of that creature that's inhabited me for some time, a creature that takes over me sometimes and pushes me to commit acts of cruelty, to seek vengeance. I remembered all those weird habits I cover up, but that are visible sometimes because I just can't help it, those rituals I perform right before someone comes in. My lucky numbers, my compulsive blinking, walking staring at the sun, touching the ground three, six, or nine times, the temptation to obey dangerous impulses, the strange sounds that come from my throat, all those old childhood ceremonies meant to ward off death and disgrace. I struggle tirelessly to conceal them so my mother won't upbraid me. But she thinks calling me out on them in front of others is a way to correct me. The very opposite happens. All she manages to do is embarrass me.

All we managed to do was embarrass Don Feliciano. Try to understand human actions, Domi, the tame revolutionary, says, and I feel him looking into my eyes. Strange bird.

———

Last year, we went to Mallorca at the end of the school year. It was the first time I'd returned to my island since we moved to Madrid. The island of the little bookworm and her mother with the open heart. I was a Mallorcan then. Kids become from a place right away. My father says we have to let the places we live leave their influence on us. Now I'm a neighborhood girl. My accent is from Madrid. My sister signed my report card behind my mother's back because this year my grades are just all right. She told me she won't do it again because it's illegal, so I better get my act together.

I felt like the head of the class on the trip to Mallorca. I thought I'd be able to show them our Sunday beach, the Paseo del Borne, my school, the port, Calle Quetglas, but no, we never left Magaluf and a disco where I spent three nights dancing with a guy from Birmingham who sent me a photo in which he's wearing his local soccer team's scarf. My god, the guys from Birmingham are ugly in the daylight. All I remember from this trip is that we bought a bottle of vodka and took it to our room. We passed it around till it was empty. I got so drunk that I spent the whole last day in the room vomiting and thinking how ashamed my parents would be if I died of alcohol poisoning. I wonder if it's done lasting damage to my liver, cirrhosis or something.

This happens frequently. I get obsessed with what could have happened or what could happen. If I read *The Exorcist*, I think the devil might possess me. If I read one of my sister's scientific books about sex, I think I might be growing a penis and sooner or later it will pop up: Here I am. After I read it, I looked at myself every time I went to the bathroom, using the same mirror my sister used to pluck her eyebrows. From the book's illustrations, I knew that my little lump was the clitoris, but one day I started sweating, because it looked huge. This thing is growing, I thought. I'd turned the mirror around and was looking on the magnifying side. Imbecile. I live as if there were something inside me that was going to snap, sooner or later.

On the boat back from the end-of-year trip, I met a Basque guy. I told him I was thinking of joining the Communist Youth and he understood me right away. He was a good deal older than me and was already into politics. Sometimes I think I look smarter than I am, because older people always have high expectations of me. I gave him my address, and he started writing me these long letters, I don't really know about what, in a tight, slanting script full of political theories. He signed them *The Steppenwolf.* Soon I started thinking he might be from the Basque separatist group ETA, and wanted me to be his contact in Madrid. I told my brother Che-chi this, I said: I met this guy who might be from ETA, I mean, you can definitely tell he could be. And he told me: "Right. Some guy from ETA's going to tell you, of all people. Guys from ETA aren't that stupid." When I say I seem smarter than I am, I'm not talking about inside my family, obviously.

My obsession with ETA coincided with the arrest of a kid from my neighborhood called Osibisa who had a couple from GRAPO (the First of October Anti-Fascist Resistance Groups) in his apartment. He wasn't in GRAPO, he was a nobody, he was like me, just someone from the neighborhood. He didn't know the couple, but some friends of friends of friends asked him for a favor, and he lent them the room for a week. They played him like a violin. Tell it to the cops. Osibisa is still in jail, even though lawyers from the Party are trying to get him out. It seems like some-thing from a movie, but this is how it is nowadays. So I put two and two together, and then my obsession started. Besides, the guy wouldn't stop writing me. What the fuck? Didn't he have anything better to do? I'm not so interesting that an eighteen-year-old dude who only ever saw me for two hours on a boat should be spending so much time writing me. He told me he wanted to come to Madrid. I didn't even remem-ber his face. He had a beard, but who didn't back then? My question is: Can you fall in love enough to leave everything behind, a sick mother, a father like the one I had, school halfway through the year, for a guy who might get you caught up in a criminal enterprise? Could love blind me so much that I could plant a bomb on my uncle Angelito, the colonel, for example? When time erases the obsession, I can see how dumb it was, I see it, and I think I won't succumb to such nonsense, but when I'm in it, I'm stuck. I get this guilty look on my face—in this particular case, the look of a terrorist.

When I get obsessed with something, I imagine I can't control myself, that I won't manage to rein in my impulses, like when I thought that if I ever got pregnant, I'd throw myself off the Vallecas bridge before I told my father. That bridge is next to the home of a comrade from the Communist Youth, and I go there with him sometimes when his parents aren't around. He tried to convince me to f. u. c. k., and I told him, "I'm not ready," which is a phrase I use to say no without seeming like a tight-ass. Figure it out on your own, Amanda tells me, but don't be a tight-ass. It's so hard to find balance in life. I told the guy I wasn't ready as I looked out his bedroom window at the Vallecas bridge, "I'm not ready," and I felt like a little girl surrounded by mystery.

———

I write poetry on my father's Olivetti. I've got two books already. One is called *There's Always Something Hidden*. Estrella saw it on my shelf and cracked up laughing. Strange bird, she said. Lolo published a book with the help of the Party. On the cover, he's smoking a cigarette, and he signed copies of it at a booth at the Vallecas Fair. I don't know if there have ever been two poets in the same family. I type with ten fingers because I took a typing course. My friend Raquel won a prize in our old school with one of my poems. I lent it to her to present. I told her: Take it, I've got more than enough. I reserved for myself what I thought were the best ones, but hers (i.e., mine) won. The jury sucked. My father bought the Olivetti for his law classes because no one can read his handwriting. He's in his third year of continuing education, the college for people over twenty-five. He gets better grades than us. And he can type as fast with two fingers as I can with ten. Nowadays my father likes Red poets and reciting them; he reads poems aloud and I record him. He loves to listen to himself later, and for us to listen to him:

How sad
I cannot sing the way
The poets sing who sing today!

How sad
Not to croon in cloying tones
Those bright ballads
To the glory of the fatherland!
How sad
To have no fatherland!

My father's gone Red. In part because the Party helped my brother publish his book and get his life together. My father thinks you've got to have some project to organize your life, be it Dragados or the Communist Party. He says he's always been a Red, but when he turns around, my mother shakes her head. From sheer gall, my father wants her to become a communist like him. But my father doesn't want my brothers getting mixed up in political nonsense, and he always tells them that if the police ever stop them and ask for their documentation, to say their uncle is a colonel in the Civil Guard. Chechi's been arrested a few times leaving concerts, not for his politics but for his hair. My father admires Santiago Carrillo, the secretary-general of the Communist Party of Spain, because he has authority, and my father likes authority.

My mother has turned ironic. It's like she doesn't believe in the truth of anything anymore. I don't even think she trusts God. Nothing surprises her anymore. She reads the newspaper, and when my father talks

about the elections, she raises an eyebrow as if to cast
doubt on everything he's saying. She often insists to my
sister and me that we need to study and make money.
She even dares to say this sometimes in front of Dad,
and he takes it as a criticism of their marriage, of him—
as rancor. He's right, because now my mother wishes
her life had been different. She's spent her life asking
my father for money and it's obvious she can no longer
stand it. When they're fighting, she sends me to ask him
for it. He doles it out just a tiny bit at a time.

I knew her when she was content, happy, I'd even
say. She had a smile I've never seen on anyone else. Not
even on the most beautiful women you could imagine.
When I first knew her, when I first remember her, when
I was four, five, nine years old, she looked serene to
me, she stood out from the other mothers. I adored her
smile, her broad hips, perfect for crying in her lap; I admired the beauty she radiated, the beauty of a person
who follows the dictates of her character and doesn't
try to draw people's attention because she knows she
doesn't need to. Even when her scar was still tender
and I thought I could cure it by running my fingers up
the spine of that centipede which in the early days had
stiff strings sticking out of it like the legs, even then she
smiled with hope.

Now she looks at us over the tops of her round reading glasses, which look like those of John Lennon or

Janis Joplin on one of those rock records my sister's boyfriend brings over. She's a lady with rocker sunglasses observing her family as if she were already looking down on them from the other world.

There are Saturdays when I come home from the Communist Youth meeting and the apartment is dark because it's wintertime and night falls early. I smell of everyone else's hash, I have the faint vapors of my last drink on my breath, and my clothes stink of cigarette smoke. I'm scared my mother will smell me and interrogate me, but all the lights are out. I ran out of the Communist Youth offices, leaving Manolo the Goon in the lurch, still hoping one day I'd return the favor and feel him up, maybe give him a hand job, but I'm not ready, my sexuality is still confined to fantasies I can't manage to materialize. I read and reread page 120 of *The Godfather* and it gets me hotter than when any boy touches me:

> *It was getting late and they went up to their room.*
> *She mixed a drink for both of them and sat on his lap*
> *as they drank. Beneath her dress she was all silk until*
> *his hand touched the glowing skin of her thigh. They*
> *fell back on the bed together and made love with all*
> *their clothes on, their mouths glued together. When they*
> *were finished they lay very still, feeling the heat of their*
> *bodies burning through their garments. Kay murmured,*
> *"Is that what you soldiers call a quickie?"*

"Yeah," Michael said.
"It's not bad," Kay said in a judicious voice.

A *quickie.* Up to now, all reality has offered me is smells that gross me out, clumsy caresses, and internment in a childish world that prevents me from giving myself over to a sexuality that both fascinates and terrifies me. Page 120 is a pleasant refuge. I want to live there.

A memory comes back into my head, one that always surprises me: in this same apartment, when I was nine years old and I spent the days taking care of my mother just after her operation. The cleaning lady's little boy followed me to my room, and without saying a word, touched my pubis and grabbed my hand and put it on his penis, which was stiff as a board, and I just sat there cupping it like I was holding a bird. He was a short, thin gypsy boy, handsome, with long hair, precocious and sly. And I was a tubby little girl. I remember I was wearing pajamas, blue polka-dotted pajamas. His hand on my pubis and him guiding mine to his dong. The two of us standing there, not doing anything else, shaking the way children shake in Japanese cartoons in moments of tension. When we heard his mother or mine walking by, we retracted our hands and went back to other games. Is it possible that the discovery of pleasure remained back there, arrested, trapped?

I wander through the dark apartment, not turning on the lights, passing through the girls' room, my room, making sure she isn't there, then going, ill at ease now, into the little room, the dark little room where my father goes to study for his degree on certain afternoons. A small bed pokes out between shelves, like a drawer, for short-term visitors, and my mother's there in the drawer giving off muffled cries that mingle with the pulses of her agitated heart. Its beats sound like the plastic chest cavity of a doll when you shake it hard. It's a clipped sound overlaid with the sighs of a person in deep pain. I smell like tobacco, hash, horny boy sweat, but she won't notice now, she's steeping in her pain, and I lie down next to her, almost falling off the bed because the mattress is so narrow, and I know I can't do anything but hold her. I won't be able to save her. I don't know if I even want to anymore, and that tortures me. Inside, I just want everything to end, for this Saturday and every Saturday like it to end. Where's my father? While I hug her, my mind travels toward Monday, to the still-confused aspirations certain teachers have awakened in me, to those days of strikes when instead of studying we play Johnny-on-the-pony, roughhousing and hurting each other, sweating, to lazy naps in El Retiro and our first draft beers at the bars in Atocha; I'd like to follow in

Amanda's footsteps down those streets in the center of town that I still don't know but that contain the promise of danger and freedom. Peligros and Libertad, dangers and freedom, those are the names of two of the streets I know. I'd like to see myself walking through abandoned lots on a Monday, crossing hills surrounded by roads where we bump into guys who will never go to school and creeps like the one who attacked Estrella. I want desperately to escape this Saturday and expose myself to danger.

Raquel's father bought her a scooter. He wants to make up for her having to play housewife since her mother's gone. She leaves dinner on the table at night. She does everything without protest, as though it required no effort, but I know sometimes she stays up till the morning hours studying the things she couldn't get around to during the day. We take the scooter back and forth from school now. At first, when we were heading downhill on the curves in the Barrio del Niño Jesús, I would cover her eyes a moment and we would shout from pure excitement, as if we were both ready to die. Then one day a guy saw us and got out of his car at a stoplight and shouted: "Are you girls idiots or what? Let me call your parents and you can kiss that fucking scooter goodbye!" My mother is scared I'll fall in with the wrong crowd and doesn't realize I usually *am* the wrong crowd.

My father gave my mother a box with a ring and a pair of earrings inside. My mother doesn't want them. From what I could grasp from what my mother said in the bedroom (I was behind the door eavesdropping), if her husband's giving her jewelry, it's because he's got a guilty conscience. The jewels are proof of guilt. The box stayed there on the nightstand that's between their two mattresses now. And even though they went to a Chinese restaurant the other night to a work dinner where the wives were invited, she didn't wear the ring or the earrings. My sister and I noticed. She wore a dress she bought when we arrived in Mallorca. Nowadays my parents have to go socialize at night. The women wear long dresses, and my mother thinks they are stupid and frivolous, people from another planet. I think she has some kind of hang-up and doesn't trust women who aren't as discreet as she.

I remember when I was nine, sitting in the corner of a velvet-lined dressing room in a boutique in El Borne while my mother was in the mirror trying to decide on a dress with a low neckline. I looked at her with admiration, because I'd never noticed my mother had boobs, the kind you would show off, the kind you'd be proud of. And she looked at herself as if staring at another woman.

"Close this up a little," she finally said to the shopgirl, "my husband won't like it so open." The shopgirl told her it would lose some of the charm if she did, and that it was flattering to my mother's chest, but my mother's stiff, she doesn't give in, just as she refused to accept this gift from my father that for her has a very precise significance. And no, she's still not ready to forgive him.

She's shrunk a bit in the past year. Now she always wears pants, flats, and turtleneck sweaters. While the neighbor teaches her to make a bouquet of flowers out of white bread, they talk on and on, unaware that I'm in the hallway listening. I always spy on her. I have since I was little, and that's why I know all the things I know. They can't pull one over on me easily. The two of them went out for a bite yesterday, that's what they told me, ha ha, now I find out they were watching *Emmanuelle*. They remember scenes from it and laugh. My mother says, "He knows how to do all that and more. Where did he learn it?" The neighbor wants her to go into more detail, but my mother is reserved, even if she does let slide the words "Everything, everything." The neighbor always tries to convince her to clean up a little, show off her good side, seduce him, she says, but my mother doesn't feel like seducing anyone. She no longer believes in him, no longer believes in God.

———

I go with her to vote. She was going to go with him, but they got into a spat at the last minute. She didn't want to vote for the Communist Party, no sirree. I should have taken my father's side, since I was a member of the Communist Youth, but even being in the Party, I can't be so insistent, so bossy. We climb the hill together to the voting site, holding hands as always, though I keep thinking maybe I'll let go if I run into a comrade. She's got her ballot in her hand, she's going to vote for the first time in her life, for Felipe González of the Spanish Socialist Workers' Party, and she's happy to be choosing for herself. I can't understand what she's so proud of, but I think what she feels is satisfaction. It's strange and slightly intimidating to me. As if she were transforming and I didn't know who she was going to become. She doesn't like me growing up, I'm afraid of her not being what she always has been.

One morning this summer, I go to the doctor with her. I've never been to Concepción Clinic, where they operated on her. When they brought my brothers and sister and me from Palma to see her, she was already back home, just out of the hospital, and so I've never fully laid eyes on the famous Dr. Rábago. I idealize him as much as my mother does, but for me, he's a mystery. I imagine him like Gregory Peck. Tall, attentive, delicate. In a lab coat that shows off his broad shoulders. Auscultating my mother with his eyes half-closed. Slightly in love with her. I don't know why I'm supposed to go with her this time. Maybe my father couldn't skip work and my sister has an exam. It's a checkup. One of many these past five years. A doctor comes down the hall and my mother gets up. I thought I would recognize him when I saw him, but no. Dr. Rábago isn't Gregory Peck, even if my mother stares at him with such devotion that I end up seeing him through her eyes until I do believe they resemble each other.

We go to his office, and after asking her a few questions about how she feels—my mother says she's very tired—he asks her to lie on the bed behind the screen and open her blouse. I get up to go with her, but he tells me to stay seated.

"How old were you when we operated on your mother?" he asks me.

"Almost ten," I say.

"Have you been taking good care of her?"

"Really good," I say.

"She's getting older now, and...she doesn't look after me like she used to," my mother says, smiling.

It's not true, I think. It's not true! She can never stop acting like she's been disappointed. Well, I feel disappointed a lot of the time too.

I see shadows through the fabric of the screen. The cardiologist is bent over her. Asking her things about her mood, her pains, her arrhythmia, her breathing, her tiredness, her depression. He talks about depression, a word I've never heard before. The conversation is long. They treat each other formally. The doctor listens to my mother. Even without seeing him, I can tell he's a good listener. When she's answered all his questions, he stands there for a second in silence, as if needing to analyze all the information she's given him. I follow parts of their conversation. Sometimes I don't understand why they're talking about such personal issues; at other moments, I just get distracted. My mother is usually so reserved, but here she is opening her heart to a man who actually held it in his hands. Is that why he knows her better than anyone? My father would be horribly jealous if he were here. Dr. Rábago tells her surgery has made great progress in recent years. There are better valves than her current implant. He explains it to her carefully, as though worried about upsetting her. She responds timidly, but also worried about letting him down. No, I won't go through another operation. He warns her something's giving out. No, I'm not strong enough to try again. I hear them talking there so tranquilly that I absorb their words without alarm. No, I don't want them to operate on her again either.

We catch a taxi and my mother says: To Goya! And we both chuckle, overjoyed not to be going back to the neighborhood. At Parriego she buys me red sandals, and at Cels García something she calls *outfits*, a little big so they'll fit me this summer and the summers afterward. I'm sixteen now, but she still harbors the hope that I'll keep growing and eventually be taller than she is. It's natural. We go to a restaurant, the California, for our pancakes with whipped cream and chocolate. It's just like when we used to go out in the morning. What are you going to be when you grow up? she blurts out. I know there's another question behind this one, something she really, desperately, wants to know: What's going to become of me? As if she foresaw a catastrophe. We don't talk about what the doctor just recommended. And since we don't, we wind up forgetting about it.

She'll get better at the beach, my father says, and even though for days now she's only had the strength to go from the bed to the sofa, we help her pack her things. What little clothing we have is divided up into three red suitcases: one for my parents, one for the girls, one for the boys. This may well be the last summer we spend together. Inma is bringing her boyfriend, she and her boyfriend are driving there, she's taking along the music her boyfriend promotes for his record company.

I want to go with them, listen to James Taylor, Carole King, Joni Mitchell, Maria Creuza, Toquinho. A whole new universe has come through my ears. I want to have a boyfriend, a boyfriend with an old car, to drive with the windows down listening to Creedence and singing along. I don't want to spend another winter shut up in a ground-floor room behind my house letting some guy I don't like feel me up. I don't want to go home and see her destroyed.

She'll get better at the beach, my father says, but it isn't true. She hasn't managed to get out of bed. We take turns. We go out for walks at night. We try to come back soon so she won't get worried. My father goes down to the rocks to fish. She's strangely relaxed. She doesn't get alarmed if we come back late. She doesn't complain when she's left alone. You might say she's found a peace she didn't have in Madrid. It must be the sea, it lowers your blood pressure. I have a red-and-white checked bikini with embroidered edges that my aunt, the seamstress, copies from a pattern in a magazine. It's cheesy but also cute. I haven't grown, I'm still shorter than my mother, but I've got style now, and my waist is noticeable, my wide hips; you can see my pubic bone when I'm in panties. I'm not a conventional beauty. I'm not a beauty at all, but I'm cute and I like that. My boobs are brown because when my father can't see me I take off my bikini top. I want a boyfriend to touch them. I'm on my period, that's why I haven't gone to the beach today. I wanted to put in a tampon, but no matter how hard I try, it just won't fit. They say the hole closes up if you get nervous. Just remembering there was a time I thought I'd sprout a dick makes me laugh. But I can't laugh at the person I was, because my mind is still full of obsessions. My period is like a torrent, but unlike my friends, I like it. I've always been a little gross. I like my blood and I enjoy that feverish mood that overtakes me. Sometimes clots fall out of me and I flip out. They look like little bits of fried liver. I feel like that little girl with the fever that couldn't go to school, and it's a good feeling. When I'm on my period, I want to sleep with a guy. That's when I feel most like it. I've decided this is the year. It's a dare. I can't wait any longer. I found one of my sister's love letters from her boyfriend and I read it. She's already done it. Her boyfriend talks about *making love*. Amanda says fuck and screw. I don't know if these are two different things. I imagine when I actually do it I'll know if there's a big difference.

I got my legs waxed. The woman who did it said that since I was going to the beach, she was going to pay special attention to my groin. I get up on the toilet to look again because I like it. When I lower my panties, I can still see my pubic hair, thick, black, hard, and curly, and it runs up close to my belly button. Once, when I was ten, a friend from school slept over and tried to kiss me there. I would never have thought of such a thing, now I know the deal, but it really surprised me then. I let her do it, with my usual relaxed attitude, and I didn't notice much besides a tickle. When she asked me to do the same, I knelt down, ready to go, but the smell turned me off. The next day in class, she wouldn't say a word to me. It's not the only time I've been called a tease.

For a while now I've been listening to something that sounds like a machine that can't start up right, that won't get going. I open the window, but there's nothing there, that's not where the sound is coming from. I open the door to the bathroom, where I've been for more than an hour, and I stand still, trying to figure out what I'm hearing. At times, it sounds like an animal. Without knowing why, I walk slowly to the living room, where the mechanical sound turns human. It's coming from the bedroom. I move toward it cautiously, not to wake my mother, who may be sleeping and may be the source of this strange snore.

She looks at me wide-eyed from the bed. The same bed she's hardly gotten out of since we arrived. Her nightgown is open at the top, revealing the scar and most of her pale left breast. She seems to be grunting rather than breathing. She stretches a hand out and I approach her. I don't lie down beside her as I often do because I'm afraid to touch her. I tell her: It'll be all right, I'll go get Dad. She says to me: Don't leave me alone, I'm, dying. I tell her: No, no you aren't. She says: This time I know it, I know it, I'm dying, I can feel it, and I'm scared.

My mother said to me, What's going to become of you, what's going to become of all of you. And I didn't understand until many years later the meaning of that anguish that plagues a mother when she realizes she has to abandon someone who still can't go off on her own. I didn't know what death was until many years later, and I am still trying to grasp its slow, singular effects. At every age, that wound reopens, one way or another, and now I often think of all the questions I didn't ask, the reproaches I should have uttered, the explanations that might have calmed my anxiety, the infinite remorse I felt for no longer being the girl who wanted to cure her and once even had the power to do so.

That winter, I changed my routines, but I don't relate that to my mother's death. I stopped going to the Communist Youth offices and went back to tramping around with Raquel, who now had more time to waste because her mother had returned home. It was an odd reconciliation: her father never forgave her mother, and her mother pleaded guilty, even though her old bitterness toward him never went away. Amanda slowly vanished. One day she called me after returning from a trip to Amsterdam, and in her room, I helped her take off a corset made of gauze with drugs hidden inside it. I supposed it was drugs, because she didn't tell me what was in those bags. And since I was intimidated, I didn't ask. She was very thin, edgier than usual, and pretty too. She'd changed the way she dressed. She was strange, extravagant, sophisticated, capricious, and always overweening. She hugged me because I'd lost my mother. She cried, more for herself than for me, and told me to find a guy. Fucking is a consolation, it calms you down. She told me she couldn't focus on just one guy. I left her home shocked, upset, thinking I should just accept that women like her weren't for me.

Some of my old classmates spent Saturday afternoons smoking joints on the benches, and more than one started fooling around with heroin. The communist gang started to splinter, and I began to fantasize about men of the world who would take me out of my neighborhood. My sister and I examined our lives minutely, reconstructed our mother's life, analyzed our father. Well into the night, we talked about our family, all we had experienced without leaving that narrow cage our mother had built around us.

I would hurry home in the afternoons, knowing my father would be there waiting for me on the park bench because he couldn't make himself go up to the apartment alone. He never said he was afraid to, but I knew, because I was the same way. My mother's presence had been so continuous, so persistent and powerful in those hallways, that there was no way to walk down them without thinking she might appear at any moment. We were both afraid of her reproaches. Love and remorse mingled in his mind, and in mine, the guilt of having grown up and pulled away from her.

The dead appear to us in every one of life's ages, and depending on when, they confront us in different ways. Today I'm walking around these 1,300 square feet and feeling them, both of them. I'm not afraid of their ghosts anymore. I'm just trying to reconstruct all those figurines my mother threw on the floor the night I believe I started to give up. To put the pieces back together. To understand that her love decayed so dramatically because it died with the same passion that gave birth to it. We, the four siblings, secondary characters, only came into the world to make things more complicated.

One afternoon in January, six months after my mother's death, I stopped by my father's bench to take him upstairs. I was angry that he'd waited there outside in the bitter cold. I didn't like feeling responsible for his fear and loneliness. I just said hi, nothing more, and walked to the door without crossing eyes with him. I'd just slept with a boy. It was the first time, and it had been so easy, painless, natural, that the guy said to me, "You're not a virgin, are you?" I said: Of course I am, but with a malicious smile, so he'd think I was lying. Just to try to be interesting.

EVERY TIME THE WIND BLOWS

Dad comes to eat lunch every Saturday. He's so punctual that my husband puts the rice on as soon as the front door rings. Until a month ago, he'd show up at two on the dot, but after an argument we had about the three glasses of wine he'd drink before sitting down at the table, he's started showing up at two thirty, after half an hour at Navarino's Bar, drinking all the wine he pleases. I don't know how he does it, but in every neighborhood, he always manages to find a bar for "gentlemen from the seventies," which was a golden age for him as far as bars go. They're what used to be called *cafés* in Spain, and some are in the English pub style, with a special spot for clandestine dates in the back. Some are nautically themed, with framed ship's wheels and knots. Papá walks into Navarino's, and the waiter serves him his first glass as soon as he lays eyes on him. In a month, he's become a regular, and some of the men at the bar greet him by name. He likes to introduce himself with his first and last name. He's quite proud of his last name.

In every neighborhood he frequents in Madrid, Papá has a bar where he takes refuge, and each bar has its own specific group of pals, people he argues with about politics and then makes up with afterward. He used to have his favorite bars all across Spain, back when he was an auditor and visited work sites to check the books and point out falsehoods and irregularities. He'd let the employees butter him up in the steakhouse or the sea-food place, but he always had to find a bar where he could rest his elbows and spend his dead hours.

I feel bad about arguing with him about the wine. All I managed to do by refusing him a third glass of wine at home is convince him to have four at the bar, just to show he can.

It's two thirty and the door rings. My husband puts on the rice. This is a clockwork mechanism, a Swiss cuckoo clock with everyone devoted to their tasks. I hear him clear his throat as he crosses the small yard out front, stopping to take a drag from his cigarette and emitting along the way the sort of sonorous snort that tells us he's feeling crabby. Papá doesn't like our new home one bit. To reach the kitchen, you have to go downstairs, then up, then back down. Hence the snorting. When I hear it every Saturday, I want to tell him before I kiss him: You'd make it up and down the stairs better if you didn't smoke while you were doing it, and if you hadn't downed a few glasses of wine to boot. But the sway he held over me as a girl casts a long shadow, and his opinion is the one that triumphs: This house has too many stairs, damn it. Neither of us discuss something that has become clear quite recently and that changes everything, including our interpretation of his opinion about my home: he's an old man now. He acts like he isn't. And with him, I avoid that condescending attitude we usually adopt toward the old, and I never let anything he does slide.

When it's hot, he dons a little cloth safari hat that's too small for his head to protect himself from the sun, and with it a beige vest covered in pockets. He could just as well be carrying a shotgun or a butterfly net in his hands instead of a cane. His old face, tanned and cracked from his endless enthusiasm for the out-doors, has turned pale in the last year. He's grown old in a matter of months. There are signs of decline: his slow steps, the asthmatic voice that hints at pulmonary obstruction, but he can't accept that this is the last act, and his seventies' gentleman barfly act is just as excessive as ever. People praise the modernity that arrived in Spain in the eighties, but no one seems to remember the executives of a decade before, who liked whiskey, studded leather bars, hookups at odd hours, background music, blond American tobacco, and infidelity. In their contemptible way, they broke the stereotype of the office man, even if that modernity excluded women.

Papá comes into the kitchen and kisses my husband on each cheek. They're firm kisses, the kisses of a father, a godfather, a patriarch, accompanied with a soft or not-so-soft pat on the neck. He kisses his old work colleagues the same way, and my friends after the second time he meets them, and I notice how his brusque effusiveness catches them off guard.

He has a cloth bag slung around his shoulders. Inside it is his inevitable leather man-purse, which a gentleman smoker used never to be seen without. As soon as he enters, he pulls out several packs of cigarettes and lays them out on the kitchen table, as if about to play solitaire. Marlboro, Ducados, Coronas that a friend from the Canary Islands brings him, Lucky Strikes, maybe Chesterfields. He needs to look at them to figure out which is the right cigarette for the moment. In all of his vices, he conceals his dependency beneath sybaritism. More worrisome to me is what's still in the bag. There are photocopies of articles about us that he hands out to guys at the bar if it strikes him as opportune. He knows I don't like it, that my vanity shrinks as his swells, but my husband tells me it's a waste of energy struggling against the inevitable. Papá copies everything, right down to his ID, so he can leave the real one at home. He also likes to copy articles of questionable provenance defending the use of tobacco, and the columns of writers he deems more tolerant than I am who oppose the segregation of smokers in public. There's no getting around it: he doesn't care for this era. One afternoon recently, my sister and I were sitting on a terrace with him and he ordered a Cuba libre, and when the server told him they didn't serve alcohol, he asked: "What's happening to Spain?" In this particular case, it was nothing alarming; we'd accidentally sat down at an ice cream shop, but still, he'd already made it through the better part of a tirade, because everything for him is a symbol of this era, when his freedom to indulge in his vices has been curtailed. But at the same time, the relaxed nature of contemporary manners also sets him off. Every Saturday he tells us about teaching lessons to the urban youth: how he nudged a young man with his cane for putting his feet on the seat in front of him, or lectured a group of teenagers who'd climbed up on his bench, saying: Your feet are there dirtying up the place where I read my paper every day. His bench! The same bench where the neighbors go to chat with him awhile and ask his advice about their tax returns, how they should vote, or medical matters, because this old man who puts his octogenarian's health through the ringer with alcohol and cigarettes has thumbed through his medical encyclopedia till it's falling apart and is happy to look people over and offer his diagnosis. He's an autodidact. If something's wrong with him—it's almost always the bronchioles or his liver—he rereads those chapters with the smeared letters on the onion paper, and once he's detected the origin of the problem, which naturally never has a thing to do with smoking or drinking, he goes off to his doctor with a list of the medicines he needs. Here's the list. He's not just asking to ask, he knows. I'm no dummy, he says. He doesn't trust degree holders. I don't buy what they're selling, he says, this country's got a sick obsession with degrees. He doesn't ask for a diagnosis and he doesn't follow medical advice. He says, To fix one thing they screw up five others, and all they want is to open you up. He only goes to the clinic to come out with his prescriptions. I'm not going to spend the whole afternoon in a waiting room, I don't have the free time some people have.

We don't know whether to believe him, we never know whether to believe him, but to hear him tell it,

the doctor has gotten used to treating this character
who won't accept his role as patient. With time, they've
formed a bizarre friendship. The other day we had a
glass of wine together at the Azul y Oro. A glass of
wine? With your doctor? Yeah, I told him he could stay
at the house in Ademuz when he likes. Dad! Of course
I offered it to him, the guy needs to get away, get some
fresh air. You told the doctor he needs fresh air? Yes
ma'am, just like they told me in Cádiz when you were
born, and I've never forgotten it: relax, get some good
exercise, wear yourself out. I told him the very same.
So what did he say? He pays attention when I talk, he
can blow off steam with me. I'm his rock. The outpa-
tient clinic is depressing, a bunch of frail old people,
kids spreading around viruses, everyone begging for
antibiotics so they can take half their course of them
and then chuck the rest in the trash. Everybody in this
country wants antibiotics. The waiting room is packed,
it takes so long I can go outside three times to smoke.
No, I go there with my list ready. You give him your
list? Yeah, I write it down, sometimes I don't even give
it to him, I just read it out, because he can't read my
handwriting. I've got doctor's handwriting myself. Five
minutes every two months and I'm done. Papá, I don't
think it's normal for a doctor to hand out prescriptions
like that. He does it because he respects me, because
I don't just linger around the waiting room, I don't

complain and I don't demand a bunch of antibiotics so I can flush them down the toilet.

This dark episode in Cádiz has always hovered over his stories about the past, which are never very detailed if he's supposed to remember something sad. My father doesn't like sad things. He flees sorrow and edits his own biography, which he claims to be writing in snippets on napkins in Mijares, the bar he goes to in the afternoons. Sometimes my sister and I grimace, because he makes himself out to be a long-suffering father once married to an invalid. A martyr. We try to squeeze the truth, a truth we were there to witness, out of someone who's spent his whole life running from it. It's a pointless, and maybe even cruel, exercise to try and force him to remember himself remorselessly, when we know certain memories torment him when he's all alone.

He likes me being a humorist, it worries him when I go into my family history, but he's gotten used to it, because everything I write obeys the deal he forced on us when we were little: covering up things that aren't funny at all with humor. Not long ago, I published a story about my mother's open-heart surgery, and that's what I called it, "Open Heart." When he got home, he said, "It's well written, but it's really sad." That conjunction contained a tacit reproach, a petition: Write about what you want, but not the things that cause me pain. Don't break our pact. There were things I felt I couldn't write about till he died. Cádiz comes up because it had to have marked him, but how precisely was always vague and fragmented. As with so much, it's as if his children had to intuit everything from his short, abstract statements. I'd like to tell the full story of the past, a past I don't remember but that I was a part of, but all I have are inconclusive phrases and the shrouded past of an always-irritable man.

DAYS OF MADNESS

A few days before I'm born, my parents hit it big in the New Year's lottery. They use some of the money to buy their first car. My father learns to drive on his own, without classes, and with the family inside. If he dies, why should his children live? He waves his hand out the window because he doesn't yet trust his abilities, and those beginner's gestures will never go away, even when he's as comfortable driving as walking. To relieve my mother's weariness after my birth, and maybe the loneliness of being a mother of four, Papá decides to take us to spend some time in the family village. It's our first trip in a car, from Cádiz to Teruel. My siblings, ages five, four, and three, are in back, and I am in front, just a few months old, resting in my mother's arms next to the erratic driver with the cigarette in his hand.

Papá leaves us at our grandfather's house, which we're supposed to treat like our own, and we spend a gentle spring there in the country, surrounded by fruit and vegetable plots and being coddled by aunts and neighbors. He goes back to Cádiz alone. He's thirty-two years old, and his aptitude as an accountant has helped him rise fast in the company. He's ambitious, he doesn't care how many hours he spends in the office or on the job site, and sometimes he even brings his account books home. He's lucky, because he knows she's waiting there for him, and unlucky because he has a baseless fear that she'll vanish. She knows about his apprehensions, and since she realizes they'll only grow worse during those days of solitude, she knows he can't be by himself, and she starts worrying he'll look for someone else. In their first letters between Ademuz and Málaga, there's a desperation in my mother's writing that reminds you of a romance novel: *I love you more than ever and better than ever. I've already told you many times, if you leave me, I'll die, I'll die.* They are made for each other. They share a disproportionate love that might end in disgrace at any moment.

My mother is docile, she couldn't be any other way, her traits are delicate, harmonious. When she's serious, she looks frightened; when she smiles, she does it so warmly, showing off her perfect teeth, that you can hardly resist giving in to her kindness. These two expressions—one of timidity, the other of tenderness—captivated my father from the moment he first saw her in the courtyard of the Civil Guard station in Málaga, where she had gone to help the captain's wife, her sister, raise her children. My father saw the girl smile, then turn serious as though hiding some sorrow, talking with the clear accent of that prodigious city that would eventually be his, and thought, I want her now, and said: Marry me tomorrow. When she returned to the village, he grew frantic, got scared, wrote her father to ask for her hand, and two months later he went to the village for the first time for the wedding.

In the photos taken by the young village photographer who would become the unintended chronicler of that universe in the countryside, you can see them looking stern as they enter the church, surrounded by the poor kids that show up at any and all festivities; there they are in front of the priest, formal and on edge; now they're smiling as they cut the wedding cake with the obligatory bride and groom on top and the beaded curtain in the background, at a cousin's bar where the makeshift banquet was held. Everything humble, everything poignant, sincere, a consequence of imperious desire. He had years of loneliness behind him, he'd never gotten much tenderness, so he didn't know how to give it: product of a childhood thrown from place to place, two years as a youth in the Civil Guard patrolling the Málaga Sierra on horseback, cold nights, boots too small for his feet, with a partner just as badly off as he. He didn't like that life, and without studies, he'd never make it past captain. He doesn't like having a doormat for a father. He doesn't want a wife like his mother, who fears more than she loves. He tries to emigrate to Canada to be a lumberjack, but it doesn't work out. He prepares to take the police exam, but it's called off, and so he puts to good use something that for him was like a game, a talent he never guessed he could make a living off of: numbers. Numbers, for him the most comprehensible language, like sheet music for a musician. His teacher at the academy tells him, *Oh, if only you could go to college.* And that phrase, that lack, will torment him throughout his life. Arrogance will be his way of hiding his sense of inadequacy, his resentment against his parents for sending only his little brother to school.

When he writes to his future father-in-law to tell him he wants to marry the man's daughter, he says, I want to marry her but it has to be soon, she, too, seems to be in a hurry. He has a place to offer her a first home: Ceuta. The day after the wedding, with a hangover evident in the bags under his eyes and fright you can see in hers, they head south, where she will give birth to a new child every time they move. The first time she gives birth, she gets scared and travels pregnant from Ceuta to Teruel to take shelter with her sisters. Málaga will always be the city of her dreams, Málaga, the El Palo neighborhood, the fisherman's quarter where she wished she could stay forever, cozy, familiar, where the sea is gentle and where you can go down and walk by the beach in the evening. There, perhaps, her clear accent might have taken on the relaxed sensuality of the south, there she could have been another woman, could have transformed and left the village girl behind, but these wishes aren't worth bothering with to him. His drive to prosper has no room for weakness, and nostalgia is a luxury they can't allow. Málaga will get left behind to become an eternal symbol, the place where she wanted to set down roots. Málaga is where she gave birth to her third child, Chechi.

Cádiz is a different story, nothing else is like it. Woman, how could you not like Cádiz? He introduces her to new cities like a real estate agent or a local reporter. Everything is perfect. He loves the people shouting without a care, the constant hubbub, as if the street were at once a vast household and a marketplace. If it wasn't for the wind, which bothers him and drives him indoors, this would be the place for him. But with her brood of children and another one on the way, she stays holed up in an apartment without its own neighborhood or its own street, in a solitary building outside of town, at the mercy of the winds, situated along Cádiz's Industrial Highway, and to make a nest of it, she reproduces with their scant furnishings the first home they lived in as a married couple—their apartment in Málaga—which was in turn a re-creation of where she had lived before, and she will do this forever, forging a domestic homeland to make nomadic life less painful for her.

The young mother closely studies the photos taken of them in the attic of the building a few days after my birth for their accreditation as a large family, which makes them eligible for a number of social benefits. She's drained. As a girl, she suffered from fevers that left her with a heart murmur. Only now, after four pregnancies in a row, has the doctor told her to be prudent and try to avoid a fifth one. Papá grimaces, because he's long dreamed of a house full of kids, seven, eight maybe. He likes tiny children because they don't talk back, they're funny, they're primitive, like puppies, and they adore him. He likes to say: My brood.

After leaving the family at Grandpa's house, he returns to Cádiz in his car. He stops at the bars at the crossroads and has a drink at each of them. For him, the road is a place to meet people, a safe, familiar emptiness. He's in the prime of life. He's not alone. He's got a woman who loves him, admires him, tolerates his jealousy, submits to this nomadic life, where everything can change from one day to the next, and who deals—albeit painfully—with the sorrow of never really liking to be anywhere. Four children have emerged from her womb, and she recognizes their father in all four of them.

He enjoys an undisputed masculinity, a fieriness his children haven't quenched. The sight of his pregnant wife reinforces the idea that pleasure is greater when it bears fruit. That is why he struggles to accept the idea that I, his youngest, will also be his last. He arrives in Cádiz and enters the apartment. It smells like her. Like a bloodhound, he also sniffs out the scent of children, but stronger than the Number 2 pencils and baby food is the aroma of his wife. It's the natural scent of her very pale, round breasts, soft, full of milk, prettier after starting to sag a bit in that ruthless period of motherhood that started five years ago. This perfume her flesh emanates lodges in the man's olfactory memory, and he will describe it to his second wife eighteen years later, when his first one is no more.

———

The apartment smells of privacy disrupted. He opens his suitcase and leaves it on a chair. He goes to the kitchen but doesn't know what to do, he doesn't know how to do anything. He steps out onto the large balcony, where he used to sit in his pajamas every afternoon with the children. He's struck now by how isolated the building is, from neighbors, from Cádiz, the untamed city that branches off in streets like hallways where people mill about with cramped familiarity; Cádiz, always buzzing, gregarious, rowdy, so open it's nearly impossible to suffer or enjoy a single morsel of solitude; Cádiz, like a picture postcard colorful against the skyline; Cádiz, how far Cádiz is from this apartment surrounded by cranes and gigantic concrete blocks where on Sundays he takes neorealist-looking photos of his children peering out from inside a gigantic pipe or sitting on top of it. He later develops these images in a darkroom, absorbed in one of many fleeting pastimes that reveal his unsuspected, fickle talents.

The city far off, the open sea out front. The home exposed to those winds that, they say, give rise to madness. She isn't afraid of the wind, the storms, or the heights. My mother is serene and peeks over the railing to contemplate the sun's rays glowing in the sky, the waves breaking menacingly, the bellicose roar of thunder. She's enjoyed this spectacle since she was a child, when she and her father and sisters used to look over the living room balcony to admire the rainwater rushing through the village and clearing away the debris. She smiles to herself, laughs at my father, but eventually gives in to his fears, not calling them fears because another of his preoccupations is that she'll think he's a coward. They usually close themselves up in the bedroom facing the courtyard to wait for the sky's fury to die down: the children watch their father smoke and stare at the floor while their mother concentrates on something or other, familiar now with these eccentricities she loves but can't understand.

Sensing menace in the east wind, Papá briefly asks himself why he brought her here to this solitary building where she feels isolated and unprotected, and immediately he turns this flicker of guilt against her, imagining her off in the village surrounded by love and affection and himself here unbearably alone.

He sits down in a chair in the living room, as tense as if he were in a hospital waiting room. He goes to bed that night without dinner. He drinks a brandy and smokes in the darkness, trying to imagine how he'll fill his time and give it order. When the morning light enters the bedroom, he washes and shaves with a meticulosity that distinguishes him from other men. He passes a straight razor over his face and remembers seeing her reflection in the mirror when she would bring a cup of coffee into the bathroom every morning. How long did she say she was staying in the village, a month? Ridiculous.

He goes outside and strolls with long steps till he reaches the city. Everything's different in the light of day, and he loves seeing the city reborn, smelling of coffee, of washed cobblestones and the coarse leaves of geraniums. Cádiz seduces him. He thinks how few times she's visited this paradise on earth. It's as if the two of them lived in two different universes: him working hard and frequenting the raucous bars downtown, and her in that apartment that's like a ship moored in the port. The scent of coffee fills his nose like a promise before he enters the bar Brim, where they know him; the owner doesn't ask before greeting him with a coffee and Inés Rosales biscuits. Just two breakfasts or two glasses of wine are enough for the quick-witted waiters in this city to consider you a regular. His pale suit shows he's an office man, almost a gentleman with his stature and his noble looks, even if he does come down to the people's level, where he's relaxed, a fish in water. They talk about the east wind kicking up, you can already smell it, and soon the city will be dry and covered in sand.

He unlocks his office and waits there for his colleagues while he works. The routine of work envelops and protects him. He smokes constantly, goes downstairs for another coffee, goes out to munch on something, gets back to work. He doesn't visit the work site, the cranes aren't moving today. When it's time to go, he grabs a glass of wine with a colleague. Then the guy leaves, and without meaning to, as though impelled by necessity, he starts wandering. In some of the bars they know him, in others, he makes himself known. The nocturnal bachelor's life, with him dragging out his time on the street until the dawn broke and he crawled back to his room at the pension, ended when she came into his life, but sometimes his old impulses carry him away, his willpower flags, and he returns at sunrise to find her there crying. He hugs her, perspiring nicotine and alcohol, and murmurs: Come on, now, what's wrong with you, dummy?

He can feel his beard growing in. He walks down the street as if he had somewhere to go, the way he learned to do as a boy to pass unnoticed or not look lonely. His steps take him to the Pai Pai, a place he's been going to on nights without her when the need for escape overpowers him. There are two men inside him, one tenacious and one distractable; one reliable and one unruly; one puritan, the other anything but. The first one restrains the other's madcap tendencies as a defense mechanism; my mother hates the out-of-control one, wishes she could erase him from her life, but her aversion provokes the opposite effect: stubborn, disobedient, he takes off again.

A woman with a manly voice is singing a bolero. That harsh masculine voice imposes itself in his memory over the voice of my mother, who sings when she does the housework so softly it seems like she's whispering, into her children's ears, into his.

Every time the wind blows
It carries a flower away
You'll never come back, I know,
My love.
Don't abandon me
At nightfall
The moon rises late
And I might get lost.

He hates the savor of melancholy, and alcohol helps him break down barriers and shorten distances, and unsure how he wound up there, he finds himself at the next table over, chatting with guys who at first were maybe as lonely as he. The dim lights of the cabaret, the laughter, deform the faces of his new friends, dim the sound, distend the hours, which expand amorphously into an endless early morning. He remembers himself as a young man with a shifting identity before he met her, at the mercy of a wild streak that guided his impulsive character. When he leaves, he feels the wind's lash and the weight of the overcast sky. Two or three coffees shared with the last of the night owls, and he takes a bus back home. He falls asleep and dreams fitfully of her voice threatening to not come back. When he gets up at his stop, his beige linen suit snags a bit on a nail sticking out of the seat. Once on the sidewalk, he writes down the tag number of the bus.

Back in the apartment, he doesn't want to go to bed. A blanket of light dust has covered the table, the dresser, the bed, the crib, the children's toys. He left the window open. After closing it, he sits in the dining room, immobile like a Pompeian figure caught off guard by death.

He's never remembered the days he spent without sleeping, three, maybe, in his head the bar tops file past one after the other, disordered, out of time, the

Manzanilla, Casa Manteca, conversations in clipped phrases in La Viña, quick naps at some point or other in the office. He opens his eyes, emerging from a long, deep sleep, and the first thing he sees is a man in a white robe, his same age, his same build, with almost his same face. He looks so similar that for a moment he wonders if it might not be him, doubled in a dream, telling himself to get his life in order, watch out for his deliriums, tone things down for a while, take up a sport, call his wife and tell her to come back as soon as she can. Why don't you take up fishing, buddy, the guy tells him, "fishing forces you to meditate and concentrate on the simple things." They've always told him he looks like the director of the psych hospital in Cádiz, people have even confused them with each other before, and that's it, there he is, signing a sick leave authorization and treating him like a child even though they're contemporaries.

When Mamá, alarmed by the telegram, goes back there in a taxi a few days later with the kids and her father and brother, he tries to smooth over his breakdown. He has had the house cleaned, washed and shaved, waited for them as though nothing had happened, but she eyes him up apprehensively. He's skinny, trembling, ashamed. His older daughter approaches. Papá, Marisol's coming, take me to see her. Papá, she's coming for carnival. And he strokes her braids. Marisol, Papá, the girl repeats, sensing that her father is listening to her from somewhere very far away. The older daughter, who's barely six, takes a seat on the sofa, responsible beyond her years, holding the youngest one, who's a few months old, and singing her a song, *Chiquitina, chiquitina*, and their father feels overwhelmed by the wish that they'd all just die, her, the children, him, so no one and nothing could affect their lives in this refuge.

Slowly, the human presence in every corner of the house salvages him from unreality. In the pocket of his raw-linen suit she finds a piece of paper with numbers scrawled on it in a jittery hand. He stands there thinking, trying to remember, until he puts the torn jacket on again and it hits him, and he leaves home to find that bus. He looks at the numbers he wrote, wavy and disordered like a child's chicken scratch. He waits for the bus, looks for the seat with the nail sticking out, and sits there, ill at ease. He feels a suppressed urge to vomit. Before getting off, he tells the bus driver he's just ripped his suit. The driver tells him to go to the office and put in a complaint, there's nothing else he can do for him.

He undertakes this mission as though it were the sole cure for the ailment that nearly drove him to the one thing he's always feared, losing his mind. Every morning at office hours, because he's on leave and has got nothing to do, he visits various claim windows seeking compensation. In the afternoons, he descends to the rocks to fish. At first, following his impulsive, expansive nature, he tries to strike up conversations with the other fishermen, but seeing that they're uninterested and that silence is a precondition to joining their group, he reticently, docilely adopts this discipline, and for the first time, he learns the joys of shared silence. After a month, city hall sends him money to buy a new suit.

When he tells this story, it always stops here, with the happy ending, pushing everything else down till it's invisible, modifying the tale at his whim to erase little by little others' memories of the signs of madness in those days.

Who's going to clean the mud the kids' shoes leave on his bench in the wintertime? They don't know a thing, he says, they don't know the price of the water they drink, they won't know where they get the water for the plants in that park that he watched emerge from the dust in front of their building when they arrived in '73, Darwin Park, as it's called. He talks to whatever young people will listen to him, sounding like an old nutcase, about the Atazar reservoir and how the trashmen need it to clean all the shit they leave behind, stomping like they didn't know any better right where he comes to catch his breath in the morning, in the August heat or the January cold, reading his newspaper and chitchatting with the neighbors. He talks to the kids about the workers who died at the dam, victims of ruthless nature, all so that they could come here and get their filth all over everything.

The kids look at him as you look at a lunatic, or at least that's how I imagine it, I rested my boots on this very same bench, and I was perfectly aware of the miraculous origins of Madrid's tap water.

Papá wants his bench clean. He feels nostalgic for a world where an old man could talk down to a group of badly behaved youngsters and they would look at the ground and tamely obey him. I don't know if the world ever was like that, but this is how it looks to him in his memories, which are inevitably distorted. He walks down the street now trying to recover the lost time when people were more considerate, pointing out how crass people are and cursing whoever's around. Dad, Dad, someday someone's going to answer you back and there's going to be trouble. Talk back to me? He says, as if the warning were an insult. His inner violence, which I remember breaking out in his old fits of rage, roils vigorously now but is sterile in his thoughts. An authoritarian without vassals, he stomps down the street like all those Mr. Sammlers on the Upper West Side whose paths I cross in the wintertime in New York, just as ruminative, just as bitchy, head full of diatribes, hypnotized by his minute observations of a present he can't grasp but which he studies with entomological relish.

I think he takes pleasure in imagining conflicts where he's forced to intervene, if necessary with aggression, to restore a lost harmony to the world. I've never known a more quixotic man. My father wields his cane like Quixote brandishing his lance, and is often on the verge of poking anyone who dares shatter the serene cityscape. He wants to keep the world in balance, but there's no way for him to do it. At the stoplight, he murmurs the same old crabby melody about mothers clutching their cell phones and pushing their baby carriages into traffic, forcing the cars to screech to a halt. Maybe he really did see this once, but it's turned into a classic now, on permanent repeat. He grumbles when a cell phone rings on the bus, when children play ball next to the patio where he has his wine and does the sudoku in the afternoons, when they call him an old fart and don't respect his authority as a man of a certain age. He has a tireless urge to be recognized because he feels his presence diluting. I can't help reproaching him, but I often feel sorry for this boss without subordinates, this father who lost his undisputed authority many years back. Sometimes I'd like to commute his sentence and say, Dad, you can boss everyone around all day to your heart's desire and no one will argue with you.

When I serve him rice, he lights a cigarette. He doesn't have the same hunger as in the old days, and any old thing distracts him. He'll even lean his cheek on his hand like a boy in a school cafeteria who can't finish his meal and feels the food lodging in his throat. I want to grab that head of his and kiss it, but I don't, I've lost the habit.

He doles out optimism and fury in equal doses. He loves his neighborhood, his apartment, his balcony, where he goes to smoke at night and breathe in some much-needed fresh air. It's the only balcony in the building that's still open. The women in his building close theirs off when they become widows. It's as if standing in the open somehow represented disloyalty to their dead husbands. His building is full of widows who have closed off their balconies with aluminum, but he resists, out there on his third-floor balcony—he didn't get a higher unit because he suffers from vertigo. He's a widower twice over, and ironically used to live in a luxury apartment in front of Maudes Hospital, where he went so many times as a boy just after the war's end to pick up his aunt, who was a nurse for wounded soldiers. He's still not alone: a lady he calls his *squire* sleeps at his home so he can feel a human presence and so the spirits and demons his mind gives birth to won't harass him. He doesn't put it like this, but I know. On Saturdays, she leaves him, and my sister and I take turns going to see him, because, to quote him directly, "You know I can't eat by myself."

He likes rice, he likes the rice with bouillon his son-in-law makes, but he smokes a cigarette and lets his food get cold and with every deep drag the ash grows longer, and he forces us to stare at this burning tobacco we hope won't fall into his meal. Papá, Papá, your ash. Papá's hand is on the folder he's brought over in his bag. He tells us he's got something surprising with him. He laughs, he enjoys the mystery. It's something to do with a speeding ticket he appealed months back. Since he retired, his primary activity has been appealing and complaining: it used to be a hobby, now it's an obsession, fighting abuse and corruption from his humble corner of the world, as he calls it. And his roguish intelligence shines through his knack for numbers. "Half insane, full of lucid intervals," as the Knight of the Green Coat said of Quixote.

My brother called me the other day to tell me he'd come across an old colleague of Dad's from his Cádiz years who had inquired after him warmly before spinning a finger around by his temple and asking: "And the thing that happened, he never had any problems with that again?" That thing, that thing. My brother is more tactful than I and didn't dig any deeper. I realize every time I've gone for some kind of therapy, because my anxiety keeps growing, I've wound up talking about him, as if discovering the origin of his mental state might give me access to my own. Dr. Michelena, attentive and perceptive, ventured a fitting verdict on my father, similar to the one uttered about Quixote: he's intelligent, with a tendency to delirium, which he kept under control in his productive years, when he had work and family obligations. Now, since he's retired and his schedule is open, he spends too much time in fantasyland.

A few months ago, he found an oil painting in the trash, a homemade copy of *The Girls on the Bridge* by Edvard Munch, and took it home. When I asked him what he was doing picking worthless things out of the trash, he took offense at my questioning his judgment. The following Saturday, he brought the painting for us to look at. He'd taken it to Navarino's first and shown it to his new colleagues at the bar. What if Munch painted several copies of the same work? He asked. Couldn't it be? He sought the support of my husband, who answered sarcastically, "Could be, could be," without falling into the trap, "but for that Munch to end up in a trash bin in Moratalaz would take a good many more coincidences."

Maybe his son-in-law's humor is more effective than my ire. I told Dad to stop going around talking

ELVIRA LINDO

nonsense, people might think he's crazy, but even if,
in this particular case, his reasoning bordered on the
bizarre, my doubting it only made his delirium worse.
My husband, who's funny and tolerant of Dad's eccentricities, lent him some Munch catalogs. Later,
I scolded him for indulging these delusions. "Leave
him be, he's keeping himself entertained, and besides, this way he's concentrating on just one obsession." And entertain himself he did; for months he
used his allotted time at Saturday lunch to inveigh
against corruption, astutely analyzing, with his old
accountant's soul, Spain's endemic ailment, before
somehow managing to divert the conversation to
the recurrent theme of Munch. The excuse for mentioning the Norwegian could be a date or figure (my
birthday—*Congratulations, dear, by the way, you were born
the same day Munch died*—or a record set at an auction
of his art—119 million dollars—but, as my husband
told him, "not for yours, Manolo"), or some essential
facet of the human condition: angst, death, solitude.
For months, all roads lead to Munch. Eventually he
dropped it, after my many attempts to cut his tirades
off, but without showing irritation or averseness to
them; probably he had just grown bored of this odd
foray into Nordic expressionism; and at that point, he
at least appeared to consider the remote but not entirely implausible possibility that what he had leaning

against the wall in his apartment might not be one of the great works of twentieth-century art.

It would have been more practical to ignore the first sparks of his delusion, to let it go or maybe even pretend he might be right, and thus to make it easier for him to pull back from the ledge, because quixotic deliriums are a common feature of authoritarian characters, who can't stand mockery or opposition to their ideas, however absurd they are. But perhaps I only managed to grow up by casting doubt on my extravagant father's ideas and unrealizable plans: Dad's talking to us about alien beings, Dad's spotted UFOs, Dad wants a castle, Dad's bought a country house and wants us to see it, Dad's found some Roman coins that will make him rich, Dad knows who's responsible for that unsolved murder in the paper, Dad knows where a kidnapped child is, Dad's going on about some crime triangle on the coast; when there's a famous criminal or a disturbed woman who stabs her friends, Dad does what he can to establish some connection to the case, Dad knew the parents of the girl found guilty, Dad used to have coffee with the gangster known as El Solitario, the Loner. Dad is always tugging at the thread, and all of humanity comes unraveled in his mind. The crazy thing is that sometimes what seems like utter nonsense to us winds up being true, or almost true.

The appeal against the speeding ticket on the free-way is a subject we've heard about for some time. He sits down in the chair in his office, where he used to work on his company's files, and analyzes invoices, fines, or the bulletins of his condo board. Paperwork. He has tons of imagination, and he embarks on impossible projects. For a while, he was trying to get Madrid's municipal government to sponsor his building's bathroom repairs through a program for historical conservation. "Why not? The building's fifty years old now. The other day I heard on TV they need to keep them in good shape for movies set in the seventies." Luckily, this matter was forgotten when the corresponding institution issued a resounding no. He devotes his unchained intellect to paying nothing or as little as possible for any and all goods and services. From the very first, he was unwilling to pay the speeding ticket, and eventually he winds up pulling out a letter he sent to the transport secretary. "This is my last shot," he says. He reads it aloud in his still-gallant voice, which is raspy and muffled from the tobacco. He tells the transport secretary why, in his opinion, the fine is an unjust one, entering into details we have a hard time understanding, some of which seem confusing, others deceptive. In the next paragraph, he alleges humanitarian and personal arguments, making clear to the aforementioned transport secretary that his driving record is impeccable and that, as an auditor for Dragados y Construcciones, he has traveled to every corner of Spain with four children in tow, never failing to show prudence and responsibility. He generously offers his help with the eternal problem of urban congestion. He's no passive citizen, he's ready to make a change. This issue of traffic circulation is one that has always occupied him, so much so (he clears his throat), so much so that I may as well mention that my daughter, at eleven years old, with my help, won a children's writing competition you yourself sponsored. She's a writer. You may know her. He clears his throat because he knows he's entering dangerous waters. He names me. And he goes on: I helped her write an essay which offered several solutions to relieve traffic in the city, and she, he adds, being the diligent girl that she was, understood, and she received said prize in 1973. Cordially.

My husband and I are dumbstruck.

"Papá," I say desolately, "you can't do that. Don't you realize the position you're putting me in?"

Without listening, my father pulls another letter out of his hat. The more important of the two, the one that makes him laugh like a little boy, the one he uses to convince me that everyone else understands him, that everyone else thinks he's the tits, that I'm the only one who thinks his behavior is strange or out of place. The transport secretary answered him. He looked over the ticket. You're right, he writes. The whole thing's baffling. The transport secretary has ordered the damned ticket expunged. And he ends the letter with an affectionate greeting to my father and his daughter, with congratulations for the prize in '73, and another to his illustrious son-in-law. My father doesn't capture the irony here, or maybe he does but doesn't care, because in the end what he wanted was not to pay the fine, and he got it.

"Not bad, eh?" he says. "Right?"

He knows there's nothing funny about this, but he keeps repeating himself to avoid my anger. And my anger will soon melt away, just as it did when I was a girl. I'll forget the bad mood he's put me in, the shame, the discomfort. But later, when he repeats this "Not bad, eh," I'll respond that I disagree and that my name is only mine to use. I'm convinced I'll manage to turn the whole damned thing into comedy: his bad behavior, his mischief, like a senescent little boy's. We'll wrap the whole thing in humor so it's bearable, we'll accept it the way parents accept a child's neediness.

I've done this many times before, turning his eccentricities into farce, into a comic strip, but making his strength, his fury, his brutal intelligence and indomitable character into something tender, incidental, a cause for laughter that reduced his personality to the stereotypical grumpy old man. I didn't know how to translate his amiability into words, his neighborly willingness to strike up a friendship with whomever, his need to shoot the breeze with strangers. When he saw himself transformed into a comic character, I know he found it deeply strange, because he takes himself so seriously and likes to inspire respect and even fear. Seeing himself in writing, his manias and his authoritarianism on display, voicing inappropriate thoughts that make him ridiculous, traumatized him. He's sensitive to ridicule, needs to reinforce his masculinity at all times, and seeing himself as the butt of a joke in other's eyes shook him to his core. But vanity is a balsam that heals all wounds. Going to his usual bars and hearing people laugh at the stories I told about him made him feel popular, and that was compensation.

When he leaves, after putting on his ill-fitting hat, returning his cigarettes to his man-purse and his man-purse and xeroxes to his cloth bag, I watch him walk, big and clumsy, to the door, and I imagine the hangover from all the whiskeys he drank after his wine at lunch. When I empty the ashtrays it feels like I'm struggling to breathe. As if I'd smoked all those different brands of cigarettes piled up one over the other. We open the windows and rest, exhausted. He always leaves a feeling of weariness and defeat behind him. He always wins, whatever the argument, whatever the contest.

At the award ceremony for that essay prize, they handed me an envelope with a voucher for a sporting goods store in Puerta del Sol. My father took me there one Saturday morning. The place was immense, and it did honor to its name, All Sports: they had whatever you needed to practice any sport you chose. But I didn't need anything. I had two left feet, I was tubby in my early teenage years, and physical activity didn't interest me. I'd once gotten the notion to take part in the intramural track and field championship at school, but the differences between the events eluded me. In the relay race, I didn't hand the baton off to the next runner; in the discus, I almost split open the heads of a couple of girls running on the track; there was basketball too, and I got hit in the face with the ball and still didn't manage to catch it; my long jump was no more than a few centimeters. Still, that shop fascinated me— the possibility of cashing in my voucher, the athletic wear, the beauty of those accessories for sports I would never understand. My father told the clerk to find me a polo, a Lacoste polo shirt, which brought back to me memories of Mallorca, when I'd wanted to be a prep. Pleased with my maroon polo, I followed my father to the fishing department on the second floor. I watched him clutching my voucher eagerly. He showed me one tackle box, then another, then another. The voucher was enough for one rod and one tackle box. "And the polo, don't forget!" he said, in case I got the idea to complain. He told the clerk, maybe as a justification: "The thing is, the girl doesn't like sports." And we left All Sports, the two prizewinners, each with our bag, and walked to the parking lot. Even if it never entered his head to feel anything like gratitude toward his little girl, I did feel vain rather than generous for buying my father something. He tormented us with that gift on the highway, stopping whenever he saw a river that looked promising enough to cast his line. A gift bought with a voucher I now understood he considered more his than mine, since, according to him, he wrote the essay, and beyond that, he's the one who made me who I am.

THANKS, EVERYONE!

There the time lived was so alive
That it always survives life itself
And every day I think its splendor
Of fruit and promise will return.

SOPHIA DE MELLO BREYNER ADRESEN

My brother held the remains in their winding cloth in his two hands. Time had left so little of her, she looked like a baby in the apprehensive arms of a first-time father. My cousins, no strangers to dealing with the dead, oversaw the procedure. After removing the nameplate, they had pulled my mother's coffin from the columbarium and handed my brother César (aka Chechi) the bones, which the gravedigger nimbly bundled in her shroud. A phrase kept echoing in my memory. The question my grandmother Sagrario asked when she came to visit after my mother's death. How did they wrap the body? she asked. And I took this, like everything she did, as a symptom of her coldness, a mind that only knew how to stress prosaic details, being incapable of comprehending feelings.

In my memories, my mother wears her suit with the brown jacket she put on when she took a trip with my father one long weekend in May. It was the last trip they took together. I took it to mean they were reconciling. The mood in my house hinged on my parents' quarrels and reconciliations. It was tiring, molding to them: after a period of silence and confrontations, you would suddenly hear them in their bedroom talking excitedly. I would hate them for conscripting me in a war and then signing a peace treaty without my input. I never got used to them being relaxed, and their moments of togetherness irritated me.

I remember that trip because Chechi's friends invaded the house, smoking and blasting music and taking over all the rooms, including my parents'. I walked down the hall as frightened as if I were alone in the forest: in the shadows, I saw a naked girl come down from the top bunk in the boys' room, a couple was making out under the covers of the lower one, my parents' room was locked, two guys were smoking a joint in my sofa bed, another was sitting on top of my father's law notes on the coffee table where he studied, and in the kitchen, several more, among them my brother, were frying eggs with sausage, cracking up laughing, jumping back every time the oil popped. In the bathroom,

I closed my eyes and peed hovering over the seat, as I did at bars.

My sister had taken off with her boyfriend, and my other brother, Manuel, whom we always called Lolo, was gone doing something or other for the Communist Party, so I wandered down the hall, looking askance at all that was happening in the rooms and uncertain where to take refuge, trying, as always, to take my brother's side, to be loyal and not disappoint him, as a co-conspirator rather than a participant—I didn't feel old enough for that. I watched the people there with fascination and envy. They ignored me the way you ignore a cat, and like a cat, I hugged the wall as I passed. I didn't know if I was being rejected because of my age or if I'd ever be comfortable letting a bunch of strangers into my home. A few hours before my parents got back, I helped my brother clean up. Evidence of revelry clung to the floor and the walls. We couldn't help but laugh when we walked on the parquet and the sticky layer of grime made noises. My parents' arrival came as a relief; I still had a bit of that old loyalty to authority that turns so many younger siblings into traitors and snitches. At fourteen, I'd mostly stopped tattling, but I still didn't like people getting between my mother's sheets.

It rained on the way back, my parents said, but they still got out of the car to spend the afternoon by the river. That was typical, we did it almost every time my father took us on a trip, so he could fish. We'd wait in silence to keep from spooking his prey. A few days later, my mother told the neighbor that instead of fishing, they'd taken a nap in the grass. And they laughed the way they always laughed when there was something they couldn't say openly in front of me.

The rain or whatever it was, a shower in a roadside motel, swelled the curls of her thick and ungovernable hair, that sensual mane that appears in photos of her when she was young and that the fashions of the time would later distort, when she started teasing it up or perming it. My father used to block her path to the bathroom, touch her thick hair, and tell her, laughing: "Don't comb it, don't press it down, leave it like that," and he would call her by her corny nickname from the postcards they used to send each other before they married. Just then, all that worried me was my mother figuring out what had gone on in their absence, and I observed them with the contempt children feel when adults flirt and refuse to act their age. Ignoring me.

My mother is also the woman I see now in a surprise Super 8 film we just rescued from the deep in one of my father's cabinets. It's the first time I've seen her in motion since she died. She comes close to the camera, waving, greeting me. Suddenly, she's back in the world of the living. She walks with that characteristic sway in her step, that lax movement of the hips. She's wearing bell-bottoms and a blouse embroidered with flowers, half her face is covered by sunglasses, and even if her hair is back-combed, it's longer than usual, and reminds me of the way Italian women used to wear their hair. She's very thin, girlish, and is enjoying the use of her heart, which is fit again a few months after her operation. There she is, waving to me thirty-five years after she left. This is her, before disappointment crushed her and the imminent end came, the one I now realize she foresaw.

Thirty-five years later, I responded to my grandmother's question in my mind: They buried her in a white winding cloth. Like my father, whom we held a viewing for in the funeral home in Madrid before heading to the village. Who could have dressed him? My sister? Me? We wouldn't have known how to capture his negligent air, his way of wearing expensive clothes without looking stiff, his shirt buttoned halfway up and his pants eternally sagging. How could we dress him for a funeral without betraying his style, tie loose, the way he always knotted it, respecting his unkempt white hair. Prim and proper in his coffin, my father would have looked like a capo, a dictator, a tyrant; alive, he looked like a Russian poet, a Bernstein-style orchestra conductor, a luminary, an Upper West Side eccentric. In my memory, he appears sometimes in fisherman's garb, with his brown rubber waders and a tackle box full of bait and lures slung over his shoulder. Smelling of trout and tobacco. This is the image from his glory days. Joyous, expansive, mind reined in by professional ambitions, child-rearing, his wife's respect.

This is how the two of them appear to me, capable of protecting me. I have to force myself to remember their decrepitude or decline, even though that's the nearest and last part of this story.

While the son held the mother, small, wrapped in a shroud, in his arms, the other men opened the husband's coffin. We were honoring a wish expressed a few times after meals, when alcohol had dissolved his inhibitions and he said things that mattered to him. Distrusting his children, worrying we'd disobey him for the sake of comfort, he'd left his will, the stubborn bastard, in writing on top of his desk:

Children, if something happens to me, take me to the village with Mamá.

With Mamá. Under that phrase, the date. His handwriting, geometrical, erratic, moves me. The note was there nine years before his death, waiting for the moment, under a letter opener. He was canny like a dictator who fears all respect for him will vanish upon his death, or like so many old people who suspect—and rightly—that their children just don't take them seriously.

We obeyed his request to the letter. My brother put Mamá in the coffin over his chest. I smiled when I thought of this forced interruption of my mother's eternal rest, though I'd like to think that the two of them, relieved from the spiritual agitation of life, would find a way to return to the years of happy togetherness before I came into the world. I can't stand being alone, my father wrote in a diary we struggle to decipher. The man who left his wife alone, abandoned so many times, couldn't bear solitude, and didn't understand life without her: rocked by her absence, he cultivated an idealized image of her and omitted all trace of anything reprehensible in his conduct toward her. My sister and I used to get angry when his stories would touch on a painful moment that we, especially the girls, had shared. We'd try to correct the record, but he was incorrigible.

We leave the cemetery: brothers and sisters, kin, and friends. The children and grandchildren of those who emigrated to Valencia and Barcelona in the sixties come back to this increasingly depopulated village in July. My father used to say, "If all the people I helped out in El Rincón treated me to a drink, I'd never pay again." His vanity never went away, and we tried not to feed it, but now that he can't hear me, I admit he was basically right. In the sixties and seventies, when there were public works projects everywhere, he would show up in the village like the Godfather and people would ask him to set their children up with a job. As a crane driver, a master mason, administrative assistant, grunt. And he'd find them work of some kind or other. He'd take the time to call overseers on roadwork sites, in the port, at the reservoir, inevitably finding an opening for these young men who had never even left their village. The kids were reluctant to go, and this drove him, the seasoned nomad, crazy. His promotions had depended on constantly uprooting his wife, himself, and even his children when they were young. He couldn't understand a boy wanting to stay close to his mother. How could he, with the mother he had?

He seemed like a potentate back then, that's how I remember him, but mainly because as a girl I couldn't grasp that in essence, he was a lowly pencil pusher who used his talent and effort to rise to being auditor for huge engineering projects. He was direct about matters people normally hide, and he demanded his generosity be compensated for. I know now that magnanimity always conceals a demand for payback, however minor.

If all the people here he'd helped out with a job had shown up at his funeral, there would have been a multitude descending from the cemetery to the village. But Papá, people forget old favors, we forget the people who helped us take flight. Unless you're a daddy's boy, someone helped you out somewhere. But he wouldn't have accepted excuses, ingratitude was hard to understand for someone who had been so helpless right at the starting gate.

We walked down from the cemetery, noticing the beauty of the plains now marred by a horrible plague of new buildings. The fields were still lovely despite the bricks: against the low mountains in the background, almond and apple trees blossomed in even rows. And the rivers in the lowlands, the Turia and the little stream, choppy watercourses where we swam as children, where we went out as a family and our aunts made paellas and our uncles grilled steaks with crunchy bread lathered in garlic and oil. You couldn't ask for more from a childhood, and there I have it, encapsulated, like a treasure allowing me to grasp that even in grief or melancholy there's always a crack joy can shine through. And joy must be open to sadness to avoid becoming stupid and banal. That's what we experienced the other day, anticipatory melancholy joined to a strange sort of contentment, because we would never see my father again. I was happy not to have dragged his life out, even if my sister wasn't sure. We took the decision in a small, windowless room in the hospital next to another where he lay dying. I was happy not to condemn him to waking in an ICU with a tube shoved down his throat, terrified and unable to swear. I was glad he'd be resting eternally with my mother.

We weren't bad children, Papá, admit it. But I know you know that, I can see it here in the green notebook where you summed up your life in five pages. You toyed with the idea of writing your memoirs, but your mind couldn't face the memories, let alone putting them in order.

We weren't bad children, Father, even if these past few years you often talked about your friends' model daughters, who tended to their parents with devotion. That veiled reproach was inconsistent, coming from a man who remarried no sooner than the love of his life had died. I know the flak you got for it, that you were inconsiderate, that you skipped out on mourning, the scandal of leaving me, the little one, alone, even if you did come to the neighborhood on weekdays to have lunch with me. We'd eat, you'd vanish, giving me a kiss and reminding me you'd call that night. My father was as naive as he was strict. He'd call at night, I'd tell him I was about to go to bed, and once the song and dance was over, I'd go out for a few beers. I was a neighborhood girl, and I didn't go far. I know the neighbors said he'd left me on my own right when a girl most needed supervision, and they griped about my wild streak, which I threw in their faces, making out with some boy on the corner by our building. They said all this was because I had lost my mother. But it wasn't true, I'd been this way for some time.

I always understood you. Your independence benefited me, it was linked to mine. If you didn't need me, I could be free. I didn't want to see you out on the bench waiting for me. With no mother, and with a father in another neighborhood downtown: that's how I became independent, abruptly. Maybe with the years I've come to see this as traumatic, because now I look at that time with apprehension, knowing the dangers that surrounded me, but if I'm honest, I have to thank you, because I wasn't forced to play the widower's daughter, waiting for her father with food on the table, and you freed me from having to live with another woman I didn't know. Now and then, acting out the fatherhood others said you were failing at, you would accompany me to the doctor. I felt safe in your company, but at the same time I worried you'd misbehave. We took a taxi to the dentist one afternoon. You rode in front, as always, you might as well have been in the driver's seat, you couldn't help but tell the real driver the whole time where he needed to turn. You'd just left one of your work lunches, which stretched on till five or six in the evening, you stank of alcohol and smoke and you had your tie in your pocket. You rolled down the window to clear your head. Alcohol didn't make you groggy, it made you sociable, and you talked up the taxi driver, nosing around in his life to fill the emptiness, trying to talk over the sound of the wind.

The pain radiated through to my eyes, and I remembered another morning, not so long before when we rode in an ambulance with Mamá from the beach to the hospital. Her last trip. I was in the back with her. Her eyes were open with dread, begging me to make them give her a Valium, as though I had any sway over the paramedic, who responded to the sick woman's pain with a curt *I can't, I'm not allowed to.* My father was the only one who spoke, about banalities, the traffic or the state of the road, with that need of his to be always conversing. I remember when my aunt Concha, my second mother, my godmother, died. She was in her death throes, and my father's voice boomed like a double bass, constant and monotone from the doorway of the house in the village. My husband saw then what I'd told him so many times about my father's response to anxiety. I could never understand that need to neutralize pain with trivialities. Two years later, without ill intentions, but with a maladroitness I failed to notice in time, my husband wrote a story inspired by a family gathering where my father, a presumptuous bigmouth in the story, just couldn't stop talking. It hurt my father, he saw himself reflected there and felt ridiculous, and he stopped coming for lunch on Saturdays. Sometimes fiction, with its thumbnail sketches of a character, turns a complex person a book could never encapsulate into a stereotype or caricature. My father doesn't fit into two adjectives in a book, because that boorish, bitter man, a bigmouth, sure, lacked the malice of people who cover their vanity with false humility. This logorrheic swaggerer could sometimes be cruel, but he was also incapable of resentment. He couldn't resist the urge to see us, and so he wrote us a letter, a deep, sincere letter declaring that his feelings were above any literary misunderstanding. That letter, which I can't reread, because it hurts, with that mixture of love and remorse it provokes, exists as a photocopy among his papers, xeroxed like everything, because he was determined that nothing in his life should be forgotten.

My psychologist asked me: Did you ever think that he talked so much because he was terrified when things got tense? That he used banality to try to ward off horror?

That afternoon you went to the dentist with me, you walked into the office and greeted every single person in the waiting room. I wondered why I hadn't come alone. The truth was, more than his company, I needed him to pay the bill. They called my name and he followed, telling the nurse, I'm going in with her. Cigarette in hand, words fraying, I noticed, he sounded like he needed a nap. He greeted the dentist overeffusively, and sat in a chair against the wall. Out of the corner of my eye I could see him looking for somewhere to ash. For a moment, I was afraid he would grab one of those little basins the dentist gives you to spit in and use it as an ashtray. I closed my eyes, but I could hear him clearing his throat, coughing, moving the whole time. The doctor, clearly irate, made the gentle suggestion he return to the waiting room, but my father said he preferred to stay with me, that I was easily frightened, apprehensive. He talked about me as if I were a little girl, one he knew but whom I must have never met. Gangly and clumsy, he reached out to catch his balance and accidentally turned out the lights. He sat there in the dark in the consulting room while the dentist had his drill in my mouth. Now, not waiting for a response, the doctor ordered him: "It's best if you wait outside." I would have asked forgiveness the way you do for an ill-behaved child, but my mouth was open and my eyes were closed. We took the taxi home in silence. Without asking, he gave the driver his address at Maudes. His wife was waiting for us, affectionate, wanting to do something to relieve the pain. They gave me a painkiller and told me to lie down on their bed. The walls were covered in mirrors. I could see myself through the shadows in the faint lamplight, my pain multiplied in those sepia-toned, artificially aged panes of glass. This place looks like a whorehouse, I thought. I sank into the softest mattress I'd ever lain down on, bundled in a nearly weightless comforter, in a sorrow that gave way to sleep. Now they're going to come in, I thought, and I'll have to get up and move to another bed. I closed my eyes, and when I opened them, the midday light was seeping in through the cracks in the rolling blind. I got up, and dozens of girls like me got up in their bra and panties too. Breakfast was waiting in the dining room. They were gone. I don't know where they slept. I felt like the girl my father had described.

I walked down the steep cemetery hill listening to my brothers and sister and dialoguing with my father before I'd even had time to miss him, confessing the kind of things you never confess when someone's alive. I had been doing this with my dead mother since I was sixteen. Sometimes, feeling bitter and hurt, I'd recriminate her for feeding into my insecurities, or for her lack of understanding or her intolerance toward my neuroses. There was a time when I obsessed over these unresolved issues, but then my wound, which throbbed so intensely, gave way to a slow reconciliation, and that's when I missed her terribly, at last showing signs of my orphanhood years after her death.

Many times, stung by some public attack or private deception, I've asked my mother: Are you finally going to take my side? Every time I fought for respect, for consideration, to not be treated condescendingly, I'd address her: Will you back me up this time, Mamá? When I got an abortion, when I stood up for the right of others to do so, when I was abandoned, when I got lost in the night, when disorder swallowed me, when I was negligent, when life overwhelmed me, would you have rubbed my face in it or would you have helped me up? All those times I cried alone so my little son wouldn't see me, all those times I thought: Mamá, don't you know how much your sobbing harmed me, don't you know how my heart hardened and I turned cold toward people who cry too much? And when I've gone outside and walked past other women, some old, the way you would be now if you'd made the effort to live, I tried to imagine if you'd concluded that journey of liberation you began a year before dying. I look at those old women who transformed in the third act of their lives and I wish I could see you, changed, renewed.

My poor mother, shedding her vulnerability, her unfair dependence, her victimhood, my mother, old and free. How often I imagined one of those shrunken old ladies, still coquettish, like Japanese figurines, taking my hand to walk down the street. And me saying: Mamá, what's the point of all that suffering over a man, dying, missing this?

No, we weren't bad children. To the contrary, we agreed to play the secondary parts in your story. And even now, when you've left us, we're still standing loyally, mulishly off to the side. We live in a world of constant, implacable judgments, and I could say to you: Papá, you made me anxious, unstable, obsessive; you stole a part of the self-assurance I deserved, put your wishes before ours, your example made me think any man would abandon me as soon as I showed the least sign of weakness. But even if all that's true, what would be the point of wasting my life complaining? Your character still attracts me, unstable, irate and capricious, because the greater truth, the one that weighs heavier than all reproaches, is that you loved us so furiously that sometimes it hurt; you loved us, even if your love was sweet and violent. I could reproach you, Mamá, for not seeing the damage you did to me, that need of yours to have a girl, and that's what I was then, a girl, who would take your side and obey your contradictory commands, never grow up and stay by your side, but also be an adult and fight for you. But I recognize now in you a profound depression that didn't permit you to act otherwise. And I can distinguish and appreciate the legacy you left me, a delicacy that impregnates everything it touches, a subdued sense of humor, the warmth of that physical closeness that makes love possible.

I don't believe in God, even though I tried, but I do believe in those memories that rain down on us endlessly, taking shape as ghosts that accompany us. I hear them, these spirits, and I pay attention to them, because I fear forgetting will rob me of the color of their voices. Sometimes they torment me, other times they shelter me from the storm. My father's death fills me with a pure sadness, free of any fear or remorse. With her, it's the opposite. Maybe this is because my adolescence covered up the pain or rejected it, leaving nothing but rage behind. I didn't go to the cemetery when they buried her. I felt the weight of my aunts' reproachful stares, and I whiled away the afternoon on the village streets, seeing nobody because all the locals had gone up to say goodbye to the woman who was their friend, aunt, sister, niece, sister-in-law, or neighbor, the girl who, until that day she left on the arm of a handsome and determined boy from Málaga, had grown up and matured on those steep streets, thinking she'd never change this landscape for another.

I spent the afternoon of my mother's funeral climbing hills and descending them on the loneliest walk I ever took, knowing that I was abandoning my duties, in mutiny against the obligatory sorrow that would plague me all summer in the midst of my family, detesting my orphanhood and the looks of pity it aroused. I'd grown up attached to my sick mother, and she'd chosen to die when I had plans, some of them ridiculous, to break away from her and be free. Hadn't she chosen the very worst moment to go? Her death was a form of giving up she'd been gestating for a long time, ever since she lost her will to live.

My character condemned me never to share my grief with anyone. I learned to admit that. I wanted return back to Madrid and take refuge in my invisibility there, to stay home alone, put on a record, lie down on my sofa bed, close my eyes, *How deep is your love, I really mean to learn, 'cause we're living in a world of fools,* imagining someone would rescue me someday from this state of ghastly apathy and bring me back to life.

My father's funeral was calm. His death doesn't wreck a household or leave any unsettled scores. It's the death of an old man. As children do, I miss not looking deeper into certain chapters of his life he found painful: not being the child picked to go off and study, having to leave for Madrid with nothing at age nine, all the plans he couldn't realize because of bad luck or a lack of support, his fears, the days of his nervous breakdown in Cádiz, which he always blamed on the east wind to keep from admitting he was mentally fragile and prone to delirium...Now, I try to imagine what I don't know, all that mystery, my parents' life full of unknowns, and I walk among a few certainties and very many uncertainties.

He didn't care to expound on personal matters, it distressed him, that was the typical attitude for his generation, his sex, and his character, which couldn't stand

playing the victim. He could go on tirades about corruption, politics, plummeting educational standards,
the tax office, debtors, crooks, and the wealthy. His accountant's mind was very sensitive to these matters, but
if you dug deeper, you'd see that here, too, there was a
personal connection. When he saw a politician brought
to trial for corruption, he used to say, "Why doesn't
he kill himself?" He could never have accepted public
humiliation. He used to boast he'd never stolen a thing
in his life. We never understood why not stealing was
something we should congratulate him for. But he'd
spent his life holding back, feeling the inevitable strain
of life on the margins of the black market, disgust at
his mother's dirty dealings, her rapacity, and then,
once his professional life had begun, he had to constantly buckle under to abusive authorities. Arrogant
superiors—no child of the war escaped their influence.
But an accountant—who if not him?—must learn to
resist the urge to stick his hand in the till. And it's hard
when you watch others get rich with less merit and less
effort. The spectacle of corruption was a pattern in his
life. When he wrote in his little green diary that Spain's
problem was corruption, he meant the ways he had suffered from it.

His monologues also centered around the disgust
old people often feel for a world that excludes them.
The growing nihilism that makes them sensitive to

every sign of chaos they see in the street or on TV. Watching the end of their lives approaching and interpreting it as the end of the world.

After the funeral, we spent two days walking through the fields and stuffing ourselves. Not like in those French films where the diners remember the deceased with witty comments and mordant replies. We gathered around a paella my cousins made and washed down with bitter wine the same old stories as always, the ones everyone knew by heart, that have survived the onslaught of time, ancient tales dramatized with the same words to fill the silence and keep emotions in check. My brothers smoked cigarette after cigarette, same as during Christmas, and the same low cloud of smoke I grew up in formed around their heads. I imagined my father's big nose poking through the threads of smoke the way God in religious movies parts a gray, stormy sky, my father with his astute eyes approving, appreciating the vices he's handed down to his boys.

When the food was gone, we talked a long time, and this is surely the finest homage we could pay a man who relished doing the same. As evening fell, we poured a dash of anisette into our cups of mint tea, and at night we drank homemade liqueurs and lost track of time. I knew this was a deeper form of saying goodbye. You can't go back to a place and air your melancholy over something no longer there—it's an insult for those who stayed behind. The only one of us who ever adapted to the village as an adult, enjoying it the way my father did, is César, who loves walking through the country-side and the brief but affectionate daily contact natural to people who live in proximity. He reminds me of my father, moving tirelessly from place to place, planning excursions, prey to inner frenzy. Like my father, he had an aptitude for math and became an accountant, but in his heart, he was a country boy and he would have pre-ferred a life devoted to nature. My brother, who should have been a vet, a country doctor, draftsman, farmer, or all of those at once, who inherited his father's en-ergy, who was driven to venture off into the country in his free time, searching for some kind of apple that thrived in these sulfur-rich gardens; my brother be-came an administrator too, and that unpleasant job forced him to become a nomad. He dreams of freeing himself from the profession my father found him when he was just eighteen, sending him away from Madrid, the neighborhood, the place where "that boy," as my father used to call him, could lose himself. Rootlessness was a secondary effect, and in a way, we all suffered it, even without leaving Madrid. My mother's death let loose the stampede.

It's the first week of August. My brothers are on vacation, and my husband and I came here a few days ago to put documents in order and clean and arrange my father's apartment. It smells like tobacco, like dirt, like thick grime. The scent is so strong it impregnates the furniture and fabrics, and even when you open the windows, it won't go away. There is a layer of scum on the surfaces. And even inside some of the furnishings, and balls of dust, hair, spiderwebs, dead skin, and fibers are under the sofa and bed.

It looks like a home its inhabitants abandoned years ago, but only fifteen days have passed since my sister and I were here for a visit. We brought dinner and went into that same kitchen, the one she and I cleaned so many times with that attention to detail my mother demanded of her daughters. Unable to avoid it, we peeked into every corner. The woman who took care of my father, who slept at his house and went with him every afternoon to La Lonja, where he would fill out the sudoku and write his thoughts on a napkin, his squire, as he strangely liked to call her, was not a particularly neat woman. But he didn't notice, all he wanted was not to be alone.

My father waited crossly for us to set out dinner on the dining room table, knowing we were snooping around, that we couldn't help feeling on our home terrain and entitled to open the drawers and cabinets with a disparaging attitude. We heard him start up with his usual routine, disapproving, suspicious that we were invading his privacy. I said: Papá, what's with all the useless things in this drawer? Why do you need two broken corkscrews? Why don't we open this new one? The one I gave you two years ago that's still in the box? He struggled to get up, impatient as ever, but short of air and unable to walk any faster. "Leave my things be! I need all that! I need all three of them!" He grabbed the corkscrew missing one of its levers out of my hand and stuck it clumsily into the cork in the bottle with such excessive force that the worm jabbed his finger and split his transparent, dehydrated skin, his poor ancient hide. Blood welled up scandalously and we hurried to bandage the wound as best we could, trying to keep his mood from getting worse. He ate the tortilla with his trembling, injured hand, and leaned his head on the other, like a boy trying to cheer up after an accident. His persistent stubbornness kept us from seeing he was dying. That night, he was already dying.

From then on, we started yielding to him. He shuffled over to his easy chair, a faded blue one where he spent practically all of his final year. We served him a whiskey and he lit a cigarette and ate a little chocolate. He didn't have the strength to bring the filter to his lips. That brief motion demanded so much strength, it left him breathless. So he just left it in his mouth. Took a little sip of the whiskey. Those had been his vices, his solace, his dependencies, and they continued to be so till the end. Though we didn't know it, these were the whims following a last supper that had condemned him to death. We were scared to leave him on his own, he was out of sorts, but we did anyway, we gave him a kiss and left, and he was free to swallow the sleeping pill he wasn't supposed to take with a sip of whiskey.

My husband has said we should put his papers in order. The house is full of them, like an archaeological dig where everything dates back to the seventies. My father has a folder reserved for each of his children, with notes, receipts, the occasional medical report. Our writings, my husband's included, are ordered chronologically. My most recent article is there, first on the pile, published on the last Sunday he was alive. He's also cut out crosswords where my photo appeared and other silly keepsakes, like when some newspaper wrote something about my birthday. Our presence, his children's presence, fills the apartment, with framed articles, ugly photos, the odd gigantic trophy like some big fat monster on a shelf at the entrance: "I keep it there because if some thief comes in, I'm not going to waste time calling the police, I'm going to grab this and crack his head open." On his table, under the letter opener, is the paper where he wrote his last wishes. There are two. The first one is taken care of. Then there's a big white space, as if he had wanted to add something and couldn't bring himself to. At the very bottom of the sheet, he wrote another request: "Don't sell the apartment, let Inma keep it and sell hers and give you each a share of the proceeds."

I smile because I see my father's manipulative character here. These aren't wishes, they're demands. The atheist wants to rest easily in the beyond by dictating the terms of our happiness after his death.

I don't know if my sister wants to live here. Probably she doesn't feel like staying in this place she used to yearn to escape, she might think of it as a step backward. But I start to imagine what it would be like to put this apartment on the market, how weird it would be to show off the rooms to strangers, detaching the space from the scenes that throb in my memory when I enter each of its rooms. And how it would be to observe this block of apartments from outside when I pass by one day on the highway to Valencia and see it rising up, the first one in my neighborhood, on this promontory with the horrible name, Arroyo Fonarrón. Will I think I can see my mother's shadow waiting by the window for me to come back from school?

Or my father's leaning on the railing, smoking on the only open balcony in the building?

Since we arrived, I've felt their presences grazing past me or moving through me when I walk down the narrow hallway. I see my father in the little room bent over the coffee table, studying for his third year of law school. The ashtray overflowing with cigarette butts, now and again he jiggles the ice cubes in his glass of whiskey. My mother is sitting on the sofa in the living room, waiting for me to watch a movie, and as always, she pulls me away from my homework, she doesn't want me to grow up, and she keeps me away from school, though later, hypocritically, she will demand I make good grades. I sit down beside her, she never needs to ask twice. I joke around with her if she's happy, enjoying that humor of hers that has turned more caustic with her physical deterioration. Sometimes she shocks me, and I think a mother I don't know has taken over my old one. My sister is studying in the girls' room. Her literature texts pile up on her table and my own desk, which I rarely use. She's the straight one, the one who keeps her commitments. I'm more tempted by fooling around, I can't resist diversion. My sister pulls my leg, saying when no one can see me I still play with dolls. It's not true. Well, it's a little true. I watch Lolo leave his bedroom in the mornings with his Che beret and his duffle coat, the same way he walked in the night before. He coughs in the hallway as he heads for the door, because he had whooping cough as a boy. We don't know where he has dinner. Sometimes he doesn't sleep at home. He inhabits another world that I have some sense of when I see him in the Communist Party offices. He changes girlfriends more often than he changes shirts, and he comes and goes anxiously, as if he were a leader of the revolution. The other day, my sister and I ran into him on the square. He was with some friends. He presented them to us as *comrades*, and he introduced us as *friends*. Since then, we've referred to him as our *roommate*. Chechi goes by César now, but he's like me, he can't make up his mind, and he's still a kid in some ways. He's started studying veterinary medicine, but he can't concentrate. Sometimes we make a pot of coffee at night to study all the things we haven't studied during the day, and we end up dancing on the chairs, with the music low to keep from waking my father, but still, we dance like crazy. When he's not with his friends, he still plays with me. He likes to propose dares, to bet money on these ridiculous challenges. The other night, he told me if he managed to fit a whole orange in his mouth, I'd have to give him three weeks' allowance. I accepted. He did it, but he couldn't breathe, he started to turn red, and I had to call my parents. It was two in the morning. My father got up, wrenched out the orange, and smacked him across the face. He didn't smack me because I ran off to my room, and anyway, he almost never hits me.

My father wakes up in the middle of the night, and to calm himself down, he eats half the chocolate bar that's on his nightstand. Sometimes he runs out of his room screaming and yelling because we've eaten it ourselves. In the afternoons, one by one, we sneak off to his nightstand. Eventually, the whole chocolate bar's gone, but it's nobody's fault. We know he might lose his mind in the early morning if he finds the wrapper empty, because he needs his chocolate to get back to sleep. It's a paradox, we fear him, but we can't help but disobey him when he's not around. My father has a nervous character. On certain mornings, when he wakes at six for work, we hear him in the bathroom saying he's going to have a heart attack and we'll be left all alone. When he says *all alone*, he means just the four of us and our mother, without him to bring home the bacon. I know it's awful, but it eases my mind when I think that at least the apartment is paid off. My father often brings his hand to his heart, he says his nerves are going to make it explode, but my mother's the one with the broken heart.

Lately, my mother's been telling him he should have married his girlfriend from Gaucín, the daughter of the chocolate manufacturer. If he had, we'd all be resting easier. She always says the same nonsense as she lies in bed and he gets up to scream at us in the morning. If he'd married the chocolate girl, we wouldn't be us, obviously. My mother would have married the village doctor, who was courting her when my father got in the middle of things, and so half of what we are would be from Gaucín and the other from Ademuz. I prefer to be entirely me, even if sometimes our situation is bad.

The six of us move around this apartment, which can be sold now that my father's dead, and time stops in my memory in those years in the midseventies, and every quotidian action repeats itself, the ones that shape our characters and define us in our own recollections and those of our family. My father, the man of action, the enemy of all sloth, stomping down the hallway; my mother, contemplative, a bit lazy, always looking for a corner to ruminate or think in. And the four of us, noisy, with friends over who make it even noisier, argumentative, insulting each other, sometimes coming to blows, especially the boys; we let ourselves abuse each other, the way many teenagers do, convinced there's plenty of space to hide secrets because our friends' homes are much more modest. We're the rich people in the neighborhood. My parents have carefully decorated our home. It's the first home they've had in forever and it's going to be forever and ever. *Forever* is a word we barely know, but my mother's health means we can no longer move. The decoration is austere: what little furniture we have is solid and discreet. With time, I'll realize they're elegant pieces arranged harmoniously. There are hardly any pictures, just one oil painting my father did in a period in thrall to one of his fierce but fleeting artistic impulses. It shows a narrow street in Ademuz and hangs in the vestibule. When visitors come, my father takes them away from it, to the living room, by the balcony, and then slowly moves them closer to the painting so they'll think they're walking down that very same street, which ends at the church. Until I was thirteen, I would get behind our visitors and take the same walk. At that time, I still managed to reach that part of the village, and imagined I was walking over the asphalt polished by human steps, hearing the hundreds of birds fly over the belfry in the afternoon, the hour in the painting, chirping and shrieking like mad. Seduced by my father's wheedling words, I could imagine myself passing through the canvas and emerging on the Plaza del Raval, where that imposing church rises up over the small village, but then one day I started to realize how absurd all that was, and following behind our guest as always, I broke out into a fit of laughter. I've never stopped laughing since. The things my father did or said started to strike me as outrageous, and I went from playing along with his flights of fancy to disbelieving and observing him critically. And yet I realize this credulity that one day up and vanished is the same thing that made my childhood a period where real and magic lived comfortably side by side.

He and his ideas, his actions, his many impossible plans, seemed made to measure for a child's mind.

Just a few decorations treasured across the years and several moves gleam on the walnut bookcase next to the book club classics and adventure novels and encyclopedias of the wonders of the world and Erich von Däniken's exposés of UFOs and other unresolved paranormal phenomena that my father was such a fan of. Half those decorations were shattered the night that my mother decided to break their life in common by hurling it against the floor.

In the diary my husband found in a desk drawer, my father wrote this biography we read now:

I'm seventy-seven years old. Since 1973, I've lived in this neighborhood, which for me is my village. The list of places I've lived runs like this: seven moves with my father and twenty on my own (twelve of these with my wife and children). Apart from these: the periods between moves we spent in the village my wife was from, which brought me happiness, a great deal of happiness. I'm a soldier's son. My father retired as a captain. I've always had a liberal disposition. I started working as a bookkeeper at sixteen years old. When I was eighteen, I reluctantly did my military service in the Civil Guard in the Sierra of Málaga, lots of nights on horseback in the mountains from '47 to '50. Those were hard years. I wore boots a size too small for my feet and that destroyed my toenails forever. I wear a size 10. But I always felt free, I took care of myself from the time I was a boy, basically, not like my siblings, and I learned to be independent and disciplined. As far as education, I tried everything: I studied accounting in correspondence school when I was twelve. Then commerce. I entered the architecture school in Barcelona. I had to quit. I studied for the police exam, but they called it off at the last minute. I wanted to emigrate to Canada, but they didn't let me go because I wasn't twenty-four yet. In Madrid, when my kids were teenagers, I studied law for three years at the Complutense University in the adult studies program. I got a couple of certificates there.

When I was twenty-four, I went back to the construction company I started at when I was sixteen. I opened the offices at the protectorate in Morocco, rose up the ranks, had my first home in Ceuta after marrying a wonderful woman. Despite her mitral stenosis, we had four children. She died after twenty-three years of marriage. I'm proud of a life marked by honesty, and of raising four children who are sincere, intelligent, and good. I remarried. It was different from the first marriage. She was a widow, she had four children too. But we relieved each other's loneliness and we were happy. The balcony of the apartment where I lived with her opened onto Maudes Hospital, where I used to go in the afternoons when my mother sent me off to Madrid on my own at nine to pick up my aunt, who was a nurse in that hospital for war cripples. The twists and turns life takes! My second wife died of cancer. Alone again! Afterward, I survived with help from others, until the woman I call my squire arrived; she's been living here for four years, and in this house she found an island of peace. Now she's gone for a month, from August 20 to September 20, to enjoy a well-deserved vacation. And that is my life in a nutshell. Thanks, everyone!

This way of telling a life, so abridged, reminds me of what Chekhov writes about the diary his father kept, which Anton and his brothers read in secret with endless amusement. In it, Pavel Yegorovich wrote so objectively of his everyday tasks, the changes in the weather, the weight of the pigs, the state of the cherry trees, the dogs' mischief, and his children's comings and goings that it seemed more like a merchant's account book than a journal meant to reflect his moods and air private thoughts. Chekhov was moved by his father's inability to tell himself about himself. The writer left evidence of the way his father's brutal authoritarianism stripped every semblance of happiness from his childhood, and though he never hid the wound in his heart caused by the cruelty he'd been subjected to, his enormous humanity led him to treat his father with affection when the man grew old. That lack of self-analysis in his father's diaries, that lack of any trace of sentimentality, didn't so much irritate him as help him tolerate his emotional illiteracy, treating him like a cripple and in this way empathizing with him.

My father, unlike Pavel, was an emotional being, and his hardness, when he showed it, was the consequence of his incredibly foul moods. Behind every phrase in this little summary of his life, I know what's real and what's hidden, the blend of love and remorse. I know how to tell the truths from the half truths. It's poignant to read that farewell, *Thanks, everyone!*, because I feel it's being uttered from a stage, taking a last turn, about to exit through the back door, and in it is the happy acceptance of a life shaken by circumstance but also by inner torments.

Maybe he should have died then and there. At seventy-seven, when he could still go barhopping and take refuge in his vices with a gallant air. Going out when one is still all there. Without decay and without rage.

There are folders that contain reports about colleagues who stole money. Some were friends of his. When that happened, they'd reach an agreement. The guy would give back the money, and if it was a lot, he'd get thrown out on his ear. But the crisis would be dealt with discreetly. Anything to avoid prison. Money was sweet and tempting when a person was hundreds of miles from home. He kept those reports as proof of a job well done, of a distinctive conception of justice.

There are dozens of pages with his name on the right where he's written down poems. His geometrical handwriting and the sternly typed headings make these verses look like mathematical equations. Indeed, we're surprised to find one poem written entirely in numbers. We don't know how to decipher the meaning, maybe each number had a magic significance. Anyway, he might have written it down after drinking two or three whiskeys. There are verses about solitude with an air of Antonio Machado, rhetorical and celebratory speeches for reunions with old friends from the firm. At the end of all of them, he always encourages the guests to raise their glass. He talks about freedom, ideals, friends, food and drink. There are photos that attest to a love of good meals and long talks once they're over. Young men smoking, mature men smoking and drinking. Smoke seems to waft from the photos themselves, and the people in them look swathed in fog. There are dozens of license photos, and through those photos you can follow the course of his life, his youth, mature years, old age. The last ones are from the photo booth outside the door of the supermarket. One of them is recent. Who can say what he needed it for. He looks sad in it, frightened, as if aware of the imminence of death. His commanding face turns it into a Richard Avedon portrait.

We soon find postcards from a woman writing him from Switzerland. My husband knows something about this story, he knows he was in Switzerland with her, because on the sofa, after eating and after taking a drink or two, when he thought I'd fallen asleep, he'd get in the mood to brag about his conquests. In his last years, with that lack of inhibition supposedly common among the old, he enjoyed telling the odd dirty anecdote, naughty stories reminiscent of those soft-porn movies that flooded Spanish cinemas in the seventies. The Swiss woman writes him that she hopes they can meet again. This Swiss woman with Spanish roots tries to pull him in with the promise of health advice that will help him achieve a better quality of life. The Swiss woman offers to help him quit tobacco. And to cut down on drinking. The Swiss woman says she knows what she's talking about because, many years ago, she withdrew from Spanish culture, with its huge meals and unbridled drinking and smoking. It's funny that someone would be so unperceptive as to think of my father as docile or corrigible. She's proposing to do away with all the vices that gave shape to his life.

There are women, women in restaurants, women in rooms I don't recognize but that sometimes look like bingo halls, women who must have had something like a relationship with him. He wanted to get married, he said, but the tax office made it complicated.

There are little old photos of my parents in black and white, with wavy edges on the tattered black cardboard pages of an album; I snap pictures of them with my cell phone to blow up their faces and study their expressions. I've seen them many times, but it's only now that they surprise me. All the prudishness of the 1950s, all the obligatory formality, the puritanism, the weight of the Catholic religion that condemned young people to kiss in secret and barely touch each other till they reached the altar, my mother's stiffness, her eternal restraint, all that is astonishingly swept away by the ardor of those young people in the photos who emerge from the script they were doomed to by the era they were born in to lie down in the grass together and hug, smiling with mischievous faces, unembarrassed, my mother surrendering to his arms, my father unable to control himself and placing his hand under her breast, as if to hold it up. Idiot that I am, I never noticed that expressivity, that sultriness so evident in their smiles, I never saw it, condescending, thinking like all children do that passion is an invention of the present and that they, our parents, knew nothing of it.

There are graduation certificates in the closet, the kinds of things that wind up forgotten in drawers in the homes of our parents, those resigned trustees of a past there's no space for in our own homes. There's a diploma. Wait, wait, this is the diploma they gave me for the Transport Ministry essay contest. I take it in my hands. My name there. I recollect flashes of what I wrote on those two sheets of paper. I take it to the tiny bedroom where my father studied in the evenings and my mother cried on Sundays when she was alone—a stifling, narrow room, like a third-class train car—and now I remember, now I see as I lean on the door, the way I walked over to him and told him: I have to write an essay about traffic. There was no literary pretense to it, it was an assignment I had to do for school. As though I had blocked it out, the memory returns to me with phrases, sentences I wrote with fantastical ideas dictated by an imagination not my own. Supersonic Scalextric sets, not gray and depressing like Atocha Station, with trains crossing the city as gently as the flight of UFOs, propelled by a clean energy still to be invented, streets where pedestrians could move at their liberty without disturbing traffic. Hygienic cities like those in science fiction films that already looked old even then, towns inspired by Martian communities you could imagine if you just looked up in the night sky and believed.

My father didn't usually help me with my homework, because he so quickly lost patience; he didn't understand that to teach, you have to adapt to a child's way of thinking. But since the world of cars hardly interested me, I turned to him, and now, my diploma in hand, sitting at the coffee table where he studied so hard for his third year of law school, it's evident to me that he dictated this essay to me, and then, surprised by how generous the prize was, felt entitled to keep much of the reward for himself. It's puerile for a father to insist that he wrote the essay his daughter turned in at ten, but I can admit that his infantile justification was correct, and this leads me to conclude that his deliriums arose precisely when he was contradicted or discredited, even in issues as banal as this one.

Ay, Papá, Papá, you taught me not to feel nostalgia, to repress it. And I think I've known how to live without giving in to it. I, too, could write a brief memoir of my life listing all my moves, which are no fewer now than yours. But if I'm not prone to letting nostalgia carry me away, why do I fall apart when I realize that this stage for our family's past will be stomped through, pawed—violated, I might even say—by strangers? Forced not to feel sentimental about places from the past, the only soil where I've laid down roots is the parquet floor of this apartment in a neighborhood that is not so much in Madrid as peering toward Madrid, with the same perspective as in a painting by Antonio López García. Here, in these 1,300 square feet you bought with money from the lottery in '62, on a plot where sheep still ran free in the fifties. If I lose this, tell me, what do I have left?

You want to manipulate our future, you decide after your death what's best for our happiness. Something similar is happening with me, perhaps it's a behavior I've inherited: I want to pull the strings, to influence others' desires. I'm as arrogant as you, and I think I can guess what is or isn't best for the people I love. I'd like to be God and pull the strings. I do it outside with strangers, with friends, with anyone I know who presents me with a dilemma. I ask, investigate, ponder, and then I want to act. I want to affect others' lives, improve them according to my standards, even to spite their owners, who go through life disoriented, without finding a path that leads them to serenity.

The apartment, which was ours, is packed with useless objects, pointless gewgaws you couldn't stand to get rid of. To be true to your wishes, Father, which are actually my wishes, I have to betray you. I start to imagine all the furnishings, objects, rubbish that has to vanish from my view for this to look like the austere, unpretentious home that reflected your and her good taste, and which Mamá ably dictated. I want to return this home to its origins, strip it of the mental confusion that led you to accumulate so much and lose your sense of taste.

Then I feel a kind of fever that throws me into activity, as if I were undertaking a mission I must carry out with blind faith, and with the help of my faithful Blanca, whom you would call my squire, I toss out everything pointless, unnecessary, tacky, bulky, or ugly. Yes, Papá, the corkscrews are going into the big recycling bags, you can't find loyalty in a corkscrew, in go the twisted silverware, the pots without handles, the useless objects bursting from the drawers, the old napkin rings, the keepsake mugs from roadhouses, the honey jars, the custard jars, the framed photos where we look so ugly, Papá, the objects in frames, the Munch painting you found in the trash, those prints you found God knows where and put in frames that suck up the wall space, photos of us at official events, a TV that no longer works, unused heating pads, broken extension

cords, cups without handles, lamps without lampshades or lampshades without lamps, your ratty blue
chair where you spent your last year, Father, my love
doesn't diminish if I throw that chair in the trash.

We drive a van to a dump as night falls, get rid
of the things there's no point in repairing, Papá, you
are the king of planned obsolescence, we turn the torn
sheets into rags and use the blankets to bundle up the
clothes we donate to the church. When I take some of
the pictures to the trash bin on the street, on our street,
I feel on the back of my neck the looks of those women
who closed off their balconies behind aluminum walls
when they became widows, and I see when I go upstairs
and look out on our balcony that someone's taken it all
away, because they've been watching me for days, like
when I used to make out with my boyfriend on the corner. I go out to meet the scrap-metal picker, take to the
pharmacy that arsenal of tranquilizers, sleeping pills,
painkillers, inhalers, bromhexine, and antibiotics that
made your medicine cabinet an invitation to suicide.

I know I seem possessed, I'm frantic to get my way, I
want this apartment to be the one that was ours, Mamá's
little domain, the one she hardly ever left once she'd
decorated it *forever.* That *forever* is what I want back. At
midday, my husband and I go out to eat at one of the
neighborhood bars and the waiters send us a glass of
wine in memory of my father. They've lost a customer.

And the bench—that bench that was more his than anyone else's, where the neighbors confessed to him and he faced off against the kids who put their boots where he sat and talked to them about the workers who had risked their lives to bring water to Madrid—seems to be warped on the left where he used to sit, in the shelter of the outdoors that he enjoyed so much, in January or in August, ready to interrupt his reading to converse with whomever settled down by his side. Looking at Madrid, that timeless empty lot that I used to wander through to go to school, which nowadays is Darwin Park.

And the day comes, Papá and Mamá, when your apartment looks like it used to, it's back to how it was in 1975, everything old, the upholstery, the walnut bookcase, the books in editions that show signs of their era, the scant decorations. Everything worn out. Everything perfect, for me. This afternoon, my sister's coming back from vacation. She doesn't know much about these days of backbreaking labor, doesn't suspect much about my plan. I'm tracing the line of her future. She'll come in. She'll burst into tears when she sees the changes. She won't want to stay here, no she won't, she'll sob uncontrollably and blurt out the way people do who can't cry in front of others that for her, living in this apartment would be like returning to her teenage years. I'll pretend to understand her, I'll tell her we can hang the For Sale sign from the balcony whenever she wants. We'll sit on the couch. We'll remember those nights after my mother died, when we analyzed my father through to the morning hours. We used to lambaste his selfishness, his sudden fits of rage, his alleged lack of concern for us, nobody would have imagined we were the same children who would receive him with a smile the very next day, me hanging his suit, Inma chatting him up, the two of us laughing when he told us sternly: "I don't want you agreeing with me about everything, I need someone to argue with!" We knew just how to drive him up the wall.

I know that tonight, my sister won't be able to sleep, that she'll keep thinking about returning to the apartment where she studied, where she mediated between my parents, where she took care of me, telling me stories from movies and novels night after night, a young woman with too much responsibility in this chaotic home. It will sadden her, too, that someone will violate our memories. She can't see herself showing the girls' room to strangers, where Mamá used to look out the window and wait for me to come home from school, where we listened to American folk music, where she and Mamá told secrets behind my back. How much money could we ask for in exchange for this place my mother decorated for *forever*?

Tonight, about to fall asleep, I, too, will think of what my sister is turning over in her mind. I'll only have to wait a couple of days until the decision to take over this house grows in her thoughts, as though she'd come up with it herself. We are executors of others' happiness, Father.

And thinking this, I lie on the sofa, examine the living room that looks like it did then, and fall asleep. I'm fourteen, I sleep as deep as a teenager. Soon, Mamá will come to ask me why don't I go to Gloria's bakery to buy some cream buns to snack on?

THE CHILD AND THE BEAST

María, a distant cousin from Aranjuez I never knew, came over one July afternoon in 2016. She sat down in front of me and looked at me with those big, never-blinking eyes that I now know so well. I tried to find some hint of our genes in her traits, but María's face is so sweet that it's hard to square it with that side of the family, with its big noses, square jaws, and hard eyes. The similarity came later, or maybe I just wanted to believe in it, when I discovered how stubborn she is: stubborn, unbending, resolute.

She introduced herself to me via email, telling me she lived in Berlin, played the English horn, and had been adapting works for that peculiar instrument; she wanted to establish a repertoire, since few composers write for this strange variation on the oboe, which is surprising, because its sound is capable of transmitting a penetrating message, full of depths, like a voice telling truths from the beyond.

María told me she met with her colleagues sometimes to take a break from classical music and try something a bit more experimental. Her husband, the bassist Ander Perrino, had organized a sextet with the intention of exploring literary works. A spoken opera, she said. One told in words and music. With the voice as one more instrument. María asked me for a text for her project, and wanted me to participate as well. She'd heard people in the family talking about me since she was a child. When she heard me on the radio, when she saw my name on a book cover, she imagined meeting me and reestablishing a tie broken by my parents' nomadism.

My father had died three years earlier, and I'd been toying with the idea of writing something about him. I didn't want something nostalgic, I'm not really prone to nostalgia, and I didn't want to write a memoir or a purely sentimental text. I wanted it to be the natural continuation of an exercise I had engaged in since I was a girl: observing, observing my father, trying to understand his erratic, unpredictable behavior, which could go from gentle to incensed before you had time to react. There's no one I've devoted more hours of conversation to than my father. From the analysis my sister and I subjected him to, with our mania for mulling things over until the words run out, to those hours in therapy where I've stilled my anxiety, letting the subject of my father suck up the time and space I should have devoted to my own neuroses. I could draw a straight line from his obsessions to mine, from his misgivings to mine, because you can't help reproducing the mental schemas of the person who raised you, but that never affected my love for him. I'm hard, like him, and I don't blame others for my shortcomings. They say when people die you end up missing the tics that used to drive you crazy more than who they were as such: what I'd never wish to erase from my memory of him is all those things that used to mortify or exasperate me. This habit so many families have of idolizing the dead speaks to a mendacity that infuriates me.

When María came to our house that summer evening, I'd just written a story about the first time my father was hospitalized with COPD; the second time, he died. I devoted a few paragraphs to childhood sorrows my father had recited many times in the course of his life. As a girl, I listened to his adventures in the ravaged Madrid of 1939 like a fairy tale, with my father as the hero. He saw himself that way, as a brave kid, bold and clever. And he was. But he was also absolutely determined that the world should see him that way, and he hid his fears as a way of warding them off. In the hospital, feeling pessimistic as death inevitably approached, he changed the story, offering a darker version of those months at the beginning of the postwar period, when he had to survive on his own at just nine years old. Concealing tragedy through humor had been a constant in his life, a strategy to keep from looking like a victim, to justify himself and to survive. His physical decline left him literally breathless and undermined that system of mental self-defenses that had saved him so many times.

María observed me with a glimmer of gentle intelligence in her eyes. When she was a child, I was one of those absent Dickensian relatives who one day make a grand entrance and restore the ruined family fortune. Sitting straight, with the formal posture of musicians whose profession obliges them to lug their instruments back and forth, María told me about her project with such tenacity that I trusted her.

I felt something like remorse for not spending time with our family in Aranjuez. My father was loyal to them. He went to visit his cousin Lázaro, and he always called on certain dates. His gratitude toward them never died. Despite the dreadful tales he told about his miseries in Madrid and how they came to an end in Aranjuez, where he found shelter and solace, we, his children, never had the time or inclination to accompany him on those visits, and the ties he'd maintained broke definitively with his death.

His absence made me ask myself why I had asked him so few questions—I, who always ask so many. Maybe he talked too much to leave an opening for our curiosity. When we listened to him, we hardly opened our mouths, ruminating instead on our personal matters in silence.

I told María I'd write a text for her, uncertain what it meant to tell a story with a soundtrack. When she left, I felt the inexplicable need to rejoin that part of the family I was only bound to through the story of my father's boyhood. And it struck me that this story, retold so many times, might make the miracle happen and bring me closer to a past full of endless questions I suddenly needed answers to. My father was gone now, and I couldn't pose him the essential one: Dad, were you scared?

Now I know he was. I worked out the timeline of the past. All those tics, those poorly dissimulated horrors, frustrations, paranoia, all the mistrust that I'd observed since I was a girl, first with adoration and later critically, his tendency to make up stories as a way of holding the world in check, his possessive love for us, the repugnance he felt for illness, his whole indescribable and overbearing personality I saw now as the best path to reach that boy he once was, the sharp young man denied affection and the right to study. The fear of solitude would never leave him, it was burned into his character. But he never uttered the word *trauma*. I write it down because I have traced the origin of his torments.

The psychoanalyst Mariela Michelena told me that when a child experiences trauma, he reacts with stupor and surprise. His one wish is to survive, and survival depends on denying what is happening. He obeys a single mandate—to keep going—and can't waste energy on feelings, fears, or self-pity. But if, years later, as an adult, this same person encounters a situation that recalls the childhood experience where pain was buried, the way my father did in Cádiz, he will relive it all the more intensely, as a pain of the past and a pain of the present. And so it was. My father worried he might lose his mind if left alone, and he avoided this torment at all costs.

When I wrote the story, I read it to my husband Antonio. I asked him to sit on the sofa and I stood at a distance from him, as if onstage. The reading lamp was on, and a weak fire burned in the gas fireplace. Seeing his emotion, I knew I'd taken the first step. I sent the story to María, who was impatient to read it. She'd left her cell phone on the nightstand, heard her email pinging at 2:00 a.m. She read it and forwarded it to the musicians. Ander started it in the train on his way back from practice, and couldn't put it down as he walked through Mitte, his neighborhood, until he reached his building in the Chausseestrasse. Lander, who plays the viola, read it on the train back to Bilbao after playing a chamber music festival in Barcelona. The violinist, Rodrigo Bauzá, read it in his apartment in Berlin. Rodrigo is from Formosa, a poor region in Argentina. He told me it made him think of his father, who felt the same emotional helplessness, in circumstances very different from those in postwar Madrid, when his family sent him instead of his other siblings to live with an aunt and uncle to relieve the pressure of their poverty. Laura got lost in the story between the clarinet classes she teaches at the Frankfurt School of Music. Jarkko Riihimäki, the Finnish pianist and composer, told me that he read it repeatedly one morning at a residence in Arenys de Mar, then took a long walk after breakfast, in a contemplative mood, and tried to imagine music for certain of its paragraphs. And one day inspiration came; he heard the melody or, to put it another way, a gathering of musical sensations.

I wanted Madrid to sing beneath the feet of my little hero, for us to experience that defeated city in 1939. Jarkko came to see me. He'd never been to Madrid. We walked around the neighborhoods the boy had ventured through, and soon I was listening to the first few pieces, their titles filling me with emotion: *El Rastro, Reminiscence of My Father, Atocha, Manolo, To My Brother, Funeral March.* I was amazed he'd felt such a connection to the text, and in his notes I sensed the living presence of that intrepid, helpless boy, walking through a city he barely knows.

I'm finally in Berlin. It's November of 2018. María has worked conscientiously on the project, and we're now about to present our spoken opera in the Admiral Palast, a beautiful theater built in 1910 that survived the Second World War. She's convinced the Spanish embassy to include our show in its commemoration of the sister cities of Madrid and Berlin. I'm staying on the Friedrichstrasse, the same street where the theater stands, with a week of rehearsals ahead of me and uncertainty about how to deal with them. We had dinner this evening to get to know each other. My sextet is the Linien Ensemble, so named for the Linienstrasse, a famed street in Berlin that evokes infinite lines crisscrossing in space: we know where they begin, but we don't know where they'll end, just like this project we've undertaken. The Linien has a violin, viola, piano, bass, clarinet, and English horn. Or, to say the same thing differently, Rodrigo, Lander, Jarkko, Ander, Laura, and María. I'm afraid of disappointing them, of all the effort they've needed to make it here, all the trust they've placed in me, going up in flames. I've been listening to recordings of their concerts, and am impressed by their enormous talent. I'm the oldest one involved, I could be their mother, yet I don't feel I have anything to teach them. If only I could resuscitate my ear from my childhood, the ear of that girl with the soprano voice that could fill a room with the sound of angels.

I look at the city from my room in the Eurostars hotel. A huge floor-to-ceiling window seems to float above the elevated train tracks. It's an expressionist vision, evocative of Berlin as I conceive of it, at once cinematic and pictorial, and I take it as a good sign for our upcoming performance. In the morning, I take that train to RBB, Radio Berlin-Brandenburg, where they're lending us a studio because Ander plays in the orchestra. I'm careful not to get lost, as I tend to, especially as I'm so excited about the unforeseen gift of this new stage in my life, when I'm already past fifty and should be happy writing my books and articles, just being a *writer* and carrying on predictably. But my true vocation isn't literature, it's adventure. I like action, I like revealing myself, even if it leads to flare-ups of a million obsessions I keep hushed, latent, hoping they'll go unnoticed in the calm periods when my fears are kept in check.

Every morning before I leave for the radio, I engage in those numerical rituals I imagine will free me from approaching disaster. I'm prey to my old superstitions again, but maybe this is a weakness I share with actors and should just accept once and for all. The anxiety of revealing myself and the need to be heard.

When I reach the studios and the musicians' warmth envelops me, my nerves ease and at times I seem to float above the notes. They encourage me to sing, and I do what I can with my voice, which is a shadow of what it once was. We eat lunch in the radio station cafeteria. The classic tray where the worker scoops out globs of fatty meat, mashed potatoes, pasta. We stuff ourselves, because acting makes you tired. I hear them speaking English, German, Spanish. I try to follow along, to pay attention. Pay attention, Machado wrote. And Raymond Carver followed his advice half a century later, as he wrote in his poem "Radio Waves." I'm the only one who doesn't know how to read music, so all I can do is pay close attention, listen studiously.

The night before the debut, my loyal friend Lali arrives, along with my husband, two of my children, Elena and Miguel, and my sister, whom I told nothing about the story she'll hear tomorrow. She reproaches me: she always has to find out what I'm doing from other people. Now that she knows what the story's about, she complains that I kept her in the dark. I had a sense that I should come, she says. The story is also hers, in part.

I'm horrified I'll lose my voice, get a stomachache, stumble over my words. They told us the theater's full, and far from calming me down, the good news about the four hundred spectators upsets me. Half are Germans, half are Spanish, and they have family stories like my own, about starving little boys wandering aimlessly through ravaged cities, playing in the rubble, indigent.

I'm still not onstage yet, and my mouth is already parched. My palate is like cardboard and my saliva is thick. But I can't run away. When the musicians finish tuning up, I walk slowly to the center of the stage and stand before the microphone. After a week of rehearsals, I can no longer conceive of my tale without music, without this music that's about to start. I don't know who I am, what my profession is, what rules apply to what I'm about to do. Hearing the opening applause, I look up at the spotlights as if I could talk to God, and think, Papá, be a father this time, protect me.

And I start to read.

EL NIÑO
Y LA
BESTIA
Elvira Lindo
Jarkko Riihimäki
María Lindo
Linien Ensemble

My hand in his feverish hand,
I think, this is the last time I'll know this
Raspy, noble touch.

The hand
As though sculpted in wood
The cruel, protective
Hand of my father.

Through the white curtain
Seeps the hospital noise
Scent of drugs and disinfectants,
Of decadence and trembling breath.
A thick and vaporous scent
That envelops the dying
And those who this time give death the slip.
Steps come and go,
Adjusting IV drips, checking heartbeats
All of it infected by the imminence
Of valediction.

But something sacred is evoked behind
This thin white curtain:
The intimacy of the end
Which needs nothing more
Than a scrap of fabric
In a corner of the ICU.

—Father, do you hear us?
Your children and grandchildren are here.
We're all around you.
Our hands resting on your body,
As if engaged in a makeshift exorcism
That might yet
Cleave you from the ailment that is killing you.
Father, I've taken your right hand.
Do you feel my hand in yours?
Like when I was a girl,
I think I can communicate with you
Without speaking.
With you or with God.
Remember, my father,
When you rescued me from the wind
That almost tore me from the earth?
I thought about you while I held on to the ring
Of a manhole cover to keep
The mountain wind from sweeping me away.
I was waiting for a miracle
And you showed up.
I see your body bent
By the storm, running toward me,
Veiled in a cloud of dust,
And your hands
Pick up your five-year-old girl,
Squeezing her against your chest

Returning safe and sound
To home.

Like God, you are a savior and implacable,
Fierce enough to hurt
Your children
Who were both children and servants,
Adorers of the paterfamilias
Until we managed to free ourselves
From your powerful influence.
Or maybe not,
And you remain forever
Overseer, Judge.

Father, my father,
I wish I could go with you
To wherever it is you're going.
Perhaps you've already taken
The stony path of memory
As they assure us
The dying do
In a rite to seek the light of eternal repose.

Father, my father, let me join you on this journey
On a journey through a time
When I don't yet exist.

I see the boy leaving Atocha Station, escorted by two Civil Guards who look like they've arrested him. People look at them from the corner of their eyes, because no one dares stare at things they aren't supposed to. Maybe the boy's an escapee, and was trying to hide out on the train, or maybe his parents told him to run away. So many people dream of fleeing this defeated Madrid!

The boy tells the officers goodbye with little ceremony. One of them motions quickly toward the road he needs to take. Now the boy's alone. And when a boy is alone, he looks smaller, more tender, more dispossessed. But it's a serene, sunny day, and in his hand the boy holds a scrap of paper where his mother wrote down his aunt's address. The aunt didn't come to pick him up. She's a nurse, single and eager to find a boyfriend, but she agrees to take care of this boy she doesn't know for a while.

Manuel is the boy's name. Manuel's never been in Madrid, but he's not scared. He's been scared so many times already that fear has disappeared, leaving behind a state of permanent alert that will last his entire life. Manuel is nine years old. He's thin like all the war children, and tall, like very few of them. His head is big and noble, his traits prominent: a large nose resting over his fleshy mouth; an emphatic, square jaw that reveals a resolute character; and eyes with an intense stare, sharp, somewhere between timid and aggressive. His ears seem to jerk back from his face like those of an animal on the prowl. If he were an animal, he'd definitely be a fox.

The journey he's just completed was a long one, but he walks with pep in his step. He's well-dressed if you compare him to the other boys he passes on the Ronda de Atocha. He's got shoes with soles, which distinguish him from the children in espadrilles; a jacket inherited from an older brother and already too small for him; short pants; and in his hand, a box tied with a string which he calls, vaingloriously, his suitcase. He thought his aunt would come pick him up, but she's not there. He doesn't mind. Another boy, any of his brothers, would be terrified, but he isn't. He's sharp. He's sharp when he wants to be, and always bad, so says his mother. His mother is sharper than he is, and he can tell she's not like other mothers. Recently he had to punch a kid who told him, "Your mother's nasty." When she found out, his mother laughed and said, "Better nasty than stupid."

A year ago, his hair fell out. They thought his father had died in the war. He thought he'd lost him, and he had even had dreams about it, where his father would show up in his dirty captain's uniform with blood soaking through where his heart was. Then one morning, when he was playing in the town square, he saw a man in brown rags, looking like a beggar. He didn't recognize him at first. He stood paralyzed, just as when his father appeared to him in dreams. The ragged man crossed the square and walked over to him, picked him out among the children, put a hand on his shoulders, and said in a whisper: "Son." The boy was so frightened that within a few hours, his curls started falling off in his hands. He remained bald several months. People called him mangy, but he knows it wasn't mange, it was shock. Later a witch gave him a magic ointment and his hair grew back. His scalp itched, and his mother would slap him hard on the head to make him stop scratching. He's a bad boy, a rogue, he's got a mean streak. If there's a fight, he's the first one there. His mother knows he's the only one in the family who can survive being alone. And she sends him with an escort of two Civil Guards traveling to Madrid on official business.

He can't get used to his father being alive. Since his return from the dead, he's looked to the boy like a phantom, uncertain whether he really belongs in the realm of the living. He thinks about him, walking through this city he doesn't know, remembers him, wonders if he's alive or dead. The uncertainty will make him afraid of ghosts and closed spaces for the rest of his life, will keep him far from churches and shrines and allergic to silence and solitude.

Madrid, 1939. You breathe the breath of the dead as you walk through the streets. Those who fell beneath the bombs, or who were lined up by firing squads against walls on the outskirts of town, the daily dead from starvation, tuberculosis, childbirth, poverty, infections, fear. Those who die from fear.

Manuel lives in the Plaza del Campillo del Mundo Nuevo. His aunt and he share an apartment with a dining room, a bedroom for her, and a niche for him, barely big enough for a cot and a washbasin. He's pushed his bed over to the window, and the noise from the inner courtyard accompanies him when he falls asleep and wakes. She calls his name before she goes to work, and it wakes him up, but he stays in his little room until she's gone. His aunt is freer with her hands than his mother, to put it lightly. Sometimes she has a reason to hit him, other times she does it because she feels like it. She hit him one day when he ate all that their rations card entitled them to—his part as well as hers. They'd gotten beans, he couldn't help himself. He ate them knowing his aunt would smack him across the face, and that knowledge made him eat them all the more avidly.

When he's alone, he shuts the door to the balcony, though it's already warm and dry and a sweltering summer seems to be in the offing. He's afraid he'll follow that impulse that tells him to throw himself off. He doesn't know where these thoughts come from. He's also afraid he'll jump on the subway tracks or stand in front of the tram and close his eyes. The one thing that torments him is the idea of suddenly going mad.

The best way to combat madness is to go outside and look for action. So he takes off down the streets of El Rastro. Every day, there's a flea market there selling shoe soles, old screws, tables without legs or legs without chairs. The washerwomen go there loaded like pack mules with bundles of clothes to wash in the river; ladies in mourning pass by with stern faces, some of them in veils as they leave Mass; he crosses old women with faces of parchment, their headscarves cinched tight, with children in black who must have lost their father or a brother. Even the little girls are wearing mourning. On Mira el Río Baja hill, people come and go in a huff. Old women bent over, rag-and-bone men, children in frayed espadrilles who quit school before the war and are headed off to work.

His aunt told him not to go around with his hand in his pockets, it makes him look like a dimwit and the cops might stop him. So he tries to pretend he's got something to do, a plan. He worried about looking like a hayseed, coming from the village and showing up in the capital, but even if he has nothing but the shirt on his back, in the La Latina neighborhood, he looks like a little prince. When he arrived in Madrid, he didn't know whether his aunt would send him to school. "She might send you to school," his mother said. He imagined walking there every day, imagined his teachers and classmates. He's always been good at his studies and bad at games. He fights too much, he's a sore loser. But his aunt never said a word about school, and he didn't ask.

His first day there, she sent him off to stand in the welfare line with a lunch pail, and that's what he does in the mornings. Wait in line. He goes home, eats his rations, looks apprehensively over the balcony, and goes back outside.

He walks fast, as if he had an objective, a mission. People who wander around for no reason are suspicious. And he has the whole day to arouse suspicions. His aunt warned him that if he gets in trouble, she'll send him back. And for his mother, that would be almost

like him returning from the dead, he thinks. Another
fugitive from the beyond.

He's got a cheerful nature. He waved to some stranger,
and now he's won over the owner of the bar on the
square. Sometimes he delivers a message and gets a
soda in return, and then he'll spend a while leaning on
the bar, like a little man, surrounded by war cripples.
He needs to kill time until afternoon comes and he can
go pick his aunt up from the hospital. His aunt has a
name, Casilda, but he christened her the Beast after
the day she beat him, and he'll go on calling her that
every time he tells this story, over and over, until the
end of his life.

The Beast abused him, but the boy who doesn't
know how to lose thinks he's getting vengeance on her
every time he uses that nickname, even if only in his
mind. This private form of vengeance, degrading his
enemies by erasing their names, will become an unfal-
tering habit of his.

He's not afraid of beatings, but he is afraid of being
alone, and he's very alone on Saturdays, when his
aunt takes walks with her friends to Puerta del Sol, or
on Sundays, when she goes to Mass. He follows her
at a distance, like a dog, stopping and looking at the

ground if she turns back and motions to him to beat it, to leave her in peace. He's insistent, and he waits for her like a beggar at the doors of the church. Begging for companionship.

At the door to San Isidro church, the old beggars reserve their spot and shout to scare off the poor boys who come there looking for alms. The boys buzz around like flies: they run away, but soon they return. He laughs at how they get past the guards and beggars: they've got nothing to lose, and they don't feel fear. Manuel knows he doesn't look like a panhandler, but he isn't proud of this, it embarrasses him, because it means he's got no reason to be there. He's just a boy waiting on the stone steps for his aunt to come out.

He only ever entered the church once, and it was a torment.

The fearless boy who can't bear solitude, the view from up on the balcony, the screech of the tram's brakes, also worries the doorwoman's niece will infect him with tuberculosis.

The doorwoman's niece wears black too, and sings very softly while she does, because she's consumptive and her voice is weak. They used to have a doorman, the girl's father, but her aunt says they came for him one night during the first summer of the war and took him for a walk and he never came back.

The doorwoman's niece sings a ditty he knows well. The organ-grinder on Calle Carretas plays it, the one in Delicias too, he also heard it on the radio, everyone's humming it these days. But the girl sings it in a way that moves him, and he stays in the stairwell listening to her, very still so she won't know he's there, embarrassed of the stirring his heart feels. He has to restrain another impulse, to go to the room where the girl sews, kneel down, and hug her, pressing his face into her lap. This isn't something a boy should be wishing for, he thinks. He doesn't know why he wants to press himself into her skirts. It's a longing he can't put a name to.

Like the birds whose presence tells of spring
the violet sellers appear in Madrid
and hawk their goods
like swallows chirping, chirping.

If only his little brother were here, he'd have the courage to sing. His little brother, even if he's a wimp and a coward, is a genius when it comes to learning songs, carols, verses. If you ask him to sing, he'll do it without an ounce of shame. If his brother were in Madrid, at least he'd have someone to defend, someone to fight for.

Sometimes he walks for hours. He crosses Madrid all afternoon to kill time before he goes to the hospital where his aunt works. Once he followed her without her knowing, and that one time was enough to learn the way. If he were a dog, he'd surely be a bloodhound; like a bloodhound, he recognizes how the different scents of the city change from one neighborhood to the next. From the scent of cheap wine, old wood, and rag paper in El Rastro to the scent of rubble in Antón Martín to the sweet effluvia of Sol; from the aroma of caffeine and ink in Gran Vía to the dark stench of the Calle Desengaño, where women made up in a way he's never before seen wave to the passing men from the doorways; from the scent of schools and cologne in Chamberí to the odor of fever and disinfectant in Maudes Hospital.

The Moroccans leaning on crutches take walks outside the hospital to get some fresh air, and some of them give him a tip for the cigarette butts he's picked up off the ground at the movie theater entrances on Gran Vía. He's been going to Callao Cinema because they're running *Tarzan Escapes*, with the real Tarzan who grew up in the forest and was raised by apes.

He waits for the session to finish looking at the photos in the marquee. The first day, he watched the children picking up cigarette butts from the ground and he does as they do, because this is another way of not being alone. He envies the ape-man living with all the comforts of the jungle, where the weather's always good; there are lakes with crystal-clear waters, vines you can swing on as fast as a car, and delicious fruit all round. All that paradise, radiant, offering itself up to our hero, who's made his home in the branches, and lives in glory, accompanied and protected by the band of Mangani, who communicate in a language the white man, always menacing and greedy, can't understand. How welcoming, how homey the African jungle looks to him compared to Madrid.

The military hospital smells like dry blood, bleach, and gauze. In the background, you occasionally hear a sick man crying in furious agony. He's seen his aunt walk past quickly in the hallway, and the sight of her in her nurse's uniform provokes an unusual admiration for her. He imagines a future when he, too, will have a mission, something to do, a uniform, a schedule, and his name embroidered on his breast pocket. He's counted the number of people who have uttered his name since he arrived in Madrid, and there are three of them: his aunt, the bar owner, and the doorwoman's niece. The doorwoman calls him *Casilda's nephew*.

His aunt never asked him to go meet her at the hospital, but after seeing him a few times in the doorway, she's gotten used to his presence. Now, if he's late, she slaps him on the back of the neck. He takes this as a greeting, as a way of acknowledging his existence. Not long ago, his aunt bought a paper cone of roasted lupine seeds and they ate them on the walk home. At last, he thought, his efforts to be loved were paying off. Next to her, walking in step, he enjoyed feeling protected like a little boy, but also feeling mature like a man.

He's written to his mother. On the right-hand side of the sheet, in a schoolboy's diligent hand, the date and city appear. Madrid, May 25, 1939. Dear Mamá. Mamá, not Mother, which is what the other boys say. It's the one remaining scrap of tenderness when he writes her. He tries to impress her, telling her he was in front and saw Franco when they drove him through Cibeles in a car with a twelve-cylinder engine, though the truth is the feverish masses had flooded the streets and he didn't even make it as far as Atocha. But he did see the dictator's portraits in all the shopwindows, with signs that read *Franco, Franco, Franco* and *Glory to the Caudillo.*

He tells her he knows Madrid like the back of his hand. He makes a point of mentioning the names of streets to show how much he's learned. He tells her about his chores. The lines he stands in, the messages he delivers. He tells her he has a friend in the stairwell, that the bar owner gives him free soft drinks, that there are neighbors who greet him by name. And he tells her about walking home with his aunt eating lupines from the same cone, as if they did this all the time.

He carefully licks the stamp he brought from home. What he leaves out of the letter are the terrors that plague him every day: the fourth-floor balcony, illness, death roaming the streets in the form of people in mourning, grim men with missing arms or legs, hungry faces in the ration lines, his own hunger the day he ate his aunt's rations.

He also leaves out the hours he wanders around with nothing to do, waiting on the stairs of the church, at the door to the hospital for war cripples, at the gate to the school in Embajadores, where he lingers until the children come out. Then he plays soccer with them with a ball made of rags. He recognizes the little ramblers like himself, who hide their poverty walking like dogs along the walls as though trying to be invisible, the ones who startle when they hear a noise and take off running around the corner.

He doesn't tell his mother something he heard on the radio before the parade that keeps coming back into his mind now, when he least expects it. A man on the radio said with a great deal of authority:

"The war isn't over. The war's still going on. It's going on in silence, on the invisible front."

The invisible front, he repeats to himself, trying to decipher these words. He wonders if this is the same war he sees every day: the rubble of the Church of San Sebastián, the girls in mourning, the children starving and in rags, the mutilated, the men his aunt says are killed every night on the other side of the river. He's never crossed the Manzanares in case the dead are still there in the mornings, eyes open like fish.

Maybe the war is still happening and everyone knows but they're too scared to admit it, just as it's possible his father is dead and he's the only one who sees him. These suspicions torment him and make him observe the world attentively: they feed his perceptiveness and paranoid tendencies and reinforce his distrustful character.

But then the fated day comes when all the children take to the street, the coddled and the abandoned, and there's no stopping the ferment, those games incubated by warmth and long spring days in wartime as well as peace. Manuel, infected by this burst of optimism, spends the day running from the food line to home, from home to the hospital, from the hospital to go play on the promenade of Campillo del Mundo Nuevo. Imitating other kids, he's learned to jump on and off the passing streetcar, and every afternoon it's like he flies from Paseo de las Delicias to Paseo del Generalísimo. The boys hang like monkeys off the back of the streetcar, balancing and jumping off fearlessly every time they have to run from the police. His knees are swollen, full of scabs and bruises, but his gregariousness makes him join in the mischief, even if, for the first time in his life, he wants to go unnoticed.

He listens to a kid from Embajadores who tells him the House of Wild Beasts in El Retiro is open again. Since then, his wish to see wild animals like those that inhabit Tarzan's jungle has overtaken his dreams, replacing— thank heavens—the specters of war. His worries about finding his way to the zoo on his own are relieved one evening after a game, when the group leader proposes they all go together. How many join the expedition? Seven, eight, nine kids. They wrap their hands around each other's shoulders and take up the whole sidewalk, skipping along affably, excited to disobey their mothers, who've ordered them not to wander too far from home. But who needs to know about this little getaway? Madrid is too small for them. In mischievous anticipation, they sing a song they've adopted as their anthem, shouting until they're hoarse:

María de la O
What a sad little gypsy
You've got it all
You want to laugh
But even your eyes
Are dark from so much sorrow

Soon they're climbing the Cuesta de Moyano and entering that park Manuel's heard so much about. In some places, it seems like a giant scythe has mowed down hundreds of trees all at once. The stumps, thick and squat, crowns hacked away by a furtive ax, form a lunar landscape perfect for the kids, who jump on and off them.

Farther off, on the broad path that crosses the park, there's a huge number of cars abandoned some time ago. They're scrap metal now, lined up one beside the other as if there'd been a horrible traffic jam there and the drivers had just up and left. One boy says: "This is a traffic jam in Hell." And that is what it looks like. The boys pass carefully between the dented hulks, afraid they might find a rotting body in one of the seats. One boy, the leader, gets inside one of the doorless cars. The others do the same. And with that daring that nourishes fear, they shout onomatopoeias like car horns, the screech of skidding tires, the roar of an engine as it sounds to a child. But Madrid is full of cops and sour-faced men who like to scare children when they're having fun, and this happens here. A worker comes over, and as soon as he makes a sound, the boys take off running. They are audacious and timid, venturesome but well aware of the abusive weight of authority.

They take off running toward their destination. Someone says Franco has had an elephant and lion sent over from Africa, and a gray bear from the Caucasus. Manuel, the stranger in the group, finally finds a way to make himself be heard, and he relishes this moment when he can expatiate on a subject he knows very well: the jungle of Tarzan, the orphan of English aristocrats who grew up nurtured and protected by the ape Kala. The young dreamer knows everything written about the jungle in Tarzan's adventures, and what he doesn't know, he makes up, and he feels that almost-forgotten excitement of beguiling others, who notice him now and treat him as if he's important. As he talks, he finds that old self hushed and hidden since he got to Madrid. The person talking is him at last, the verbose boy with the silver tongue, selfish, anxious for people's attention. The boys listen in silence, feeling transported to the jungle by this new friend who lights up when he talks, but then one, a boy he hates immediately for stealing his thunder, breaks the spell by saying that the sons of those who fell for Spain are lucky because they'll never be orphans. Franco is their father.

Eventually they arrive. The enclosure overlooking the moat with the animals is packed with a kind of children never seen in La Latina, rich kids with white socks and laced shoes, watched over by mothers and nurses, hogging all the space as though they owned it. Forgetting his friends, he breaks madly through them and makes his way to the front, shoving and elbowing. Smiling but headstrong, blinded now by his passion.

There are many more species there than he expected: a dromedary, a leopard, a family of lions. In starving Madrid, everyone seems to have a bit of food for the wild animals. The elephant is the most trusting of all, and walks at ease outside its cage. It steps over to the adults, who place treats in its trunk. Manuel takes from his pocket a crust of his ration of yellowish bread, which is so crunchy he cuts his mouth on it. He looks at the animal's eyes and offers it the scrap of rye bread. The elephant takes it delicately, cupping its two nostrils over his hand. Manuel decides to come back every day. He will make friends with the elephant, and maybe trick its caretaker into letting him help out.

He feels he has an extraordinary capacity to communicate with these animals. He feels chosen, powerful, superior. Inspired by his hero, the orphan adopted by apes, he is certain he will learn their language and they will be able to understand him. With relentless imagination, he's already shaping his future. A future where his aunt, his ghost of a father, his cold, hard mother, and those two brothers he will always think of as spoiled are all far behind him. All lost in the past in this new life, where he'll dwell among wild beasts with no fear of being devoured, napping in the sun on the hump of a dromedary or sleeping in a cage with lions like just another member of the pride. He could stay there this very night if he wished. If he wanted, he could trick the guards going around pushing people out because the park is about to close. If he wanted, he could slip past the fence, sink down into the moat, and sleep next to the railing beneath the stars, the cold of the early morning hours relieved by the hot, powerful breath of the beasts, who will naturally take care of him like another of their kind.

His feat will teach the world a lesson: on the radio, the announcer will tell how, in a pack of wild animals, a boy found a family to shelter and love him. But he already has a family. When he wakes up every morning and what he calls his black thoughts plague him, only then does he ask himself what he's doing in Madrid. He clings to the belief that he was chosen for this adventure over his brothers because he's the boldest, the bravest, the smartest. He remains faithful to his mother's vision of him until the last years of his life, when a previously unknown, long-censored rancor rises to the surface, and he sees this episode as what it was: an unforgiveable abandonment.

———

Someone smacks him on the back of the neck. The wild-animal keeper gets his attention. Kid, are you dumb or what, don't you see everyone's gone? And he realizes that the kids have returned to the neighborhood without him, or maybe they called for him and he was too wrapped up in his fantasies. He takes off running after them along the edge of the park, because what had seemed like a thrilling adventure, sleeping out under the stars, now sounds terrifying. He sees them far away, but on the whirling carousel of his emotions, he feels pushed aside by those he thought were his friends, and winds up dwelling on his sorrows.

Night has covered Madrid with a black veil. The lights in the city are back on, but even that doesn't make it inviting: before, you walked around in the darkness, now you walk among shadows. He doesn't know what time it is or what he'll tell his aunt when he gets home. Maybe she's gone to bed and won't bother to come out and ask what he's up to. He'd like to tell her what he saw, the diabolical traffic jam, the mother elephant, the lion cub, his newfound friends—or maybe they're already his former friends. He misses his little brother terribly. And he doesn't even have anyone to tell how terribly he misses his little brother.

———

If his aunt goes off in the afternoon to run errands in the neighborhood shops, he usually sits and waits for her on the sidewalk. He likes being there watching people pass better than being alone in the apartment, sitting on a chair in the dining room, attentive to the noise behind him. From now on, unless someone's with him, he'll never feel safe indoors. His home will always and forever be the street, where he was cast out at nine years old.

The square is deserted. At the bar are two somber men, and behind it the owner, leaning down and looking out at the street as if it were another of his guests. Behind him is a photo of Franco and the chalkboard noting the drinks—what few there are—on offer. The boy climbs the stairs, smells that same old mix of reheated vegetables and the soap the doorwoman uses to scrub the entryway. He hasn't heard the girl sing for days. He asks her aunt about her, and she says that when consumptives start bleeding from their mouth and their strength fails despite their best efforts, then they have to go away. To where? he asks. To the mountains. What do they do there? Some of them get better and others die, she answers. A chill goes up his spine, same as when his hair fell out.

His aunt isn't afraid of illness. She's a nurse and she knows what to do to go on living until old age takes her away.

He puts the key in the lock. The room is dark, and he crosses quickly on tiptoe to hide in his hovel. But the single bulb hanging from the ceiling comes on suddenly. He turns and hardly has time to react or even see her or cover his face with his arm as he usually does. A dry, hard slap crosses his face and drives him into the wall. His hands are shaking when he brings them to his mouth, and blood drips between his fingers. He doesn't look up at her. All he hears her say is: "This is enough. This week I'm sending you home."

When he lies down on his cot, he wants to cry, but he holds it in. He's sure his mother would have beaten him for what he did, too, but in his poignant conception of a child's rights, he believes that a person who isn't your mother has no right to hit you. He'll tell his mother this when he sees her, he thinks, and she'll forgive him. But there's one thing he can't stand: going back home a failure. He's scared to disappoint her, and to avoid it, he hatches a plan, and his eyes don't close from fatigue until the first rays of dawn are shining on the windows in the light well.

———

He takes the lunch pail, as he does every day, to go stand in the welfare line. And he goes home, as he does every day, eating his half of the rations before lunchtime. He puts the bread in his pocket. He goes downstairs, as he does every day. He sees the girl isn't back from the mountains and prays to God to save her, as he does every day. Outside, the street is packed as always with women in black, carrying loads of bric-a-brac they've bought or are about to sell at the stands in El Rastro. He goes into the bar. "You're early, kid," the owner tells him. And, trying to act as normal as always, the boy tells him his aunt has asked to borrow five pesetas; she'll give them back this afternoon when she's done with work. The man clicks his tongue, slightly annoyed, because he spends his life hearing these stories and doling out little loans, but he's trusting, and he lets the boy have it.

Manuel goes back home. He takes out the cardboard box he calls his suitcase from under his cot and puts in the jacket he arrived in, back when it was still cold, his other shirt, and two changes of underwear. He still has the photo inside of his parents with his older brother and another of his little brother, Angelito, from just after he was born; the authorization his father wrote for him in lieu of an ID; and a prayer card of St. Anthony of Padua with a prayer he must have recited every night, though he can't remember it anymore. He looks in the mirror hanging over the washbasin to see if he looks the same as he does every day. Except for his busted lip, no one would say he's on the verge of leaving forever. He puts on his mature face so no one will think he's a little boy. He's got that expression mastered. The one detail that's off is his pants, which are short.

He writes a note:

Dear Auntie:

I've gone to Aranjuez to my aunt and uncle's. I'll write my parents. I have a stamp for the letter. Don't worry about me. Thanks for everything, and goodbye.

Manolo

He leaves the paper next to the food with the house key. And he hurries off with his box in his hand. There's no need to pretend he's carrying a suitcase anymore. Not even for him: it's just a box tied with a string. When he passes by the bar, he dares to wave at the owner, who looks at him now slightly askance.

He goes to a store on the corner and buys an apple. He calculates how long he can live with a crust of rye bread and an apple. Two days, easy. He likes to think he's planned everything down to the last detail.

He climbs the same street he descended a lifetime ago. He's gotten used to the city's poverty, and also to its incessant noise. He no longer notices the barefoot kids he comes across, the others whose toes poke from holes in their soles, and he's not scared anymore by the metallic shriek of the tram as it heads toward the Paseo del Prado; he doesn't flinch when he crosses through the cars ignoring the brand-new stoplights. He knows now as he leaves that he's started to become one of them, that he's not a hayseed or an outsider anymore. He doesn't realize he's come a long way on his own, without anyone's help, learning by observing others and going along with others. Handsome, tall, and singular, with the bearing of a young aristocrat whose parents' sudden death has left him alone in this impoverished, dry, sterile forest of people desperate to survive, too hungry and scared to be generous.

He enters Atocha Station and goes straight to the counter. He asks for a ticket to Aranjuez, and the salesman gives it to him without even looking. At home, in the family home he left behind, he had two postcards from his uncles in Aranjuez. His father's two brothers. In one, you could see the colored photograph of a palace, in the other, a regal garden. He knew his uncles weren't rich, but he always imagined them living in

that palace. In his imagination, Aranjuez is a paradise
where his father was happy as a boy. And not all little
boys are happy. That name, Aranjuez, echoes in his
young mind like a dreamland, part Eden, part African
jungle. He doesn't know where his uncles live, but his
father has always said everyone who bears his name in
Aranjuez is family, and they help each other out and
protect each other. He's always known he'd go to Aranjuez one day, but he couldn't imagine he would take the
decision on his own.

He sees the guards wandering on the platform and quiv-
ers. They might ask him where he's going and why he's
traveling alone. He sees an old woman carrying several bundles and sticks close to her. He tells her he can
carry one for her. She looks at him. Who could mistrust
a boy she sees for what he is: a handsome, formal child,
very tall, with a clear, expressive gaze, a broad smile,
and nice clothes for the time. They enter the train as
if traveling together, and sit together like grandmother
and grandson. He tells her he's going on vacation to see
his uncles, that his father is there, and he's been dream-
ing of swimming in the river. The train takes off, the
racket relaxes the boy, and he closes his eyes, nodding
off, accidentally resting his head on the woman's shoulder. The old woman studies him, sees his lip split from

a recent blow, and for some reason we will never know, when the official comes through to check their tickets, she tells him they're traveling together.

The air coming through the window is warm and caresses his face. The boy keeps drifting off, aware of what he's leaving behind and anxious for what awaits him. The old woman wakes him, Young man, you need to get off, this is your station, and Manuel tells her goodbye, the way you take leave of a person in a dream. He leaves the station and walks for a while. When he reaches a square, he asks a man about the family that shares his last name, and the man nods. They take off walking and cross the small city under a blazing sun. It's a humbler place than he expected. On his first walk through it, he doesn't see the river or the palace or those regal gardens from the postcard. For a moment, he thinks they've left the city limits and are in the countryside, and he's alarmed. He looks at the man out of the corner of his eye to see if he's a plain-clothes cop about to arrest him, but right then, they turn into a neighborhood of low, crumbling homes surrounded by barns. The man calls to a boy and says: Hey, you, take this kid to your house, he says he's your father's nephew.

————

The boy, who turns out to be his cousin Lázaro, takes him home. Lázaro's mother is there, and she sits my father in a chair and listens incredulous to everything he has to say. He says he's there to stay. Or wants to know if he can stay. He doesn't explain much, just that he's spent the past few months standing in the welfare line and feeling lonely as can be. His cousins gather around him. In two days, he'll know all their names. Alejandro, Lázaro, Ángel, Isabel, Amado, Lucio, Anselmo. Manuel will always remember that he ate a tomato salad that day.

And our little hero stayed there for some time. What did his aunt from Madrid think when she read her nephew's note? We don't know. We don't even know how his mother reacted when she received a letter from her sister-in-law in Aranjuez that read: Your boy's with us. When he grew up and found a girl who loved him a way he'd never known before, he understood: sometimes you're cast into misfortune, and other times, bravery, desperation, and good luck can take you to the promised land.

My father used to say that under the brutal sun of the Meseta, the children would run across those gardens of Eden, whose produce stilled the hunger of the poor. He never saw the royal palace or the prince's gardens until he returned to Aranjuez as a full-grown man.

My father, I would like to leave you here forever
In this garden.
I would like this to be the end of your journey,
For you never to remember or see beyond this land,
Not to face the fact
That you, too, were hard and unjust.
You were.
But how could you not have been?

I observe you, beaming and trustful,
At last dwelling in the universe of your
Nine tender years
After living with the beast of war,
That war
That as you well know
In your apprehensive distrust
Was not entirely dead.

This land should be the place
Where the lives of the innocent
Pass.

Don't keep walking
Toward the future, Papá.
Where better than this garden
For an eternal life?

Here you will forget
What you never should have known.

You're losing the warmth
Of the living.
Before the cold the dead leave behind
Invades me
I kiss the back of your hand,
This hand
Sometimes protective,
Sometimes cruel,
Which I always loved so much
And I tell you goodbye.

How sweet to leave you here
Playing
With the other children
With your name shouted
Constantly
By the mouths of all:
Manuel, Manuel, Manuel!

ACKNOWLEDGMENTS

I always wanted to make my parents characters in a novel, because this is how I saw them, sometimes with admiration, other times with fear, when I was a girl. I can only thank those people whose support during this research into myself has lasted years or an entire lifetime, almost. My sister, Inma, lent me the good memory that I lack, adding important details, and my brother César was always willing to accompany me through the landscapes of our childhood. My friend, the psychiatrist Aurea Lamela, responded sensitively to questions I had about the writing of the present book. My conversations with the psychoanalyst Mariela Michelena about the nature of delirium and the consequences of childhood trauma were essential. The economist Emilio Ontiveros spoke to me of the unrecognized importance of administrators in large public works projects, and this gave me a different perspective on my father's job. Elena Ramírez, my editor, has been infinitely patient, often pulling me out of the distraction I'm so prone to and bringing me back to the flow of this story. And nothing would be possible without the help of my husband, Antonio Muñoz Molina, not only because of his literary advice but because he loved and listened to my father so generously.

I should name all the friends from my father's neighborhood, his debate partners, his old colleagues from Dragados, who always talk about him so warmly, and all those waiters and bartenders who came by to offer their condolences after his death. They lost a good customer, I lost a father. Being both was very important to him.

CREDITS

SONGS

"Amapola" [Poppies] on page 103 by Joseph Lacalle, 1920

"Chiquitina" on page 119 by Augusto Algueró, 1962

"Mirando al mar" [Looking at the sea] on page 152 by Marino García González, lyrics by César de Haro, 1949

"Yo te diré" [Every time the wind blows] on page 235 by Jorge Halpern, lyrics by Enrique Llovet, 1945

"How Deep Is Your Love" on page 277 by Maurice Gibb, Robin Gibb, Barry Gibb, 1977

"La Violetera" [Like the birds] on page 333 by José Padilla, lyrics by Eduardo Montesinos, 1914

"María de la O" on page 340 by Manuel Quiroga, lyrics by Salvador Valverde and Rafael de León, 1933

POETRY AND PROSE

"Sonatina," poem on page 186 by Rubén Darío, 1896

"Qué lástima!" poem on page 192 by León Felipe, c. 1930

Excerpt on page 195 from *The Godfather* by Mario Puzo, copyright © Mario Puzo, 1969

"O tempo vivido" poem on page 257 by Sophia de Mello Breyner Andresen